RETRIEVAL
An Academic Murder Mystery

Linda Blackwell Billingsley

ISBN: 9781071093665

Cover design by Ron Johnson

To My Husband and Family
and
All the Other Friends
who have encouraged and helped me through the years

Thank You

Table of Contents

Chapter One

Wondering when the Marquis de Sade had gone into furniture design, I shifted in my plastic seat. Until this event, the Library Advisory Committee had seemed a painless way to fulfill my service obligation to the English Department. However, I now found myself present, by invitation, at the celebration of two questionable events: the dedication of a new library wing to house the Smythe Center for the Study of Government and the installation of a robotic Library Retrieval, Tracking and Technology Assistant—LORETTA, for short.

Squirming in my seat, I heard someone ask, "Is this seat taken?"

I looked up to find Marshall N'Dour, from Chemistry, towering over me.

"No, let me move over so you can have the aisle seat." I may have thought de Sade had it in for me, but I knew no suffering compared to Marshall's efforts to fit his 6' 6" frame into the chair.

"Thanks."

He smiled, pushing his chair back slightly and angling his legs into the aisle. We were in the back row because I had been hoping to make a quick escape although I now realized the crowd was too small to cover an early departure. I felt sure Marshall always sat in the back row because he knew no one could see over him.

"So why are you here?" he asked quietly.

"I'm on the Library Advisory Committee."

"You approved the Smythe Center for the Study of Government? And the Smythe Archive?" he asked quietly.

"God, no! The committee was never asked. We were simply presented with the plan."

"So I guess they won't be studying democratic governments," he said drily.

"I don't even want to think about what they will study. So what are you doing here?"

"I'm a sucker for technology."

"Me too, but I'm a little sad about putting books in boxes instead of on shelves." Marshall surprised me by nodding. I suddenly remembered he was up for tenure. "So how are you doing with the tenure-year pressure?"

"Holding up as well as can be expected. I constantly think about alternative careers."

"Yes, I understand. Something eight to five with real earning power and clear demand."

"My current favorite is auto repair."

"You look more the electrician type to me!"

"Too damn tall for either."

"Basketball in Europe?"

"Been there, done that, and too old to do it again."

We were laughing as Dr. Maureen Shaughnessy, the University Provost, the President's second-in-command, came to the microphone. She introduced Senator Samuel Smythe, a silver-spoon conservative who consistently voted to give women, children, and minorities the short end of the stick.

"He put a million of his own ill-gotten gains into this project, but he also dipped deep into the pork barrel," I murmured to Marshall who grimaced.

"The fellowships for students and that creepy director he appointed are what worry me," whispered Marshall, frowning.

Smythe began to blather away about what a great opportunity this was to benefit the university, a premise that led shortly to a ten-minute campaign ad. I snorted softly, and Marshall laughed. I could barely restrain myself from acting like we were in seventh-grade assembly where I was always in trouble for making people laugh.

Smythe finally wound down, and the Provost introduced the Director of Libraries. He sucked up like a vacuum cleaner and then introduced LORETTA, the retrieval system, explaining that each box would house from 50 to 150 books. On command, our robot (as yet nameless) would fetch the box.

Every time I heard the acronym LORETTA, I imagined a socially-awkward geek who wrote line after line of the computer program to the sorrowful country voice of Loretta Lynne. I was smiling at this image as a student assistant stepped to the computer and ordered a biography of George Washington, an innocuous, patriotic choice for LORETTA's first public performance.

"Want to have dinner after this?" Marshall whispered as the robot set the box on a platform next to the computer terminal.

Before I could say "yes," the student assistant had opened the box and begun screaming.

The Head of Circulation and two reference librarians dashed into the glass-fronted room where LORETTA was housed. They took one look in the box, blanched, and dragged the still-screaming student into the adjacent office.

Everyone in the audience stood up. As one of the librarians returned to close the box, I felt Marshall sag. His café-au-lait complexion had paled, and he was about to faint.

"Sit down," I commanded, tugging at his arm. "Sit down!" He crumpled into the chair.

"Put your head between your knees!" I pushed his head down. "Take deep breaths."

"Oh, my God," he moaned. "Oh, my God."

I sat down, fumbled in my bag for a bottle of water, and put my arm around his trembling shoulders.

"Drink."

He raised his head and drank. After a few sips, his color began to return.

Around us was complete chaos. Clearly no one knew what had happened.

"Are you okay?" I asked.

"Yeah, I guess."

"What happened?"

"There was a dead person in that box," he said softly and swallowed hard. "Or part of a dead person.

Chapter Two

Marshall and I, along with the rest of the audience, were not released until early evening. A strange silence descended as we lined up for our individual police interviews. The older woman in front of me was a Classics professor. She explained twice, with growing irritation, that she did not have any identification with her because she had not expected this event to involve "meeting with the local constabulary."

I finally stepped up to the table and said, "Officer, if it's any help, I do have identification, and I can vouch for Professor Landau. Her office is right down the hall from mine." I put my driver's license and university picture-identification on the table.

"Thank you, Dr. Brinkman," said Professor Landau.

"I'm sorry, ma'am, but we have a job to do," said the young police officer, rising from his chair with a conciliatory and respectful nod.

I had read about "snorts of contempt" but had never heard one until Professor Landau emitted that sound before saying, "If that's all, I will be going now." She swept off, and I sat down.

"Thanks," the officer said.

"No problem." I gave him the required contact information and retrieved my identification. Marshall was next. Thirty minutes later we were walking in the front door of Castillo del Mar, a local tapas place.

"I'm sorry, but I don't think I feel like eating," he said, after we were seated in one of the high-backed booths.

"Let's order a bottle of wine and maybe a cheese platter just in case."

"I know that I should eat, but I keep seeing…." He choked up, looked away, and took a deep breath.

I did not know Marshall well. We were not friends, just acquaintances, through university committees and campus politics.

The server brought our wine, and I ordered, requesting an extra basket of bread. I tried not to think about my almost-maxed-out credit card. We sipped our wine in silence until I said, "Is it better if you keep this to yourself, or do you want to tell me what you saw? No pressure either way, but I think you're actually the only person in the audience who could see what was in the box. I'm not prying and don't need to know, but if it would make you feel better...."

Marshall smiled, and I found myself wishing him a few years older.

"I'm sure the Provost saw too. I saw the look on her face. That librarian who closed the box also saw, but I feel so sorry for that student worker."

I nodded sympathetically while thinking perversely that she would always have the ultimate work-study story. I restrained myself from sharing this thought.

Marshall ate some bread with herbed garlic butter, and then reached for some of the machego. I smiled as he forked some thinly sliced cheese onto his plate.

"I must be coming out of the shock," he said, signaling our server. "I think we need an order of chorizo and the gambas in garlic sauce. Also, would you please bring some olives? Is that okay?" I nodded happily, trying not to worry about my credit card.

"It was LouAnn Bond," he said.

"What?"

"I wouldn't swear to it, but the face...," he stopped and took a large drink of wine. "You know, LouAnn Bond, the President's assistant."

"She can't be that short!" I protested, and we both burst into unseemly laughter. In fact, we laughed until we cried, and that was my first indication that the wine had gone to our heads.

"Do you know her?" he asked, wiping his eyes.

"No. Just by name. Do you?"

"A bit." He did not elaborate but insisted, "I'm sure it was her."

We ordered a second bottle of wine and a delicious salad, followed by flan and coffee. I figured tomorrow I would race to the bank and make a payment on my credit card from my meagre savings account. "Emergencies will have to be small," I thought and added a quick prayer for my twelve-year-old car.

When I awoke the next morning, I remembered how much Marshall and I had laughed throughout the evening and during the cab ride home. I did not have classes that day so I walked to the bank and then the two miles to retrieve my car from the restaurant. En route I stopped for a plain coffee, congratulated myself on my economy, and read the local paper. The incident was reported, but the victim was not identified, "pending notification of family." It was, as Marshall had surmised, only part of LouAnn Bond. The library was closed indefinitely while the police forced LORETTA to surrender the rest of the body.

When I got to campus, it was clear that everyone knew it was LouAnn Bond in the box. Rumors were rife—LouAnn had been cut into a hundred pieces, her heart, kidneys, and liver were missing, and so on. Every student I bumped into was in a panic over a different rumor and hysterical about work that might require a visit to the library. Everywhere LouAnn Bond was the subject of conversations that often began, "Not to speak ill of the dead...," as the speaker proceeded to tell some first-, second-, or even third-hand tale of an unpleasant encounter with the deceased.

I had lunch with Miranda Lopez Gianinni, a professor in Spanish and a woman of great kindness and gentility, who surprised me by saying, "LouAnn Bond was an absolute bitch."

I raised my eyebrows and waited for her to continue.

"You know I was on the Athletics and Academics Committee for years." I nodded. "I got off last year because...." Miranda paused and finally said, "Long story why I got off, but James is a huge sports fan so this fall we did what we have been doing for years and travelled with the football team for one of the away games. We flew down with all the trustees and people we know." I nodded again, thinking how Miranda and James, childless and both full professors, could afford to pay several thousand dollars for a weekend outing, designed for and enjoyed by rich people except for the lone faculty representative on the committee whose expenses were paid.

"We were so looking forward to the trip, but we got to Memphis and discovered that we were not with our friends. We had been put in some remote hotel with people we didn't even know," she fumed. "I found out that LouAnn had made the room assignments. I had always been on good terms with her so when we got back, I called her and left a message asking if there had been a mistake. I told her that we had always been in the main hotel and were disappointed not to be with our friends." Miranda stopped, her face flushed with anger.

"What did she say?"

"She didn't bother to return my call but sent an e-mail saying that since I was no longer on the Athletics and Academics Committee, my room assignment was not a priority for the President's office." Miranda paused and then added, "I had heard a few things over the years about her, but I had dismissed them because she had always been perfectly polite and helpful to me."

"That's so...," I searched for the right word. "So rude. So insulting. Did you complain?"

Miranda looked at me as if I had just admitted to believing in elves.

"Now who would I complain to?"

Her question haunted me for the rest of the afternoon. When something was wrong at the university, when someone was treated rudely or even unjustly, the question of where to lodge a complaint always came up. Although my tenure case had involved a carefully defined part of the university's business, when the process went badly awry, I had found there was no one to whom I could complain or from whom I could receive formal, unbiased advice.

Curious, I went on the university's web site to check Bond's title. She was listed as a "Special Assistant to the President." Salaries were a matter of public record, and the local newspaper had been listing them ever since it had gone online. Bond was

6

making the same amount as the President's assistant who kept his calendar. This seemed odd since Bond's position carried much more responsibility.

The day after my lunch with Miranda, the newspaper identified the body. The next of kin turned out to be a brother doing jail time in West Virginia for armed robbery. LouAnn Bond was 59 when she died. She had been born and raised in Holloway Springs, West Virginia. I assumed that the President had paid for the fulsome obituary which detailed Bond's career at the university from her undergraduate degree in English to her first job in the Controller's office to her thirty-year career in the President's office under two different presidents. Aside from her mother, who had predeceased her, and the brother, the obituary listed no other relatives.

As I read the obituary, I thought ruefully that at least Bond had belonged to a church and imagined how my obituary would read: "Celeste Brinkman, Associate Professor of English, non-practicing Catholic, unattached, workaholic, only child of older parents...." I stopped and reminded myself of my friends and the aunts, uncles, and cousins who popped in and out of my life like we were living in prairie dog town. At that moment, the phone rang, and Marshall asked me to have dinner with him on Sunday. I happily said yes and then remembered the woeful state of my finances. I had made a vow to stop eating out and economize, but Marshall was the first man who had held my interest in a long time. I told myself that I would economize in other ways.

"Did you see LouAnn Bond's obituary?" I asked, as we were about to hang up.

"Yes. It made me sad. Family is so important, and, except for her brother, she had no one.

Chapter Three

Two weeks after LouAnn Bond's death, the absence of news suggested that the police did not have a clue. A young police officer had appeared at my office door one morning to ask some general background questions about where I was from (here), where I had studied (Beloit, St. Louis, Wisconsin), where I had lived and worked (Los Angeles, Albuquerque, and now here for ten years), and when I had arrived at the library (ten minutes before the ceremony). When she asked whether I knew LouAnn Bond or knew of anyone who had a grudge against her, I replied that I did not. She also asked questions about where I had spent the weekend before the ceremony. I told the truth: I had been holed up in my apartment finishing an article except for several quick walks to clear my head. If I needed an alibi, I was out of luck. I was happy to see that the officer did not seem disappointed or unduly alarmed, but she did murmur, "You people work a lot of weird hours."

That afternoon I picked up the independent student newspaper, always an example of the highs and lows in journalism, and found a full-page spread entitled, "Who Was LouAnn Bond and Why Would Someone Kill Her?" The paper had a picture of Bond taken at a recent reception for alumni, and I realized that while I had not known her, our paths had crossed. At least a year ago, I had attended a meeting in the building that housed the university's upper administration—the President, the Provost, and the Vice Presidents for Finance, Development, Research, Academic Affairs, and Student Life. On my way to the meeting, as I was climbing the stairs, I heard voices on the landing above.

"I can't believe this shit," a man was saying angrily.

"Well, Frank, there is no need to use that language," a woman replied in a measured, holier-than-thou tone. "It's a fact that the President and Provost don't trust you."

I thought about descending quietly, but my curiosity got the better of me, and I paused to listen.

"What do you mean they don't trust me?" the man demanded hotly. "Why in the hell would you say that?"

"Just think about it," she said smugly. As she moved to descend the stairs, she looked back over her shoulder and said in an insinuating tone, "Remember Lila Daniliov, Frank? Why should they trust you?" She was not upset but smiling as she almost collided with me.

"Excuse me," she said with the faintest lilt of a southern accent.

"Excuse me," I replied. "I wasn't looking where I was going."

We nodded politely and passed on.

When I stepped onto the third floor landing, I found Frank O'Donnell, Vice President for Academic Affairs, standing at the window and staring out over the campus. I cleared my throat, and he turned, nodded briefly, and started downstairs. I was sure neither of them knew I had overheard their conversation. I now realized that the woman had been LouAnn Bond.

I had told the police officer that I did not know Bond. This was an accidental lie, but in not telling the officer about my conversation with Miranda Lopez Gianinni, I had deliberately withheld information. Miranda and I had been friends ever since I came to the university. I could not imagine her, a petite woman barely five feet tall, murdering anyone, much less moving and cutting up the body. I wondered how the dismemberment had been done and then chastised myself for my grisly curiosity. That day Frank O'Donnell had sounded furious, but did furious translate to murderous? Probably not, or we would all be killers, so why should I make trouble for him? And as for the Lila Daniliov of O'Donnell and Bond's exchange, I had no idea who she was. My conscience, while not exactly clear, was not killing me so I let the conversations go, just as I had let the other gossip surrounding Bond pass.

I had agreed to go to the mid-year family reunion that weekend, and was sure my cousin Harold, a police detective, would drop in at some point. I decided to run the situation by him.

Because the March weather was uncertain, our family gathered in the school's multi-purpose room at Our Lady of Hope. Part of the family belonged to the parish so we got the space for free as long as we cleaned up. I usually timed my arrival for an hour or so into the potluck when the food was plentiful and cousins thick on the ground, but this Saturday, not wanting to miss Harold, I arrived promptly at one. Aunt Christina put me to work laying out food and locating serving utensils.

We all put in a few bucks for the meat, beer, and soda, and we each brought a dish. I had made red pepper hummus. Janey, who is my life-long best friend as well as my cousin, had sworn that she would bring green salad so we would have something to balance out the jello, macaroni, chips, and onion-soup dip. I have ten first cousins, but Janey and I are the only girls. She is three years older than I am and ten years younger than Harold, her next oldest brother. She found me as soon as she came in and unveiled a gorgeous salad.

"How are you?" I asked, hugging her.

"Going nuts. Middle school!" Janey is married to Dominic, and they have Daniel, who is 12, and Clare, my goddaughter, who is 14.

"What's wrong?" I asked with some concern.

"Didn't you hear me?" demanded Janey. "Middle school! Clare is in eighth grade and Daniel is in sixth. Do I need to say more? My only salvation is that this year no one is in seventh grade, the ultimate pit year!"

"Are they coming?"

"Princess Clare may dain to drop by for a few moments after her softball practice if nothing better comes along. Daniel is somewhere here already."

"Rough?"

"Yeah, someone is always yelling or crying, and a lot of the time it might be me," replied Janey, laughing. She would be forty this year. I felt my biological clock ticking like a time bomb, but I always reflected that as a doting "aunt" and godmother, I shared much of the best time with the kids and experienced few of the headaches.

"How's the new job?"

Janey had recently taken a part-time job in a large, suburban parish. As the Director of Religious Education, she was finally getting paid to do the work she had done for years as a volunteer.

"Too soon to tell. It's weird working in a parish where I'm not a member— there's a lot to learn about the people and their expectations. I'm also not used to having money to do things!"

I was interested in what Janey was saying, but suddenly I spotted Harold across the room and excused myself.

"Hey, Cece." Harold, my oldest cousin, thirteen years my senior, has always been sweet to me. When I was little, he gave me piggyback rides and always took time to talk with me at family gatherings. He called me "Cece Baby" until I was thirteen and explained to him that he had to stop: "It makes me feel embarrassed, and Mom said I needed to talk to you." He did not laugh but listened and promised to try. He dropped the "Baby," but I will always be "Cece" to him, and now it just makes me smile.

"It's good to see you," I said, hugging him. "How are you?"

"Actually, I'm getting ready to retire. Six more months."

"That's great. What will you do?"

"I have some leads. I may go into a landscaping business with a buddy of mine."

"Sounds great. You're the best gardener in the family." He smiled at the compliment.

"I need to talk to you."

"Sure. What's wrong?" he asked, immediately concerned. I took the beer Harold offered.

"Nothing, but can we find someplace quiet?"

10

"Follow me." He took me through the fire doors to a quiet stairwell. "What's wrong? It isn't about that woman who got killed at the university?"

"Are you on that case?"

"No, but I've heard about it." He eyed me curiously.

"I was in the audience when they discovered her body."

"Unpleasant, to say the least."

"I didn't actually see the body—I was in the back row, but my friend who is over six feet tall could see in the box."

"Not a pretty sight," murmured Harold, taking a sip of his beer.

I had fully intended to tell him everything I knew and ask his advice, but I still felt uneasy about causing trouble for Miranda or Frank O'Donnell.

"How's the case going? There's been nothing in the news."

"Not well. Apparently a lot of people disliked Bond, but the detective in charge told me that it's hard to get a handle on who might have hated her enough to kill her."

"No leads?"

Harold sipped his beer for a few minutes in silence.

"Just between you and me?" I nodded encouragingly. "It had to be someone who knew how to run a power saw."

"The murderer brought a saw in?"

"Didn't have to. They were still working on the new wing. Back behind that new storage system, the contractor had set up a workshop with all sorts of power tools including a table saw like your dad has but bigger."

I suddenly felt sick.

"Fingerprints?"

"None. In fact, when the workers came in on Monday, they thought the janitors had cleaned up their work area. The sawdust had all been cleaned up, and the blade was gleaming like new. In fact, it was new."

"So how did you figure out the saw had been used?"

"There was blood and a bit of fiber stuck under the guard, but not a print anywhere. Gloves probably. Some drop cloths had disappeared, but they are probably deep in the landfill by now. We checked all the campus cameras and got no one unusual putting anything like drop cloths or trash bags into a dumpster."

"Cameras?"

"Didn't you know?" Harold looked surprised. "Since 9/11 and that Virginia Tech thing, there are surveillance cameras all over campus."

"You're kidding, aren't you?" I looked at him closely.

"No, I'm not. Honey, there are cameras all over the place now, not just at the university. Unfortunately, the library cameras are only focused on the public entrances so there are several doors where you can get in or out and not be filmed. But the cameras have been absolutely no help. Of course, we're sure it's a man."

"Why?"

"Moving the body."

"Bond was small. She couldn't have weighed a hundred pounds."

"Sure, but a hundred pounds of dead weight is heavy. That and the power saw. Women don't use power tools."

"Some do," I protested. "There are courses now that women can take, and my friend Cass built the entire addition to her house."

"I know," Harold said, "But your friend is still the exception."

I nodded thoughtfully.

"You need to keep all this under your hat, Cece. I shouldn't even be talking about it."

I crossed my heart and put my fingers to my lips. Harold smiled.

"How was she killed? I mean, you can't just run someone through a power saw." I shuddered.

"Strangled."

"Can you get fingerprints from flesh?" I asked.

"Sometimes, but she was wearing a turtle neck, and, like I said, whoever did it wore gloves."

"So it happened downstairs?"

"We don't know. Forensics didn't find evidence of a struggle anywhere, but whoever did it planned carefully and clearly knew how to clean up."

I pondered this statement for a moment.

"Anything else?"

Before answering, Harold again swore me to silence.

"We have a time frame of sorts because the computer recorded someone accessing the system around ten on Friday night of the weekend before Bond was found."

"Wouldn't someone have had to sign into the system?"

"Good question, and the answer is no. The workstation was left open because they were loading so much stuff into the system, and the room is kept locked. The techies are all kicking themselves for not locking the system down, but it was convenient to have it open, and they were still debating who should have access and how to set the log on."

"So you know when and how but not who or where."

"Yeah. .500's only good if you're a batter." Harold sighed. "So what did you want to talk about?"

I had decided not to tell Harold about Miranda or Frank O'Donnell lest they end up victims of the unfocused investigation.

"Actually, this. Idle curiosity," I assured him. "I was wondering how the investigation was going. You know how I've always loved mysteries, and since I was there when she was found, I guess I feel a special interest."

Harold studied me for a moment with his cop's eyes but did not press the point.

"If there's anything else, Cece, just give me a call. You ought to come to dinner, and I'll walk you through the garden. In two or three weeks, it should start producing early lettuce. I'll have Jeanette call you."

"How are the kids?" I asked as we stood up.

"Larry seems to be on one long party. We don't see much of him, but I'm worried. I wish you'd talk to him."

"I haven't seen him this year at all. He used to stop in for lunch sometimes last year. Is he still at the university?"

"Supposedly, but his grades were in the toilet last term, and I doubt they'll be any better this time around."

"Maybe he needs a break, some time to grow up. A lot of young people take much longer than you and I did to grow up." Harold frowned. "How's Karen?" Now he smiled broadly.

"Great, and those kids of hers are the light of my life."

"Are they going to be here today?" I asked as he opened the door.

Suddenly, two small children wrapped themselves around his legs, squealing, "Papaw! Papaw! We didn't know where you were!"

Their mother, a slim brunette with Harold's clear blue eyes, came up and kissed his cheek.

"You're the main attraction, Dad!"

"Hi, Karen." We hugged. "Your dad and I were just catching up. He sure thinks the world of these two."

"It's mutual."

"What are you doing these days besides chasing these kiddos?"

"I'm still working full time at the accounting firm, but I'm hoping to go part time when we can afford it, or maybe even start my own business. Full time is hard with the kids."

I spent the rest of the afternoon visiting with my extended family. Karen took me aside later and also asked me to talk to her brother. She was clearly worried that he was moving toward some serious trouble so I promised to talk with him. I saw my parents and promised to call and make a dinner date for later in the week. I ate hummus and green salad but also jello salad with marshmallows, Frito pie, three-bean salad, macaroni and cheese, and lots of chips with dip, not to mention having both cake and pie for dessert. On the drive home, I assuaged my guilt by telling myself that the family only gathered twice a year, and the meal had only been four bucks plus humus and crackers.

My phone woke me at ten on Sunday. No caller's name popped up so I answered hesitantly.

"Is this Dr. Brinkman?"

"Yes, this is she."

"This is Maureen Shaughnessy."

"Who?"

"Maureen Shaughnessy, the Provost."

"I'm sorry, Dr. Shaughnessy, but I'm not quite awake."

"I apologize for waking you."

"That's okay."

"I'd like to talk with you today. I was wondering if you could come to my house for lunch."

"Of course, but I don't know where you live."

One o'clock found me ringing the doorbell of a painted brick house in one of the city's expensive, older subdivisions. Once I was fully awake, the invitation seemed even weirder so I had spent the morning researching Maureen Shaughnessy. Although I had met her a few times during her three years at the university, we had never done more than shake hands and exchange a pleasant greeting at a large function. She was an impressive speaker, partly because of her low-pitched, husky voice but mostly because she had the "gift of the blarney." Her wit was quick, and her warmth always felt genuine. No matter how large or hostile the gathering, she was able to make people feel she was on their side, catching even cynical faculty members in the web of her charm. I suspect her earlier experience as a prosecutor explained her rhetorical skills.

For no discernible reason, after beginning a successful law career, she returned to a prestigious graduate school where she completed a doctorate in history. Almost as soon as she earned tenure at a large mid-western university, she had been tapped for administration where she had quickly risen to the rank of Vice President for Personnel, a big job. A profile of female college administrators in a national publication informed me that she was 55, had two grown daughters, and described herself as "long divorced." I found out that Silvano DiGiorgio, her former husband, was 65, and for an impressive thirty-five years, had been the head prosecutor in the office where Shaughnessy had once interned and then worked.

Maureen Shaughnessy opened the door herself and immediately held out her hand, saying, "Thank you so much for coming."

"Not at all." I shook her outstretched hand.

"I hope you won't mind, but I just made us salads and threw some cheese on a platter," she said, leading me into the kitchen. "Just put your purse and jacket there." She gestured to a small desk and chair in the corner.

"Do you like to cook?" I asked, surveying the pots and pans that hung over the island which was about the size of my entire kitchen.

"I do, but I have so little time these days. Come sit down."

We sat at an old, oak, farm table in a small alcove with bay windows overlooking the yard.

14

"What would you like to drink? I've set out Prosecco and water, but if you would like a soft drink or iced tea...."

"I love Prosecco!"

"Good." She poured two glasses of the effervescent wine. "We'll have coffee with dessert." She sat down across from me. We each had a large bowl of several kinds of lettuce, artichoke hearts, small tomatoes, hard-boiled eggs, and grated Parmesan cheese. In the center of the table was a cutting board with three wedges of cheese and a basket of crackers.

"I didn't even ask what you like to eat. This dressing is a homemade vinaigrette with citrus, but if you'd like something else, there are other dressings."

"No, this is fine. So much better than what I would be eating at home."

I dressed my salad and passed the bottle to Shaughnessy. Her fingers were slender and well-manicured. She wore a diamond ring on her right hand and pearl earrings but no other jewelry with her dark pants and casual sweater. She had a nice, slightly plump figure and striking coloring: dark hair which she probably dyed, dark blue eyes, and long black lashes all set off by porcelain white skin.

"Black Irish," I thought, amazed as always when anyone in our great melting pot country exhibits the clear look of their ancestors. Her face had what my mother would have called "Good bones." Even the further passage of time would not erase her high cheekbones and fine jaw line.

"Please help yourself to the cheese and crackers," she urged me with a smile. "I am trying to restrain myself. I love cheese, but the dinners out are putting on pounds I don't need."

We ate for another few moments in silence, and I realized that she was studying me as much as I was her. I decided to wait her out, and when half my salad was gone, she finally spoke.

"You must be wondering why I asked you to lunch."

"My sparkling personality?" She let out a surprisingly unladylike guffaw and in that moment, I began to like her.

"Thanks for making me laugh. I haven't been doing enough of it lately."

"When I need to laugh, I just think about the Cannibal Deli."

"Cannibal Deli?"

"One day this English professor went into the Cannibal Deli and looked at the menu board. English professor brains were $2.99 per pound, Math professor brains were $1.59 per pound, Film professor brains were $5.99 per pound, but college deans' brains were $12.99 per pound. The English professor was insulted and asked why deans' brains were so expensive. The owner said, 'Do you realize how many deans it takes to get a pound of brains?'"

When Shaughnessy finally stopped laughing and wiped her eyes, I explained, "I just fill in the professions and prices according to the situation, and I can usually make myself laugh."

"Thanks so much for sharing a tool I will be using almost every day. I suspect the most expensive brains in my deli might come from either big donors or the Board of Trustees, especially this latest group."

She reached out and re-filled both our wine glasses.

"So why did you invite me to lunch? You don't even know me. And why lunch at your house?"

"Lunch at my house because I wanted our conversation to be private. I do, however, know something about you."

"My tenure case? The lawsuit?"

"Not just that. Two years ago, Sam Jacoby came to me because he had discovered materials were going out the back door of the Buildings and Grounds Division. We hired a private investigator who sent someone undercover to work there. We ended up firing five employees and prosecuting the ringleader who was selling university building supplies to a contractor friend. We discovered that when we got a shipment of drywall or paint or pipes, close to a quarter of the shipment was missing so there would have to be a second order. Needless to say, not just the materials but the job-time lost cost us an enormous amount of money. Do you know how we found out about this operation?"

"Maybe," I said hesitantly.

"Does the name Isaiah Johnson ring any bells?"

"Of course. His wife Shameka is on maintenance in my building and is kind of a friend of mine."

"Kind of a friend?"

"We talk. I like her, and she likes me so one day she told me how upset her husband was when he started working for the university and saw people stealing."

"So what happened?"

"I went online and studied the institutional flowchart to figure out who the head of Buildings and Grounds reported to. I was worried, and Isaiah was petrified that if he complained to his boss, he would get fired. He suspected the boss might also be on the take. So I figured out which Vice President that operation reported to and made an appointment to see Sam Jacoby."

"Sam suggested that I talk to you."

"Why? Anyone could have figured out what Isaiah needed to do."

"But you didn't figure out what Isaiah needed to do. You figured out what *you* needed to do. First," her voice took on the driving tone of someone used to presenting logical and convincing arguments without interruption, "You are friendly with the woman who empties your trash. Second, she trusts you enough to tell you when her husband has a problem. Third, you took the time and had the practical sense, not to mention computer skills, to figure out who to see and how not to implicate Isaiah with his boss. Fourth, you took the time to do it. Fifth, you were not intimidated by Sam's skepticism. He says he gave you a pretty hard time."

I smiled at the memory because in two minutes I had figured out that Sam Jacoby was a lot like many of the men in my family—big bark, no bite, basically a decent guy.

"Finally, and perhaps most importantly, you were discreet." She studied me for a long moment before adding, "Finish your lunch. I'll make coffee and we can talk in the den."

Chapter Four

"So what do you know about LouAnn Bond?" Shaughnessy asked as we settled ourselves in the comfortable den that opened off the kitchen. The picture window overlooked the garden, but my eye was caught by the large oil painting over the fireplace that showed two young women playing cards. They were both looking up and regarding the viewer with the same bright look of affection. The resemblance to Shaughnessy was clear in their high cheekbones and smiles, but the difference in their coloring was striking. One had inherited Shaughnessy's fair skin and black hair, but her eyes were brown. The other had olive skin and curly dark hair but the same soft, dark eyes as her sister.

"What beautiful daughters you have! And what a lovely painting."

"I took the photograph when they were in college and had come home for Christmas. Simona was graduating in the spring so it occurred to me that it might be the last Christmas they would be together in that way—at home, both students, sisters doing the same thing. I met the painter through a friend—actually," she added with a wry smile, "Someone on the Board of Trustees. They aren't all bad!"

I laughed.

"Do you see them much?"

"The Board? Too much!"

"No, your daughters. What are their names?"

"Simona and Carlotta."

"Whoa—not so Irish!"

"No. They're named for their father's grandmothers. He's first generation Italian."

I shot her a quizzical look.

"I was young and in love and definitely not in charge." She sighed. "I don't see the girls often enough now that they are both working."

"What do they do?"

"Simona's an account executive for an advertising agency in New York. She's 28. Carlotta is going to be 30. She's practicing immigration law in Los Angeles."

"You must have still been in law school when they were born."

"I had just finished and was newly married when I had Carlotta. I went right to work for the prosecutor's office when I graduated—I had interned there for two summers during law school. Simona came along barely two years later."

"It must have been tough having two so close together. My cousin did the same thing, and the kids themselves are very close, but it's been hard on her and her husband."

"Yeah, it was tough in a lot of ways," she remarked drily.

"I can't believe you did a PhD when they were in elementary school."

She looked at me for a moment and said, "You've done your homework, Sherlock." I blushed. "Don't be embarrassed. After the divorce, my mother came to live with us. She got me through. It would be no exaggeration to say that she saved my life."

"Where does she live now?"

"She died four years ago—the year before I took this job. Until then, she lived with me, and I still miss her every day." She gazed out at the garden, and I have rarely seen anyone look lonelier.

"So now you know most of what there is to know about me," she said brusquely, "And I've done my homework so I know most of what there is to know about you."

"And what exactly is that?" I asked, annoyed that she thought I could be summed up by the results of an internet search or forms in a personnel file.

"I didn't mean to be insulting." She paused, and for the first time, looked uneasy. "I need help, and I'm not used to asking for it."

"Fair enough."

"Everything we talk about has to be completely off the record. If anyone ever sees us meeting casually—eating dinner or lunch—we share scholarly interests."

"Actually we do. I looked up your dissertation on the Suffragist movement."

"Who would ever have guessed that tome would come in handy as something other than a doorstop?" We both laughed. "Okay, so what do you know about LouAnn Bond?"

After extracting an equal promise of confidentiality from Shaughnessy, I spent the next twenty minutes sharing everything I had heard about Bond in the last two weeks, ending with the conversation I had overheard in the stairwell between Bond and Frank O'Donnell.

"What a totally pernicious bitch she was." Shaughnessy spoke with real venom. "For every story you've told me, I could supply five more which is why the police are getting nowhere with their investigation."

"Did everyone hate her?"

"Only those who knew her."

"What about you?"

"I was raised Catholic and, like all good Catholic girls, I was taught not to hate people," she said primly, and then added with a grim smile, "So I just despised her."

"What did she do to you?"

"Anything and everything she could to make me look bad in the President's eyes."

"Why?"

"I was the first woman Provost, and I think that she was jealous."

"So what specifically did she do to you?"

"At first, she left a few important meetings off my calendar to make me look irresponsible, but I soon stopped her by showing her how I could and would provide computer evidence that she had never posted the dates to my calendar. So she stopped doing that. Whenever something prevented my being at an event, she had a snide way of insinuating I did not want to be there. One of the trustees tipped me off to this, and I had to sort her out about telling people, especially the trustees, exactly what I told her to tell them. I threatened to tell the President if it happened again. That particular threat worked."

"This kind of harassment should be grounds for firing someone who works for the university."

"Ah, but LouAnn did not just work for the university."

"I was wondering about her salary." Shaughnessy shot me a puzzled look. "I checked it out and $30,000 per year seemed very low pay for her job as Special Assistant to the President." She laughed briefly.

"The Foundation for University Development files aren't public. LouAnn Bond was paid another $90,000 by the foundation. The university could fire her, but to get rid of her would take a foundation firing, and the trustees for the foundation are mostly people who sit on the university's board and, of course, the President is the Chair, so it would practically take an act of God to get rid of LouAnn." A look of horror suddenly crossed Shaughnessy's face. "I can't believe I said that."

"It's nothing a lot of people would not like to say."

"I haven't told you the rest."

"What?"

"You know Kenneth—the President—is fairly old school."

"Conservative?"

"He's older than I am—in his late 60's. He was raised in a small, midwestern town, and he's a bit religious. He's not politically or educationally conservative, but personally, in the way he judges people's character, he is conservative--if that makes any sense." I nodded. "About six months ago, LouAnn came to see me and said that she was going to tell the President that Sam Jacoby and I were having an affair."

"What?"

"Big picture, Celeste. Stay with me. Last year the football coach was all over the papers for having it off with a cheerleader while his wife was six months pregnant.

20

The year before, we had that mess where the assistant registrar was trading grades for sex with his student workers."

I groaned.

"So tell me exactly what happened."

"She asked to see me late one Friday afternoon. That seemed weird, but she said it was important. By the time she came to my office, everyone was gone for the day. She sat across the desk from me and told me that she knew Sam and I had shared a room on the trip to the football tournament. I asked her how she knew this, and she said that when she called my room at 3 a.m. and asked for Sam Jacoby, he was there and answered the phone. She said that she had taped it."

"I can't believe it."

"I couldn't, at first, but when I asked Sam about it, he remembered the call much more clearly than I did. It had seemed weird because as soon as Sam identified himself, the caller had asked him to repeat his name and then hung up. Sam immediately called home to check on his wife, but everything was fine."

"Wife? Whoa. I think we had better back up."

"Sam and I have been seeing each other since my first year here. His wife has Alzheimer's. Before I got here, he could still take her to some functions, but now she doesn't recognize anyone and barely speaks. Anyway, he and I are friends."

"So how did she find out about you two?"

"I have no idea. We haven't made a great secret of our friendship and do go out, usually to plays or movies. We have orchestra and opera tickets together."

"And you sometimes get together at out-of-town athletic events."

"Often."

"So what did she want?"

"Nothing immediately. She suggested that if she told the President, he would fire me and possibly Sam. She told me how displeased he would be by our relationship and the scandal it could cause, especially among the Board of Trustees."

"Wait a minute. Scandal? The Trustees? From what I've observed, they have enough business fiddles and hanky-panky of their own going on to keep them from throwing any large-sized rocks at your glass house."

"It would seem so, but the current Board, thanks to our right-wing governor's appointments, has a block of politically powerful religious conservatives who blow hard and holy in public at the least excuse."

"So what did she offer in exchange for her silence?"

"She wanted me to convince the President to appoint Mary Beth Hays to head the President's Committee on Women although she hinted there would probably be future favors she would need in return for keeping her mouth shut."

"So what happened?"

"I went along with her, which pleased her no end. It makes me want to take a bath just thinking about the way she smiled at me as she left the office. When I was with the Prosecutor's office, I occasionally had to deal with police informants, mostly toads who would sell their mothers for money or drugs. She reminded me of them."

"So did you deliver?"

Shaughnessy laughed bitterly.

"Didn't have to. Mary Beth Hays ended up with the job—I'm not sure how, but I never said a word."

Shaughnessy refilled our mugs from the carafe on the coffee table.

"So who was Mary Beth Hays up against for the appointment?"

"Why?"

"I just wonder if Bond's interference was about her getting the job or someone else getting screwed."

"Perceptive, but I honestly don't remember all the details. You'd have to talk to Mary Beth or maybe Elizabeth Barr—she was Chair previously."

"I know Liz pretty well so I will probably talk to her first," I said, and then felt embarrassed to realize I had indicated a commitment without knowing what I was being asked to commit myself to.

"Did Bond tell the President about you and Sam?"

Shaughnessy smiled slyly.

"I told him myself. At the Christmas party, Kenneth was talking to me like a Dutch uncle—he does like to wax avuncular if you are even two minutes younger than he is and especially if you are an unmarried female. He was telling me how I needed something besides work in my life, and I figured his trips to the punch bowl were all to the good so I told him that Sam and I were seeing each other."

"How'd he take it?"

"For a moment, he was rather shocked, but then he said, 'I've known Sam and Judith Jacoby for years, ever since I came here to be president. We used to see them socially until Judith got so bad. When we marry for better or worse, we never know what the 'worse' might be. I'm glad Sam has your friendship. Just be discreet.'"

"And that was it?"

"Yes, but it made me feel bad."

"Why?"

"I had never given Kenneth credit for being at all perceptive about personal relationships. In fact, he takes me on fund-raising trips so I can provide the warm, personal touch. He just does not read people very well."

"But he's clearly fond of both you and Dr. Jacoby."

"Yes. I've always thought he was just using both of us, but I do think he cares. He's just not very good at showing he cares."

We fell silent for a moment. I was caught in contemplating "for better or worse" as a vow and remembering the words in *King Lear* about things not being the worst 'as long as we can say they are the worst," as if the ultimate horror is something beyond words—like the loss of language that comes with Alzheimer's.

"So, Dr. Shaughnessy, why am I here?"

"First, call me Maureen, and I'll call you Celeste. Second, I need help."

"Okay, but what kind of help do you need?"

"It's March, and LouAnn Bond's body was discovered almost three weeks ago. For about a week, the detective in charge of the investigation was calling me every day and reporting their progress. Now he isn't returning my calls. I don't think they have a clue, but we need to get this solved. The social media is killing us. All kinds of wild rumors about serial killers and organ harvesters in the library. How do you think that's going to play out in the next month or two when our high-profile students are evaluating their scholarship offers? Would your mother have liked you to have a scholarship to Serial Killer U?"

"Actually, my folks were hoping for me to get a scholarship anywhere!"

I laughed, and Maureen smiled.

"I know what you are saying. I hear plenty from my students. They are scared. So what do you want me to do?"

"I want to appoint you as my Assistant for Special Projects. I can get you out of one of your classes this term, and you can take that time to investigate. I will put you on a supplemental salary."

Visions of sugarplums and paid-up credit cards danced in my head, but then I thought of my students.

"I can't stop teaching one of my classes—we're almost half way through the term."

"I appreciate your dedication…"

"Don't make light of this," I said angrily. "I have a commitment, and I need to stay in the classroom."

"How about I release you from your courses next fall term? You can use that term for your research. I will pay you the supplemental salary through the summer so you will have a nest egg you can use to travel or hire a research assistant."

"Actually I'll be using it to pay off my legal bills," I said flatly. She raised her eyebrows. "The lawyer who won my tenure case did not come cheap so given the raise I got for my promotion, the victory proved rather Pyrrhic. I still owe my folks two thousand dollars, give or take a few hundred."

"I understand. If you solve this, I will settle the loan with your parents."

"What? I was just spouting off!" I could feel myself flushing with embarrassment.

"For Heaven's sake, I won't use university funds. I plan to get some work out of you for what I'm paying, but I will personally pay off your loan."

"Can we just discuss it if and when the time comes?" I murmured uncomfortably.

"Of course," she replied. "I will announce your appointment on Monday. I'll include vague things like help with recruiting students and reviewing the new library implementation. You already sit on the Library Advisory Committee, but now you'll be my liaison. We'll let your department know. Since you'll be on my staff, you'll automatically be invited to any and all events sponsored by the administration."

"That means things involving the Board of Trustees?"

"Of course. Why?"

"I have no entrée there, but since Bond worked so closely with them, I think it might be worth taking a look."

"I agree."

"What was her relationship to the President? Haven't people complained to him about her?"

"I don't know," Maureen said thoughtfully. "Your professor friend didn't complain to him. Sam and I didn't complain to him, and Frank O'Donnell didn't complain to him although she overstepped boundaries in all three cases. We also know there's something going on with Mary Beth Hays and the President's Committee on Women, but I don't think anyone from the committee has complained."

"Did Bond control the finances?"

"The President has a large discretionary fund that I am sure she had some control over although Marilyn Wilhoyt does the actual financial work."

"Is there any way someone can get a look at the books?"

"That's complicated to do on the quiet, but I'll see."

"What about her e-mails?"

"The computer people had to produce them all for the police."

"Who's in charge?"

"That kid with the pink hair who looks like he's still in diapers. I can't think of his name."

"Nathan Ramirez," I said, smiling. "He graduated last year with a double major in English and Computer Science."

"You know him?"

"He's my buddy, actually," I said. "I'll talk to him. He will need to call you--he's no pushover on security."

"I'll put his name on my assistant's desk as a call to put through no matter what."

"Can he e-mail you? He's better on modern methods of communication."

"An English major?"

"Yes, and wonderful, but he insists the old stuff—meaning literature--is just for recreation."

"Why doesn't he text me instead?" She went to the desk and came back with two cards on which she had written a phone number. "This is my cell phone. Please don't write it on any bathroom walls."

I laughed and nodded, saying, "I need to ask you something."

"What?"

"Do you suspect anyone in particular?"

Maureen laughed loudly.

"Has anyone so far had a good word to say for the deceased?"

I shook my head, thinking how many casual remarks about her death I had heard and how not even one person had expressed the least sadness about her death.

"To my way of thinking," Maureen said succinctly, "The only thing that may narrow the hunt is that she had no life outside this university."

Chapter Five

That afternoon I called Liz Barr, the former chair of the President's Committee on Women. I figured talking to her would give me a start on this bizarre research project. The possibilities of publication crossed my mind, and I chuckled ironically as I listened to her phone ring.

"Hey, Liz, it's Celeste." My mother loves old movies and especially loves Celeste Holme in *All About Eve* although, good Catholic that Mom is, *Come to the Stable* is her true favorite. One thing about being named Celeste--you never have to say more than your first name—a blessing with a last name like Brinkman.

"Hi, Celeste. How are you?"

"Good. Listen, I read about your sabbatical research in the University News and was wondering if you would like to grab a cup of coffee this afternoon. I'd like to hear more."

"I'm flattered. How about four at The Corner?"

"Great! I'll see you then."

Four o'clock found me searching the coffee house for Liz, who walked in five minutes late, saying, "Sorry I'm late."

"No problem. I hope we can find a booth." I scanned the crowded coffee house. "I see one in the back. Here, get me a large cappuccino, and I'll go grab that table."

I handed her a bill and moved quickly toward a table where three young students were stuffing papers into their backpacks. A few moments later, Liz joined me with two steaming cups of coffee.

"I love the coffee here. They've switched to Fair Trade, you know."

I nodded and meeting Liz's earnest gray eyes remembered why I did not see more of this responsible, smart, good person with whom I shared many values and interests. "Serious as a heart attack," my dad would say.

"So tell me about the sabbatical."

We spent the next twenty minutes talking about her research until I finally steered the conversation toward my real interest by asking how her research would impact her work as the former Chair of the President's Committee on Women.

"I want to form a support group for Latinas on campus. I've gotten Miranda Lopez Gianinni and Linda Rodriguez plus someone from Women United to help with the group. The Committee voted last month to fund the project."

"So did Cass Britten drop off the Committee when she didn't get the Chair?" I asked casually. I had done some research to find out who the players were.

"Unfortunately not," muttered Liz, looking at her coffee.

"Cass is a colleague of mine, and I consider her a friend, but I know she isn't always easy to get along with." I felt a stab of guilt--Cass is far and away my favorite colleague.

"That's certainly true. When the President appointed Mary Beth as Chair, Cass asked to chair the Lectures and Events committee."

"Why didn't Cass become Chair? Doesn't the position automatically go to the Vice Chair?"

"No one knows what happened. Cass just said that she couldn't do it for personal reasons, but she could chair Lectures and Events so that's where she ended up."

"Not a bad call—she has great ideas, lots of energy, and interesting contacts all over."

"And she's very persuasive," said Liz darkly.

"What happened?" I asked, feeling like I should have been paying more attention.

"That fall series on issues for transgender people that caused such a brouhaha," she began, and I nodded. "That was all her idea. She convinced the committee and recruited the speakers."

"It was wildly successful--clearly the most successful part of Coming Out Week this year."

"You went to the lectures?"

"Of course—all three. I learned a lot. I thought the lawyer who talked about legal issues for transgender people was especially interesting."

"It was successful," Liz admitted reluctantly, "But it caused an enormous stir in the community."

I remembered a single article in the newspaper which was followed by a series of right-wing op ed pieces and venomous letters to the editor.

"Of course, but sometimes this community needs to be stirred up or they'd still be living comfortably in caves," I replied, and then, fearing I would shut down further conversation, added, "But that's just my hometown perspective! Go on."

"You know there's a block of very conservative trustees on the Board now. They contacted some legislators, and there was a big conservative backlash. For the Family—you know that reactionary group—got people to call and write the President to protest tax money generally and his budget specifically being used to fund such speakers."

"I thought he did well defending the university as a bastion of free speech and marketplace of ideas."

"He did, but he also met with Cass."

"What did he tell her?"

"You'd have to ask her."

"Did he ask her to resign from chairing the Lectures committee?"

"I don't think so—she's still the chair. All the appointments on the Committee on Women are at the President's pleasure," Liz reminded me. "Before this lecture mess there was no problem with Cass that I know of. I don't know why she chose not to be Chair, but now I'm glad. I am sure we will take a closer look at her committee's proposals in the future," she added primly.

I wanted to say something about how the President's Committee on Women could be a powerful agent for change on campus, but I held my tongue.

"Besides," Liz continued, "Mary Beth Hays is doing a great job. She has the meetings down to an hour and a half a month and sticks to the agenda. I don't know whose idea it was to have thirty people on this committee."

I bit my tongue to keep from saying, "Probably someone who didn't want the Committee to address real issues concerning women on campus." Instead, I asked, "So how are things in Sociology?"

Liz launched into a long analysis of department politics that took us to the end of our coffees. We parted, promising to meet more often. Because of my new position, I felt much less guilty than usual about having the large cappuccino and eating out as I rushed home to shower and dress for my date with Marshall.

We went to Da Mama, a new Italian restaurant, and had a wonderful meal. In fact, our conversation divided itself neatly between Italian food (past, present, and future) and Marshall's research in chemistry, which he miraculously managed to make both accessible and interesting to me. We were so easy together that I caught myself almost telling him about Maureen Shaughnessy's request.

"Everyone seems to have something nasty to say about LouAnn Bond," I idly remarked as we were eating the delicious homemade gelato.

"Don't I know," he said grimly.

"You too?"

"I only had dealings with her once. It was back when I first came here."

"That's amazing. I've never had any dealings with the President's office."

"Well, your aunt isn't Mariama N'Dour." I drew a complete blank.

"I'm sorry, Marshall. My field is English literature, specifically nineteenth and twentieth century women's literature. Narrow. I know nothing, and I mean nothing, about African literature or film or culture or anything."

"My aunt, my father's older sister, is a famous filmmaker in Senegal. She is also well known in France."

"Really?"

"Yes, really," he said, mocking my tone.

"I'm still not putting this together."

"I met Ben Rosemont at a gathering for new faculty the year we both got here. When I found out he was chair of the new film department, just to make conversation, I told him about my aunt. When they started the film program here, they wanted to show a series of international films to make it clear that the program was not just about classic Hollywood movies or American film history."

"So what happened?"

"I don't know what happened exactly, but apparently because this event was to celebrate both the new program and the renovation of that old warehouse, the President's office was involved."

"Not exactly," I interrupted. "The Showalter family, who are richer than God, put up the money for the renovation, the lecture, and a professorship. That's how the old warehouse got turned into a state-of-the-art theatre and also how we got Ben Rosemont to chair that program. Trust me--keeping the Showalters happy is why the President's office was involved."

"Okay, admittedly I had no clue about any of this, but one day I got a call from the President's office. It's LouAnn Bond who invites me over for a chat and tells me that she wants me to persuade my aunt to give the keynote lecture to celebrate the opening of the building and program. I told her that I did not think my aunt would come, but I would ask her, and I did. When I talked to her, she just laughed and said there was no way she would do this."

"Why not?"

"First, her English is not that good. Second, she was in the middle of editing her latest film. Third, she suspected that both her films and lecture would be too radical for an audience of nice, rich, American donors. Most of her films, she reminded me, deal with neocolonialism and its impact on women. This includes American investment abroad and involvement in sex tourism." I whistled softly.

"I need to see her films, but not to get sidetracked, what did you do?"

"I told Bond the first two reasons."

"So what happened?"

"Over the next two weeks, she called and e-mailed me frequently to urge me to reason with my aunt. She kept saying, 'The President would so appreciate your efforts.' She simply would not take no for an answer. I finally got angry when she insinuated that my lack of cooperation could damage or, as she put it, 'cloud' my prospects at the university. I told her that the Chemistry Department, not the President and definitely not LouAnn Bond, would be making my tenure decision and that I did not think we should have any further communication."

"That was it?"

"Yes, except as we hung up, she said in this creepy, sort of threatening voice, 'Don't be so sure we won't be speaking again in the future.'"

"Nasty."

"Yes. It was my first year so I told my Chair the whole story. He laughed and said, 'Forget it. She's only dangerous if you want the President's money.'"

"What did he mean?"

"I have no idea and didn't ask because I had no interest in that money."

"Have you heard anyone say anything nice about her?"

"Only what the President said about her career at the news conference after they identified her body."

After my morning classes on Monday, I went to Cass Britten's office and rapped on the door.

"Come in," a muffled voice called, and I entered to find her looking up at me over the edge of her desk.

"Hi, Cass. New work strategy?"

"Goddamn fucking cheap-ass piece-of-shit printer comes unplugged." She extricated her six-foot frame from under the desk and stood up.

"What brings you here, sunshine? Ready to give up men?"

"If the level of romance in my life—which is currently zero—does not improve soon, I may be reconsidering my orientation," I admitted.

"Put me on your speed dial, cupcake," chuckled Cass.

"Have you had lunch?"

"Is this a date?"

"Not a date-date," I laughed, "Just a friend-date."

Cass rolled her blue eyes in comic exasperation and reached for her purse.

"Let's go eat Indian. I'm starving, and I'm parked right outside."

"Where?"

Since parking permits, at the level I was allowed to purchase and could afford, were merely licenses to hunt over distant acres of blacktop, I could not keep the amazement out of my voice.

"You'll see," she said with a wink.

"So you haven't died and been given a place of the elect?"

"Nope. I'm still very much with you, as our esteemed chair will angrily attest, but I have friends in low places," she said, her voice dropping to a conspiratorial whisper.

We rode down in the elevator, went out the back door of the building, and turned a corner to where the dumpsters and a red Toyota shared an alcove behind a brick wall. Cass backed up, and I got in as she tucked a sign, emblazoned with the university logo and "Technical Services," behind her seat.

"Who gave you that?"

"I borrowed one and made my own."

"You park here every day?" I asked, filled with admiration.

"Not on Tuesday—that's when the trash truck comes."

"What if someone finds out?"

"I take the Tech gang cookies at Christmas and occasional treats plus I help some of our mentally challenged faculty find the space bar on their keyboards—the Techies appreciate my assistance."

I was helpless with laughter.

"''Tis sport to see the engineer hoist with his own petard,'" she quoted, and I nodded in enthusiastic agreement as we sped toward New Delhi Delight, the nearest Indian restaurant. Arriving after the lunch rush, we easily found a table, went to fill our plates at the buffet, ordered chai, and began eating.

"Delicious and cheap," I commented happily.

"I hope my breath blows the little darlings out of office hours," Cass said, spooning more onion chutney onto her plate. "So what's on your mind?"

"You don't think I'm just after the not-inconsiderable pleasure of your company?"

She shot me a skeptical look as she shoveled in rice and saag paneer.

"I want to talk to you about the President's Committee on Women."

"Actually, it's called the President's Committee to Keep Pussy in Its Place," she replied sharply.

"What happened? Why aren't you Chair?"

"Why do you want to know?"

"I've been asked to consider filling the next at-large position when it comes vacant, and I want to know what I'm getting into. I'm not very good at keeping my mouth shut…"

"You're a fuckin' clam compared to me," Cass snapped, and then added, "But you're right. As a person equipped with a functioning brain and state-of-the-art bullshit detector, you might have some problems."

She had gone for my explanation without question. I felt proud of my invention but also sad about being less than honest with Cass. At 41, she was older than I, but she had come to the department two years after me and represented the next great wave of change. An out-lesbian who specialized in Renaissance poetry and Women's Lit, she was the first colleague to benefit from my traumatic tenure battle. We had immediately become allies. Although we were friends, her various romances, not to mention her rigorous training for and competition in triathlons, kept her occupied or took her out of town so often that we never spent much time together outside the university.

"Weren't you supposed to be Chair after you put in your time as Vice Chair?"

"That's the way it's supposed to happen, but we all serve at the pleasure of His Majesty Kenneth the Silver of Hair and Tongue." We ate for a few moments in silence. "He had that fuckin' Bond Bitch tell me. I assumed that he didn't even have the balls to meet with me himself," said Cass furiously, two red spots appearing on her cheeks.

"What?"

"I'm glad the bitch is dead," she said bluntly. "I almost fuckin' killed her myself that day."

Puzzled and, unsure what to ask, I waited.

"Right before last semester began, Bond called me to make an appointment with the President. I got there, thinking he was going to tell me how overjoyed he was to have me as Chair of the President's Committee on Women, since I like everything about women. Instead, when I got there, the bitch took me into her office. She told me that the President did not feel I was the 'right person' for the job. When I asked her what she meant, she said that he wasn't sure I was the 'right person' to represent university women. She kept giving me this leer like I should understand what she meant and take a hint."

"What did you do?"

"I said that I didn't know 'what the fuck' she was 'talking about'—an exact quote, my dear, and she got off on my language—she gave me a kind of Emily Post lecture on swearing and ended by saying, 'It's not just your language, it's your activities.' So I said, playing dense, 'You mean the stuff that's on my Curriculum Vitae?' She said 'not exactly' and waited like I should play twenty questions with her so I said, 'Is it the stuff on my Extra-Curricular Vitae?' I don't think she got the joke at all, but she said that I should be more discreet in my public behavior. I almost said, 'Public or pubic,' but I do have some restraint."

I snorted, and Cass chuckled but then looked at me with genuine sadness.

"I told her that I understood—and I thought I did. I told her that I would like to remain on the Committee, and she said that would be possible as long as I remained discreet about our conversation. And that was it. I was furious, but they had me over a barrel because I, like everyone on the committee, was appointed by the President. I assumed Bond was being a good little Nazi and just carrying out orders. So my plan was to cause enough trouble to make both His Majesty and that Bond bitch regret what they'd done and be very wary of doing it to anyone else."

"So you never actually met with the President?"

"Not then."

"There's something I'm not following here. What is it about your 'public behavior?' What did she mean?"

"I thought she meant that I am a lesbian and make no secret of it, but I eventually found out that wasn't it."

"Couldn't you have gotten the committee members to protest?"

Cass rolled her eyes.

"They are terrified of the President, scared shitless and witless that he will disband the committee so they don't do anything of significance. Well," she smiled lyly, "Sometimes they accidentally sponsor something that rocks the boat, but most of the time they are all just marking it down as an item on their CV and enjoying the free lunch, which, by the way, usually sucks."

"Doesn't sound much like my kind of thing since I hate meetings." I thought for a moment. "I'm still not clear on what Bond meant about your 'public behavior.'"

"Can I trust you to be more discreet than I apparently am?"

I looked at Cass and realized that she was serious.

"My mother, thank God, doesn't have a grave I can swear on, and I know from the Bard that I shouldn't swear by the moon…"

"Okay, okay," she murmured, still not smiling, and said, "When Maureen Shaughnessy first came here, she and I were together."

I almost spit tikka masala across the table.

"What?"

Cass did not say anything for a long time and then quipped, "Take a lesson, honeybunch--some doors swing both ways."

As I waited for her to continue, I wondered furiously why Maureen had not told me about this affair and whether she had lied about Sam Jacoby.

"Irony of ironies, we met at the President's Committee on Women. When Maureen first came, she visited a lot of committees, and she attended some of our meetings to find out what was going on. We ended up talking and making a date for dinner."

"The rest is history?"

"Well, it wasn't past history, as we say, until she told me that she had to stop seeing me."

"Why?"

"She was very upset and kept assuring me that it had nothing to do with me or how she felt about me. I kept demanding an explanation, and she finally said that she was afraid her daughters might find out about us. Actually, she used the word 'terrified.' They were coming to visit the next week, but it still didn't make any sense. Her daughters don't live anywhere near here or even know anyone here. I kept telling her that they would never even have to meet me, but she was adamant. It didn't make any sense at all, but I finally had to accept her decision and decide heterosexual women are a bad bet." She looked at me with a smile, "But I'm willing to make an exception for you!"

I laughed, and we fell silent for a few moments.

"I saw the announcement where you're going to work for Maureen. That's great," Cass paused. I waited. "When I left Bond's office that day, I had the clear impression that she was personally pleased about screwing me. I thought about it for a few days and then I went to see Maureen at home."

"Why?" I asked, completely baffled by this turn.

"Maureen and I almost never went out in public together, but it suddenly dawned on me that one of the few university people who had ever seen us out together was Bond. We were celebrating our six-months' anniversary and decided to go to that little Italian place in Platteville. It's a forty-minute drive from here and only has five tables."

"Bella Vista?"

"Yeah, that's it. It's in the middle of nowhere. It's a kind of hobby restaurant for the owner who is also the chef, but I think he was some kind of tycoon in his other life. Anyway, we were sitting in this booth at the back of the restaurant on a Thursday night. We were holding hands and drinking a toast when someone said, 'Well, hello.' I'll never forget that sort of dirty-little-secret tone of hers. Maureen was quick and just said, 'Hello, LouAnn. What brings you here?' Bond said in this very cool tone, 'There's an outlet mall near here and I got lost looking for it so I stopped to get directions and use the restroom. I'll leave you two to your dinner.' She went on to the rest room and left. Maureen just laughed, but I could tell she was nervous because she had told me how Bond was out to get her. She ended things about two weeks later. After I talked to Bond, I went to see her, and she admitted the bitch had blackmailed her."

"I can't believe it!"

"But it's true. Bond blackmailed her. She threatened to tell the President that Maureen was a lesbian. When she didn't seem sufficiently afraid, the perverted bitch threatened to tell her daughters."

A wave of anger went through me as I thought of all Maureen had not told me.

"She couldn't afford to lose her job, and she felt like she could afford to lose me,' Cass said quietly.

"God, Cass, I'm so sorry. But her daughters…"

"I have no way to judge how they would have reacted, but I find it hard to believe Maureen Shaughnessy could raise children so lacking in understanding," Cass said flatly. Then she added bitterly, "Just so I had no illusions about our getting back together, Maureen told me that she was seeing Sam Jacoby. I could have fuckin' killed that Bond bitch with my bare hands, but someone else did me a favor."

"That's terrible. You can't mean it."

"You think not?" she asked looking me straight in the eye. "There's another little twist to this mess."

"What?"

"When the flap over the Coming Out Day lectures went down, the President was quick to call me in. In the course of reaming me a new one, he said, 'I can't imagine what you would have done as Chair of my Committee on Women. Thank God you weren't in a position to do it.' When I asked him what he meant, he said that he had been told by someone—he couldn't remember who or didn't want to say who, but I can certainly guess who it was—that I couldn't take the Chair because my mother vas ill, and I needed to spend time taking care of her. I told him my mother's been dead for twenty years so I hope he remembered who planted that lie in his pea-brain." She paused and drank some chai. "I keep hoping I'll find out he's on the down-low so I can drop a dime and call the Family Fuckers about it."

I laughed, and smiling ruefully, she added, "I think that whoever killed that bitch did the university and probably the world a huge service."

"You aren't alone," I assured her.

I called Maureen as soon as I got back to campus, and we agreed to meet at her house later in the evening.

"I'm surprised at the quick results," Maureen said as she opened the door.

"I had lunch with Cass Britten today," I said flatly and was pleased she had the grace to look uncomfortable.

Chapter Six

Maureen led me into the den where she immediately went to the bar. Her voice was normal when she asked, "What will you have? I'm drinking scotch. Will you join me?"

"Sure. On the rocks."

"You drink with the big girls," she said, handing me the glass and sitting down across from me.

I took a sip of the golden liquid and let myself appreciate its exquisite flavor.

"Nice," I said. "Now, why did you lie to me?"

Maureen studied the glass in her hand for several moments.

"I didn't lie," she began.

"We are both Catholics so we both know sin is sin and whether it is by commission or omission, it's still sin. You lied by your silence."

Maureen started to smile, and suddenly I was furious.

"Do you think I'm stupid? Did you think that I wouldn't talk to Cass after she was screwed out of the Chair for the President's Committee on Women? Did you think I'd miss or ignore that piece of the puzzle? Did you think Cass and I didn't know each other when we've taught for years in the same department?"

"I'm sorry," she began.

"I can't do what you want me to do if you won't tell me the truth. If you can't trust me about anything and everything, I cannot begin to try to do this job."

"Are you done?" Maureen asked in an even voice.

I had heard that she was good at running meetings, easily silencing both those who would sidetrack and those who would oppose her proposals. In a flash, I knew how she did it. She never lost sight of the prey and could force her opponent back to the chase in an instant.

Just as I began to feel both demeaned and insulted, she said, "I'm sorry. I am truly sorry, and I want you to know that."

I chose not to say anything.

"Do you accept my apology?"

I met her eyes and felt myself relenting.

"I do if you will promise to tell me the truth from now on."

"I promise." She got up to freshen her drink. "Can I freshen yours?" I shook my head.

"So tell me what happened."

"I haven't told anyone."

I was surprised to see tears in her eyes.

"Not even Cass?"

She shook her head. I waited patiently, sipping my scotch, while she blew her nose and cleared her throat.

"When I took the job here, both my daughters were away. Carlotta was finishing law school, and Simona had just started her MBA. They weren't even home in the summers anymore."

"So why didn't you just reach an understanding with Cass?"

"You don't have children, do you?"

"Not yet, and it's looking like not ever."

"My relationship with Carlotta, my older daughter, has always been difficult. She resented the divorce and saw it as my fault--even now she refuses to see her father through anything but rose-colored glasses. My sense was that if she found out I was in love with a woman, she would never speak to me again."

"I can't believe it."

"Can't believe what?"

"I can't believe the daughter of a smart, accomplished woman like you would be so callous and judgmental. Didn't you tell me that she does immigration work?"

"I did. What I didn't tell you is that she is wonderful at her job. She is filled with compassion for the struggles of immigrants and their families. I could not be prouder of her. She inherited her father's talent for the law, and she uses it daily to help others, but she was very close to my husband's mother. She died when Carlotta was in high school. Like her grandmother, and probably because of her, Carlotta is very religious, and I can't trust her not to judge any non-heterosexual relationship as sinful."

"Jesus!"

"No, the Catholic Church," said Maureen ironically.

"What is your other daughter like?"

"Simona? Just as smart as her sister but much more loving and forgiving. She was very small when we divorced, but she is just much easier in all ways; in fact, much less like her mother than Carlotta, I'm afraid." She smiled ruefully, adding, "I would never worry for an instant about Simona knowing that I was in love with a woman, but I just couldn't risk having Carlotta find out."

"It never crossed your mind that Bond was bluffing?"

"Trust me--she wasn't bluffing. She hated me from the day we met during my first interview."

"Why?"

"I can speculate, but I'm not sure."

"And what do you speculate?"

"I am the first woman Provost at this university, and I think Bond had been in love with Kenneth for years."

"Was he in love with her?"

"At first, when I realized that she was doing everything she could to make me look bad, I thought about that and tried to get a read on their relationship. I could be wrong since I wasn't around them together day in and day out, but my conclusion is that LouAnn was not so much in love with him as totally dedicated to her job, and, essentially, he is the job. But his fondness for her was in direct proportion to her usefulness."

"Ouch!"

"Yes, but not an uncommon situation between powerful, important male bosses and females in close but subordinate positions. At first, I tried to win her over by making it clear that I too worked for the President, but she rejected my overtures. After I discovered that she was screwing up my calendar, I talked to Kenneth. I didn't tell him any details but told him that I thought she did not like me and was possibly bad-mouthing me to the trustees."

"What'd he say?"

"He didn't call me a liar outright, but he indicated that I had probably misunderstood her efforts and called her his 'loyal watchdog.'"

"How condescending!"

"Exactly. I have to say that if she had ever gotten cross-wise with the Board of Trustees or a rich donor, Kenneth would have let her go in a heartbeat."

"After all these years?"

"Kenneth is a politician, and with politicians, it is always, 'What have you done for me lately and what can you do for me tomorrow?'"

"Do you like him?"

I was genuinely curious.

"Personally I like his wife a lot better than I like him, but I find that's true of most couples I meet these days. Professionally I admire him. He does a very good job representing the university and raising money. He does things I could not do."

It was a balanced, political assessment.

"Tell me the whole story about you and Cass."

Maureen grimaced.

"Checking your facts, gumshoe?" she asked, her mocking tone belied by her eyes.

"Just call me Samantha Spade."

38

"Okay. I came here, I knew no one, and in the course of figuring out the job, I went to a couple meetings of the President's Committee on Women. Cass and I started talking, and I liked her. You know how she is—terrible potty mouth but so smart and funny and charming." Maureen studied her glass and then finished her drink. "I was terribly lonely. I was still grieving over my mother's death and trying to adjust to the fact that the girls were grown and gone. Cass and I had dinner a couple of times, and ..." Maureen stared into her empty glass, and then got up and poured another drink. After sitting down, she looked at me intently for a few minutes.

"I like you, Celeste, and I trust you. Cass called me after you had lunch and told me what she'd told you. She told me you are trustworthy and very smart."

"I thought she'd probably call you," I said quietly, wondering what was being left out or changed in the process of squaring their stories.

"Well, she did."

She drank another sip of Scotch.

"I don't know if I'm a lesbian. I know that once I got away from my husband, I always found women more interesting than men although I've dated men when I took time to date. Actually, I've been so busy having a career and raising the girls and then taking care of my mother that I had pretty much avoided the whole question until I met Cass." She paused to drink. "We were very private, and rarely went out in public together. Because she's always been out, that was hard for Cass, but she understood why I needed to be discreet. We thought that a dinner at Bella Vista would be safe because it was so far from here and so exclusive. When LouAnn walked in, it was just too big a coincidence. I'm sure that she followed us."

"Really?"

"That day, Cass came to my office around five, and we left in my car. Since the President's office is on the same floor as mine, I can only assume that LouAnn saw us leave together. I know it sounds weird and paranoid, but I've wracked my brain, and I don't remember seeing LouAnn get in her car or pull out behind me." She sighed bitterly. "Of course, I was paying attention to Cass and not looking for someone to follow me."

"How would she know about Cass? LouAnn worked with the upper administration. She had little or no direct contact with departments and only occasional contact with faculty members."

"I've thought a lot about how she found out about us. The only link I've been able to find is Henry Stoppard."

"The Chair of my department?"

"The very one. Cass and I ran into him and his wife at a movie one of the first times we went out together. We all said hello and made nice for a few moments."

"You could have just been friends out for a movie."

"Yes and that's what we were, but Cass is an out lesbian. I've wracked my brain for other people who might have seen us and talked to LouAnn, but this is the only connection I can come up with. In fact, Henry seemed surprised and said something about not knowing that we were acquainted."

"Oh my God! He's such a conservative asshole. It would never have occurred to him that you might be friends, not lovers."

"You know, he's independently wealthy and quite a big donor so LouAnn's been doing favors for him, his wife, and their children for years. I know he took LouAnn to lunch occasionally because I used to run into them at the Alumni Club. She was a total sucker for that kind of courtly male behavior. Henry probably thought that he was pumping her, but actually she was probably pumping him."

"Son of a bitch!"

"We're agreed on that," chuckled Maureen.

"I wish I could find some way of chatting him up, but it is not an understatement to say that he hates the sight of me."

"I'm sure he hates Cass even more."

"Maybe." I thought for a moment. "What sort of favors did Bond do for him?"

"Nothing big that I know of. Extra tickets to games. Invitations to pre-game parties or football tailgating. He and his wife are fixtures at those events. He sat on the Athletics Committee for years, and I'm sure that's how he first got to know her."

"Okay." I sighed. "Tell me the rest."

"When LouAnn saw us, we were holding hands. There was no way she could have mistaken the situation." Maureen paused, shaking her head. "We were so stupid. So naïve."

"No," I protested. "You thought you were safe."

"As I just said, we were stupid and inexcusably naïve. A few days later, I got a call from LouAnn. She wanted to see me at the end of the day. I told her to stop by my office, but she said that she preferred to talk to me privately and asked to come to my home. That idea bothered me so I asked if she would like to meet for a drink. She immediately informed me that she did not drink so I suggested that we meet for coffee at a place downtown. I knew it would be pretty much deserted at six in the evening so we would have privacy.

"When I got there, she was waiting for me. I got my coffee and asked her why we were meeting privately. She said, in this insinuating tone, 'I think you know why.' I replied that I had no idea, and she said that I needed to think back over the past week. It infuriated me that she was enjoying this sort of cat-and-mouse game."

Listening to Maureen, I remembered Cass's interview with Bond and how it had been conducted with this same coyness. I realized Maureen had fallen silent.

"So what happened?"

"I told LouAnn that I was not playing games and that she needed to come to the point. She said, 'If you don't stop seeing that woman, I'll have to inform the

President.' I said, 'Inform him of what? That I had dinner with a friend?' She kind of sneered at me and said, 'Most women don't hold hands with their friends, and they certainly don't have their friends spending nights at their houses.' I told her that the President would not care, but he might be interested to know that she was spying on people who worked for him. Then she said very primly, 'I'm sure that the President knows it is in his best interest to know what kind of people are working for him.' I told her that I agreed and would make sure to tell him about her. She then said, 'There are other people who might be interested in your love life.'"

Maureen walked to the bar and poured more scotch into her glass. When she sat back down, her eyes were blazing with anger.

"That's when I realized that no matter what she said, her activities had nothing to do with morality and everything to do with power--she was enjoying tyrannizing over me. I started to get angry and said, 'You know blackmail is against the law.' She said very indignantly in that fake ladylike tone, 'I'm not asking for money.' I was furious and said, 'So what do you want out of this?' 'Nothing. I just want it to stop.' I said, 'And what will you do if it doesn't?' That's when she said, 'I'll tell your daughters.'

"She had me, and she knew it," Maureen said flatly, flushed with anger, tears standing in her eyes. "Even if I had gone to the law about this, the damage would still have been done."

The cold-bloodedness of the threat took me aback. I knew Maureen was right. Bond was not interested in money or any other tangible benefit, but I wondered how Bond had presented this enjoyment of power to herself. Was it justified by her personal hatred of Maureen, her disapproval of Maureen's success in a non-traditional role, her condemnation of the lesbian relationship, her investment in her job, her twisted loyalty to the president, or some self-proclaimed role as a "moral" enforcer?

"What did she mean about spending the night?"

"I'm not sure, but I suspect that she spied on me at home. Cass spent the night occasionally, usually on the weekends, but I can't figure out how Bond would have known this unless she were watching my house." Maureen shuddered and took a sip of her drink. "It still gives me the creeps."

"Did she make any other threat?"

"As we were leaving the coffee house, she said in this sort of threatening whisper, Never forget what an interest the Family Fund takes in the university."

"So you think she was some kind of moral fanatic?"

"That may have been how she excused her actions to herself, but I think she just liked having power over people—any kind of power. In my case, I'm sure that jealousy also fueled her interest."

"Who worked most closely with her?"

"Marilyn Wilhoyt—the budget person in the President's office."

"Can I talk with her?"

"I'll have to figure out a way. Let me talk to the information people and see if we can put you on some sort of story about our dear friend LouAnn Bond." Maureen smiled. "I'll call you when I've got it fixed. By the way, you can call Emily Hartshorn for a library tour."

"Why her?"

"Although her title is Assistant Director of Library Operations, she's actually in charge and knows every aspect of the library operation. The Director is more or less a figurehead although he does bring in the money."

"Oink, oink," I said, without thinking. Maureen eyed me irritably for a moment and then continued, "Emily knows you are now my liaison on the Library Advisory Committee."

"Okay. I was wondering how to get in there so this should be helpful."

"I said I would be honest with you. Cass doesn't know this," said Maureen and hesitated. I waited her out. "When LouAnn and I left the coffee house, actually as we got to the door, I said something to her."

Maureen hesitated again and took a sip of scotch.

"What?"

"I swear that I didn't kill her."

"Okay, but what exactly did you say?

"I told her if I ever caught her following me again, I'd rip her limb from limb with my bare hands."

"And who heard you say this?"

"I was angry. I wasn't yelling, but the guy working the bar probably heard me. I don't think there was anyone else in there. But I didn't kill her. I swear I didn't."

As I was trying to digest this information, the phone rang. Maureen answered it, listened for a moment, and said, "Charlie, slow down. You're breaking up." Something followed. "For Christ's sake, go outside where the signal is clear." She turned to me in exasperation and said, "It's Charlie Crawford, the head of security. You'd think..." She did not finish because he came back on the line. She turned white and said, "I'll be there in fifteen minutes."

She hung up the phone and sat down, covering her face with her hands.

"What is it?"

"They've found another body."

"Who?"

"A young woman, but they haven't identified her yet, and everyone who was on staff in the library tonight seems to be accounted for. God, if it's a student...."

After sitting in grim silence for a moment, Maureen said, "I have to go."

"You've had a lot of scotch. Let me drive." She nodded numbly and did not move. "Go wash your face and brush your teeth. Gargle." All I could think was

ow much scotch I had seen her drink and how she had already started before I
rrived.

"Get your coat and purse, and we'll go."

She nodded again but did not move.

"Maureen, you told Charlie you'd be there in fifteen minutes."

Finally, she stood up, and I watched her pull herself together with an impressive
ct of will.

Chapter Seven

A few minutes later, both eating Altoid mints as if they could conceal the smell of the scotch, we were headed for the university. Suddenly I realized what I had not asked Maureen.

"I have one other question."

"Only one," she said grimly.

"Only one for now. What about Bond's attempt to blackmail you over Sam? Was that true?"

"All too true," replied Maureen, popping two more Altoids into her mouth. "I am sure that she would have threatened to tell his wife except now Judith doesn't even recognize Sam." Maureen starred out the window, muttering bitterly, "It's all so fucking sordid."

I resisted the urge to point out how appropriate an adjective "fucking" was under the circumstances, but I did not think my linguistic levity would be appreciated.

"Do you love him?" This question was none of my business, and I expected Maureen to say so. Instead, she was quiet for long time.

"It's complicated. He wants to marry me although it looks like Judith will live forever."

"So what do you want?" I asked, and she laughed.

"'Woman, what does she want?'" She cracked the window to let a blast of icy air into the car. "Do you mind?"

"Of course not. If it's any comfort, you sound perfectly sober to me."

"Thanks for the vote of confidence, but you must remember that I'm Irish!"

"So am I!"

"With a name like Brinkman!"

"Mom's side is all Donovans, O'Sullivans, and other Irish names—not a Brit or Scot among them!"

"No wonder we get along." She fell silent for a few moments. "I hope you realize how completely I trust you."

"I hope you do which is why you are now going to tell me where you were the weekend that Bond was killed."

"You can't think," she began, but then sighed. "Of course. I have two very good reasons, among a multitude of smaller reasons, to kill her."

"And you probably have a building pass key on your key ring," I said quietly.

"How do you know that?"

"Weird information comes my way. The other day I locked myself out of my file cabinet, and the university locksmith had to come and open it. We got to talking about building access. I have a class in another building and told him that I needed an outdoor key for that building so could he make one or give me a passkey. He was impressed with my politeness and interest in his work and told me that only five people have pass-keys: you, the President, Sam Jacoby, the Head of Security, and the Head of Maintenance. Even security officers only have outside keys to the buildings they are responsible for."

"Remarkably astute research, Dr. Brinkman."

"Piece of cake. My father taught me that people like for you to be interested in what they do, and most people like to explain their jobs because it makes them feel important and appreciated."

"Gift of the blarney."

"No, that's on my mother's side. Dad has just never met a stranger and is interested in everything. It used to embarrass me to no end that he would talk to anyone anywhere, and everyone from the checker at the grocery to the trash collection guys knew him by name, but now I realize it's a gift."

"One he passed on."

"Yes, but I use it a bit more selectively than he does."

"What does your father do?"

"Retired electrician, but he keeps his license and is always doing odd jobs for people in the family or people he knows or people who know people he knows—you would not believe the network. He's a busy guy."

"My father walked out when I was two. We never saw him again, and I can't even remember him. Mom raised me alone."

"Your divorce must have been very difficult."

"Understatement."

Before I could ask again where she was the weekend Bond was killed, I was pulling into the lot by the library. Charlie Crawford, Director of Security for the university, met us at the front door. He was in his fifties and looked the way you want the guy who watches your doors to look: six feet tall, a little burly, gray-haired with choirboy gone-to-seed good looks and piercing blue eyes.

"Sorry to bring you out, Dr. Shaughnessy."

"Not at all, Charlie. Have you called the President?"

"He didn't pick up, but it's late."

Maureen looked disturbed by this information, but before she could say anything else, the local police drove up, followed by a forensics van. I was surprised to see my cousin Harold get out of one of the squad cars. He spotted me immediately.

"What are you doing here, Cece?" he asked, hugging me.

"I might ask you the same thing."

As we laughed, I felt a twinge of guilt that I had not yet called his son Larry.

"The inspector on this case is a pal of mine, and we've been talking. He asked me to ride along." Harold turned as another man came up beside him. "Blake Hess, this is my niece Celeste Brinkman, actually Doctor, as in Professor, Celeste Brinkman."

Blake Hess was exactly my height, five foot ten inches, and had a trim, athletic build, jet black hair, and dark eyes. I judged him to be around forty. He wasted no time on niceties as he shook my hand.

"Nice to meet you, Dr. Brinkman. What are you doing here?"

"Dr. Shaughnessy and I were having a drink when the call came. She asked me to come along." Hess nodded and went to greet Maureen.

"All business," I muttered to my cousin.

"As it should be, but he's a good guy. He brought me along because he can't make any sense out of that Bond case. I actually suggested that he talk with you."

"Sure. Anytime." I dug in my purse for one of my cards and wrote my cell number on the back. "Tell him to call me. I'd be happy to help."

I had read enough murder mysteries to know that I needed a police contact and felt very proud that now I had two. I was already imagining how much information I would get from Blake Hess and could barely stop myself from pumping the air with my fist and yelling, "Yessss!" when I remembered that someone had died.

"What are we waiting for?" I heard Hess ask, and someone said that Simon Cranston, the Director of Libraries, had not yet arrived.

A few moments later, he walked up. Plump and pleasant is how I always thought of him, but his jovial manner hid a sharp, ambitious mind. I knew him only by reputation, one that had grown as he had plunged into politics and gotten the congressman to pull a new wing of the library and the Smythe Center for the Study of Government out of the pork barrel. As we walked into the foyer of the library, I suddenly heard the sharp click of high heels and turned to find Emily Hartshorn following us.

"I am so glad you're here," said Cranston.

"I came as soon as I could!"

"Emily, I think you already know Inspector Blake Hess," said Maureen. "And this is Dr. Celeste Brinkman from the English Department." There was an awkward pause as I realized that no one knew Harold, but Hess jumped in.

"This is my colleague Detective Harold O'Brien. I've asked him to collaborate on the investigation."

"And Cece, I mean Dr. Brinkman, and I are cousins," added Harold with a small smile.

"Okay, so what have we got?" asked Hess, turning to Charlie Crawford.

"The body was found just before the library closed. The closing bell had actually sounded so it was less than ten minutes before closing. There were only five students left in the building. They are waiting for you over there."

We had all stepped into the library, and Crawford gestured toward an open reading area where five disgruntled students were seated under the watchful eye of a university security guard.

"They have put their cell phones on the table and not been allowed to use their computers. They are not very happy, and I'd appreciate it if you could question them and let them go. None of them went to the floor where the body was found at any time today. They all claim, and the librarian on duty backs them up, that they were in this area all evening working on a group project."

"Who else was still in the building?" asked Hess.

"Two reference librarians who are in their offices. I put one of the security officers outside in the hall."

"Anyone else?"

"Two people who were working the circulation desk. I have an officer with them. Three student workers left at nine."

"I'll need a complete list of everyone who was working this evening and contact information."

"I can provide that if I can get to my computer," offered Emily Hartshorn.

"So who found the body?" Hess asked.

"Follow me," said Crawford, and led us to the administrative offices. "I didn't want to talk any further in front of the students. A professor found her on the fifth floor on the landing beyond the emergency exit door."

I thought for a moment—the fifth floor was basically a warehouse of old periodicals. As more journals digitized their back numbers, fewer people went to the top floor of the library making it seem more and more like a ghost town. I sometimes went there to work because it was so quiet. Study carrels lined one wall and there were four or five tables, but few students now went to the fifth floor.

Crawford opened the door to one of the offices and nodded to the security officer who was seated at the desk. The door swung wider to reveal Marshall N'Dour seated opposite the desk.

"Marshall!" I exclaimed involuntarily, and he looked up. He jumped up and enveloped me in a hug so tight I could feel the tremor running through him.

"What are you doing here?" I finally asked, pulling away to look up at him.

"I found the dead woman."

47

At that point, Hess cleared everyone out except for Marshall, Harold, and another officer who was pulling out a tape recorder, pad and pen. He shepherded the rest of us to the adjacent conference room.

Through the glass, we watched the hallway. About fifteen minutes later, Hess came out alone and ordered the newly-arrived forensics team to come with him. The forensics team wore suits that looked like scrubs including shoe covers, gloves, and head caps. Hess called to Harold and they both suited up. Someone from forensics examined one of the elevator cars with a light that I guessed could pick up traces of blood. She finally nodded and everyone got in. I could not see what floor they went to, but an hour later, Hess and Harold came back alone to the conference room.

"Forensics is still working," Hess said. "They'll take the body away in another hour or so, but Dr. Shaughnessy, Dr. Cranston, I must ask you to close the library for tomorrow, at least. We need time to figure out what happened."

They both nodded.

"We can put it out immediately on the alert system," Hartshorn said, and Crawford nodded, taking out his phone.

"I'm going to say it's due to unforeseen circumstances," he said to Maureen who nodded. He stepped out into the hall to make his call.

"Dr. Cranston and Ms. Hartshorn, I'd like you to see if you can identify the body," said Hess.

"Why?" demanded Cranston with a slight note of hysteria. "Must I?"

"Why don't I go first?" offered Emily Hartshorn who was clearly used to covering for her boss whenever necessary. "If I don't know her, maybe one of the reference librarians or circulation clerks will be able to identify her."

"Fine," said Hess and added, with visible irritation, "Thank you, Ms. Hartshorn. Shall we go?"

Weak with relief, Cranston slumped back in his chair.

They were gone less than ten minutes, and when they returned, Hartshorn was white and crying.

"Good Lord, Emily, what is it?" demanded Cranston. "Who is it?"

"It's Tareka James."

Cranston looked blank.

"Who?"

"Tareka. My assistant!" said Emily and began to cry again. "It's all my fault," she sobbed.

"Why would it be your fault?" Hess asked.

"I sent her up there. On Friday afternoon, just before closing, somebody called and said there was a leak on the fifth floor."

"Who called?" asked Hess. "Did this person call you?"

"No. Someone called the office and got Tareka. Her number is the public one for the Assistant Director's office. She knew I had a meeting with Simon at the end of

48

he day on Friday so she stuck her head in the door of my office and said, 'Someone says there's a leak on the fifth floor. I'll check, and if it's a problem, I'll call maintenance and get someone over.' I was busy gathering my papers for the meeting so I just said, 'Fine. Thanks!'" Emily wiped at her tears. "She was so happy and excited. She didn't get out much, and after work, she was driving to Nashville to spend the weekend at her friend's bachelorette party."

"See if anyone has reported her missing," Hess said quietly to Harold, and then turned his full attention back to Hartshorn.

"Was it usual for you to trust your assistant with this kind of task?" asked Hess.

"Definitely. She was wonderful at her job. Reliable and smart. I was trying to convince her to go to library school and get her master's degree so she could advance," murmured Emily, shaking her head. "Why would anyone would want to kill her...." She stopped mid-sentence.

"What is it?" asked Hess, and Hartshorn shook her head. He did not press her but said gently, "I'd like you to come down the hall and make a statement about what happened Friday afternoon."

Hartshorn walked with him and another officer to the Director's office down the hall. A few moments later, after Hess had rejoined the group in the conference room, Harold returned and told Hess, "Her family contacted the police Saturday afternoon when they learned that she had never reached Nashville. It was too early to file a missing person report, but the officer on duty made some notes. James called her mother around four on Friday and said that she had one more thing to do before she could leave."

"So what else do you know?" Maureen asked Hess.

I was surprised when he answered her.

"Not much. We've let the students go home. The reference librarians could vouch for all of them. Dr. Marshall N'Dour found the body when he was on the fifth floor using periodicals. He went up in the elevator. Purely by chance, he decided to walk down the stairs, and when he opened the stairwell door, there she was. She had been hit with something. That's all we know. We have no idea how long she's been there, but Ms. Hartshorn last saw her around four on Friday when she reported the leak. We need to find out who called about the leak," he murmured, and Harold wrote a note. Hess then turned to Cranston.

"What are the evening security arrangements for this building?"

"There is a security officer who checks everything in the evening right after closing, but you would have to ask Charlie Crawford about any other checks, or Emily probably knows all the details," said Cranston dismissively and muttered, "I can't believe this," an utterance which alternated with "And now this!" as if the murder had been arranged for his personal inconvenience.

"The librarians check the first two floors at closing," added Cranston.

Hess made some notes before asking, "Why only the first two floors?"

"They contain the main study areas and are most frequently used by the students. They've occasionally found students sleeping on the couches on the second floor. The other three floors are mostly stacks and not heavily used now."

"Who uses those study carrels on the fifth floor?"

"Graduate students mostly. Some faculty."

"Who keeps the keys to the carrels?" asked Hess, and I knew where he was going since the carrels on the fifth floor were near the stairwell where the body had been found.

"The grad student or professor picks up the key to the carrel at the circulation desk. Everyone signs in and out so it's easy to check if everyone is out."

"Could someone turn in the key but leave the carrel unlocked and go back?"

"I suppose so, but why would...." He stopped.

Hess's phone beeped, and he glanced at the message.

"Dr. Cranston, could you please find the carrel lists from Friday through today?"

"I'm sure Emily can tell you where they are kept," he replied nervously, getting to his feet and following Hess out the door. We were alone with Harold.

"What happened to Tareka James?" I asked.

Harold looked from me to Maureen and back to me.

"Someone hit her with something hard enough to smash her skull. I have no idea what was used or when it happened. All that's up to forensics."

Cranston came back into the room without Hess.

"Emily says the list is kept at the circulation desk, just as I thought."

"I'll go with you," said Harold, standing up. They were gone a short time and returned with the list, now in a clear bag. Harold studied the list for a moment and, after motioning Cranston into a chair, went out of the room.

"I saw the list," Cranston informed us with an air of importance. "It only had one name on it for tonight, but there were lots of names for Friday and Saturday."

Hess came back to the conference room, bringing Marshall who sat down and shot me such a forlorn glance I reached over to pat his hand.

"We've sent the librarians and circulation staff home," Hess said. "I'll let you know, Dr. Shaughnessy, when you can reopen the library. Dr. N'Dour, we will get back in touch with you if there are any further questions."

Marshall nodded. Emily Hartshorn came back into the conference room with another police officer. She looked terrible.

"If any of you think of anything that might help us, please don't hesitate to call," said Hess, handing out business cards. "We'd appreciate it if you would not talk about anything you have seen or heard here tonight. There's a reporter outside, and I'd appreciate it if you would just tell her 'No comment.' Do any of you need a ride home?" We all shook our heads. "Okay, we'll walk you out of the building now." He, along with Harold and another officer, escorted us out of the building into the cold night air.

50

"Dr. Shaughnessy, do you have any comment? Inspector Hess, have you identified the victim? Is it a student? Where was the victim found? Do you think his murder is connected to LouAnn Bond's?" Gina Tanacci, who covered the university for the local paper, asked her questions in rapid succession.

"Gina, I'm sorry, but we can't say anything. You'll have to call the University Information Office in the morning," Maureen said as a camera flashed. "And stop with the pictures, okay?" Tanacci just grinned and tucked her camera in her messenger bag.

I turned to Marshall.

"If you don't mind riding with me to take Maureen, I'll drive you home."

"That's okay...," he began to protest, but I cut him short.

"You've had a shock. We all have, but you most of all, and you still look a bit shaky."

"You do," said Maureen, coming up behind us. "Ride with us. One of us will bring you in tomorrow. Emily," she called out to Hartshorn. "Can we take you and Simon home? It will be a squeeze, but we'd be happy to."

"We're fine," said Emily. "My husband's coming for us."

Just then a car pulled into the parking lot, and we said good night.

When we got to my car, Maureen, after some polite wrangling, convinced Marshall to take the front passenger seat because of his long legs. She spent the ride talking on her cell phone, briefing the university information officer. She ended the call just as we reached her house where Marshall escorted her to the door.

As soon as he got back in the car, I asked, "So what happened?" adding, "I think it's okay to talk among ourselves."

Marshall nodded sadly.

"I went to the library to look at some old articles I wanted to use to talk about the history of chemistry. I've been thinking about doing some kind of historical essay. Anyway, I spent a couple of hours up on the fifth floor looking at the articles and thinking about how chemistry used to present itself and its results."

"You sound like a historian."

"Actually, I was a double major in chemistry and history when I was an undergraduate. I thought very seriously about doing a PhD in history, but then I decided doing chemistry would open more doors for me."

"And provide steadier paychecks!"

Marshall smiled for the first time since I had seen him in the library.

"I read the articles and made my notes. The closing bell sounded, and I'd been sitting for a long time so I decided to take the stairs down to stretch my legs. I pushed the fire door open and there she was." He paused and swallowed hard. "Her head was bashed in." He put his face in his hands. "My God! I tried to find a pulse in her arm and her neck, but I was pretty sure that she was dead. I called Campus

Security and even though I told them what was wrong, they sent some kid. He was going to turn her over, but I stopped him and told him to call the real cops."

"What were they asking you that took so long?"

"We went over my story a few times. They wanted to examine my notes, and they sent someone upstairs to find the journals I'd been using which I had left in the re-shelving area. I think they were finally convinced that I had nothing to do with what happened. I didn't even know that poor woman. They also walked me through my entire weekend which made me think I should get a more exciting life."

"But not in this way."

"Definitely not!"

"Did they say anything about the other murder?"

"No, except that they knew I was in the audience when the body was discovered."

He directed me to his apartment in a neighborhood near where I lived.

"I'm almost afraid to go out alone," he said forlornly.

"I guess you'd better go out with me," I said and was rewarded with a smile.

"I won't say no."

"I'll pick you up in the morning at eight, okay?" I asked. "We can figure out the details then."

"Thanks so much, Celeste," he said, reaching over to pat my hand before getting out of the car.

"One more question," I said. He paused with his hand on the door handle. "How old are you?"

"Thirty-six." Whew! My age. Older than I had guessed. He seemed to read my mind. "I really did play pro ball in Europe for four years after college. It was a lot harder than teaching chemistry!"

"But probably more fun."

"Sometimes, but once a nerd, always a nerd."

He got out, shutting the door and waving before I could assure him that I knew exactly what he meant.

Chapter Eight

The next morning, I awoke too early. I lay in bed thinking not only about Marshall but about what facts I now knew and wondering how the murder of Tareka James might be related to that of LouAnn Bond. The idea that a serial killer was loose in the library struck me as completely ludicrous because, as far as I knew— admittedly from mysteries, newspapers, and radio news--serial killers were compulsive about repeating certain details of their crimes. So, quickly dismissing the most sensational interpretation of recent events, I considered the possible relationship between the two victims. Unfortunately, based on my paltry knowledge, I could find no connection.

Tareka James seemed to have been well liked, pleasant, smart, and helpful. However, I had noticed an odd pause after Emily Hartshorn's heartfelt exclamation, "Why would anyone want to…?" Want to what? Kill Tareka James? There was something she had not said, but the contrast between the two victims--Tareka, helpful assistant, and Bond, hated blackmailer-- remained striking. The only clear connection was they had both worked for the university and shown up dead in the library.

Who had called Tareka James? Had the call been a summons to her death or had her death been related to something else, perhaps something she had accidentally interrupted?

In that case, the murders might be related either to the library's business or to the business of someone who worked in the library. Or perhaps the library just happened to be a convenient place to kill people. Not for the first time, I thought both the police and I were looking for the proverbial needle in a haystack. Over 5,000 people worked at the university which 25,000 students attended. The workforce itself was the size of a small town, and the student body the size of a larger town or suburb. I rolled over--the prone equivalent to throwing up my hands-- and turned my thoughts elsewhere.

I still wondered if the first story Maureen had told me were true. Had Bond blackmailed her over her relationship with Sam Jacoby? Something felt odd about the story, but the previous night there had been no time to probe more deeply. I wondered, in fact, if I were up to the task of interrogating Maureen Shaughnessy, but I had to find out where she had been the weekend Bond was murdered. Whether Maureen liked it or not, I also needed to talk to Sam Jacoby.

In addition, I had to find a pretext to talk with Frank O'Donnell who I knew, from first-hand observation, had received some nasty news from Bond. But how do you ask the Vice President for Academic Affairs what an encounter overheard in a stairwell meant? Awkward, to say the least. And who was Lila Daniliov, the person Bond had referred to? Maureen might know.

Since Emily Hartshorn was my designated guide to the library, I wondered how soon I would be able to talk with her. When would the library be open again? I felt incompetent—I had not even known the library had a second set of stairs for the staff. I comforted myself that until now I had not needed to know anything about the library's architecture beyond ordinary user information.

I rolled over again and flipped my pillow to the cool underside. How exactly was I going to find out what the police knew? Should I call Harold or Blake Hess or wait for them to call me? Hess had not seemed friendly although Harold seemed to think that he wanted my help. It made me feel slightly better that the police seemed to be as baffled as I was, but I felt uneasy over what my "help" might mean.

What if I told the police something that led them to disrupt the lives of innocent people? I shuddered, pulled the covers up over my head, closed my eyes, said a brief prayer for guidance, and slept until the alarm went off at seven. At eight, I picked up Marshall in front of his apartment.

"How are you?"

"As one might expect, I had creepy dreams all night, but otherwise I'm okay," he replied with a smile.

I suddenly realized how much I loved his smile, especially the tiny gap between his front teeth.

"Will you have dinner with me tonight?" he asked.

"I'd love to, but it will have to be late. We have a faculty meeting that doesn't begin until five, and you never can tell how many of the lonely and self-important will have to stand up and talk at length."

"Yeah, I know." He grimaced in sympathy.

"I cannot imagine that chemists regularly hold forth in the way English teachers do."

"Perhaps at less length, but they do go on, and they're a cranky bunch. They like to argue."

"Can I call you when we finish?"

"Sure. I'll be in my office," he said as he got out of the car.

I drove off to the usual distant parking lot and as I walked back in the mild, winter sun, I tried to ignore my personal morality play. I could hear my parents

54

aying, "You are being irresponsible. You cannot eat out again! You are broke! You need to use this new income to pay off your credit card, not to indulge yourself!" They would never, of course, mention my debt to them. But I heard another voice saying seductively, "You have money now and you know you like him. This might be the real thing."

Considering the damage already done, I blocked both voices and decided to enjoy the sunshine. I was passing through the ramshackle buildings of the outer campus and soon came to the more orderly brick and stone buildings that dated from the 1930s when the campus housed a boys' military school. We owed the more elegant buildings, the generous quadrangle, and the four huge, old oak trees to that long-gone private school. This part of the campus was what I loved, what made me a feel truly part of a university with all its history and traditions.

"Dr. Brinkman," called a young woman. I recognized Melissa Wagner, one of my students, as she ran to catch up with me.

"Hi, Melissa! How are you?"

"Fine. I just wanted to ask you about this research assignment."

"Yes?" There was a long pause while she looked around in embarrassment.

"Some of us were talking, and everyone thought we should ask you…," her voice trailed off.

"Ask what?"

"The assignment says we have to have books as well as articles as sources."

"Yes." I waited for her to continue, and then I realized where this was going. "The library? Is that the issue?"

"I'm sorry. I know it sounds stupid, but we are all kind of freaked by what's happened. We don't mind working on the first floor where everyone is, but what if our books aren't in the robot section and we have to go up in the stacks to find them?" I would have laughed if she had not looked so young and scared.

"I understand. Let me think about this and get back with you. Tell the others not to worry. I'll say something in class, but I am sure we can find a solution."

"Thank you," she said and started to walk away but turned back to add, "And thanks for being cool."

The rest of the day flew by. I was tired, but I had two classes to teach and tried to get in to see Maureen. No luck; I was told her schedule was full, but I had to wonder if she were avoiding me. I called a nearby private college and talked to their library director who was very sympathetic and, after pumping me for information, agreed to let my students use their library on a visiting basis.

I finally figured out a strategy to meet Marilyn Wilhoyt, LouAnn Bond's closest co-worker, who had temporarily taken over her duties. I called to talk with her about inviting the President to speak at my alma mater. I made an appointment for the end of the business day when we might have the office to ourselves. I was not sure what

I was going to ask, but I wanted to find out if Bond's closest co-workers hated her. I might not find out anything, but I figured it was worth a try.

I went into the faculty meeting and sat down next to Stephen Hope, an attractive man about my age.

"How's it going?"

He smiled, rolling his large gray eyes. He had the long, thick, dark lashes that men always seem to get and mascara can never supply.

"I meant up until now," I added, and he laughed.

"I'm doing okay."

"Have all your extra-mural reviews come in?" I asked, knowing he was up for tenure.

"Yes and all quite good so I'm very relieved."

I liked Stephen who was a gentle spirit. He was quiet—a rare characteristic among the English faculty. He had acquired a solid following among the more serious students whom he took time to mentor. This following was all the more remarkable when you consider that he taught medieval literature, not the most popular area these days. His specialty was Chaucer, and I still remembered the remarkable lecture he had given on the Wife of Bath during his job interview.

I had invited him and his wife Pamela, who worked in the library, over for dinner several times, but although Stephen and I got on well, Pamela seemed stand-offish. I had never figured out if she were shy, jealous, or just reserved, but when the third or fourth invitation was not reciprocated, I stopped inviting them. Stephen and I had lunch about once a month, grabbed an occasional coffee, and remained cordial, but when I occasionally saw Pamela on campus, I was never sure that she remembered who I was.

"How's Pamela?"

"Fine."

"Job going all right?"

"Yes, she likes it a lot better than her old job in Media, but the entire library is very upset. With this second murder, I can't imagine when they'll get back to normal."

"Scary," I offered, "My students are freaked out."

"Mine too." He pushed his light brown hair back from his forehead, a gesture I always found endearingly boyish. "It's so awful about Tareka James. Everyone knew and liked her. Pam's very upset about her death." I nodded sympathetically.

"Go, Mountaineers!" said Glenn Baird, throwing his books on the table and slapping Stephen on the back. I must have looked puzzled because Glenn added, "West Virginia cleaned Maryland's clock on Saturday. Those Terrapins looked like turtles! Did you see the game?" he asked Stephen who nodded and smiled.

"I had forgotten you were from West Virginia. Where about?" I had a vague memory of a conversation about small towns.

"You won't have heard of it. Most people in West Virginia haven't heard of it," he assured me.

"Come on—try me," I coaxed.

"Fanger Wells," he said softly.

"You're right—no idea—but great name. What's it near?"

"Nothing much. It's in the mountains. Not even big enough to have its own school."

"Wasn't LouAnn Bond from a small town in West Virginia?" Glenn asked.

"Who?" Stephen looked blank.

"LouAnn Bond, the assistant to the President. The woman whose body was found in the library," said Glenn.

"I'm sorry. I had forgotten her name." Stephen looked embarrassed.

At that moment, the Chair called the meeting to order. We spent the next two hours arguing over whether graduate students who taught freshman composition should have six or nine hours of graduate credit, and then arguing over whether we should have a set text and syllabus for the composition courses. Arguments on both sides of both issues were made eloquently and at length until past seven when someone suggested that we write two resolutions and put them up for a vote.

Glenn quickly composed the resolutions on his laptop and read them out. Probably because we were all starving, there were few objections and both votes were almost unanimous.

I walked out with Stephen. Night had come, dark and cold but shining with bright stars and a thumbnail moon.

"How old are you, Stephen?" I asked, and he looked at me in surprise.

"Forty. This year. Why? How old are you?"

"Thirty-seven."

"Ah, youth!" he said with a smile.

"You look much younger than forty," I said and meant it.

"Appearances can be deceiving," he replied. "Most days I feel about a hundred and forty."

"Teaching will do that to you," I said, and he chuckled. "I'm meeting Marshall N'Dour from Chemistry for dinner. Would you like to come?" I had asked on impulse, feeling sure that Stephen and Marshall would like each other. For all I knew, they might already be acquainted.

"No. Pamela's got dinner waiting, but thanks for asking."

We said good night, and I took out my phone to call Marshall.

We went to a Persian place I had not had a chance to try and were sharing a delicious plate of shish kebob and vegetables over saffron rice when Marshall said, "I didn't know you were such good friends with Dr. Shaughnessy."

"There's a lot you don't know about me!" I said flippantly, and then added, "You know I'm working for her now."

"No, I didn't."

"She just hired me as a special assistant. Actually, she wants me to sit on a couple of scholarship committees and act as her liaison to the Library Advisory Committee."

"And I didn't know your cousin was a cop."

"Harold was like a big brother to me when I was growing up. I was very surprised to see him last night. He doesn't usually go out on cases. He's got a desk job now and is about to retire."

"So you were having a meeting with Dr. Shaughnessy?" asked Marshall, sounding puzzled.

"Her schedule is so full that we decided to have a drink so she could bring me up to speed on a couple of projects," I said and hoped the explanation did not sound completely lame. "To tell you the truth, our lovely provost had had a wee drop too much when the call from Charlie Crawford came so I volunteered to drive her."

"If I had her job, I'd be drunk twenty-four/seven," said Marshall with a smile. "Do you like her?"

"I've been surprised to discover that although her dragon-lady reputation preceded her, I do like her. She's smart, and she cares about the university." I spoke sincerely. "Why all the questions?"

"I'm a curious kind of guy, and now I'm wondering why someone who won the prize for undergraduate teaching last year would suddenly begin working in administration."

It was an astute piece of analysis. People who love teaching and are good at it rarely cross over into administration unless they are offered one of two things: money (a commodity always in short supply among academics) or the chance either to run a program, thus changing the system in a way that will benefit students. Otherwise, administrators and faculty float along like an oil slick on a large body of water with every paycheck making clear which is the more precious commodity.

"I don't intend to join the administration, if that's that you're asking," I said huffily.

"I didn't mean to offend you."

"I had to sue in order to get tenure, and I still owe my parents several thousand dollars. Maureen offered me a way to get rid of that debt in a matter of months." I had intended to speak matter-of-factly, but I sounded angry—proof the tenure wound was still tender.

"I'm sorry." Marshall reached across the table to take my hand, making me smile ruefully. "If you don't mind my asking, what happened?"

Looking at his large, powerful hands and wondering what to say, I swallowed hard.

"Please tell me," he added softly.

"Henry William Stoppard III, the guy who is now Chair of our department, was the head of the Personnel Committee the year I came up for tenure. I always think of it as the Personal Committee because it was all male and two of the four people on it—I later found out—had voted against hiring me in the first place.

"I had edited and published an edition of poems and personal letters plus an autobiography by Flora Knight, an early twentieth-century poet who was also a community leader and suffragist—one of the many women writers who, although popular and well thought of in their time, lost out to their male contemporaries over the long haul. I had also published four scholarly articles in reputable journals on various other women's personal narratives. Am I boring you yet?"

Marshall shook his head.

"The other person who came up for tenure the same year was male. He had published a single article and edited a collection of critical essays by others. That was his 'book.' In spite of my rebuttals, no one would take a fresh look at my scholarship, mostly because the former Chair and Stoppard were such worshippers of male authors and, more importantly, such entrenched good ol' boys. To put it bluntly, they liked him better. The college committee split on the decision and the Dean, another good ol' boy, went along with my Chair. So I finally had no recourse but to hire a lawyer and sue. Now here's the truly bad news."

"There could be more?"

I nodded.

"Treating us differently was their big mistake, but if they hadn't tenured a male colleague on less defensible grounds that same year, I might not have won because the prejudice, the double-standard, might have been less evident. It has made me wonder how many women have suffered the same form of injustice and did not or could not fight or fought and lost."

"What a horrible story."

"It still hurts a lot," I admitted. "But working in administration, ironically enough, is a way out of writing a check that is a monthly reminder of how I was totally screwed in my job."

"I understand."

"No, you don't." I spoke flatly. "Not really. As a chemist, you can do other things, but an English teacher—someone who loves teaching literature—doesn't have a lot of choices. It hurts to be betrayed in the place where you have a chance to follow your vocation." I grimaced at the Catholic quality of my explanation. It was the first time I had ever been so nakedly honest with anyone but my cousin Janey about what had happened.

"To have some good ol' boy and his gang of bullies go after you because he doesn't think women's literature should be taken seriously and then to have a bunch of sexist fossils decide that you, as a teacher and scholar of that literature, should not be taken seriously and also driven out of academia rocked my world."

"You're right that I don't understand, but having been a smart, bi-racial jock may give me some small insight," he replied in an equally flat, matter-of-fact tone.

"You're right. I need to remember that I don't have a corner on being fucked by the ignorance and prejudice of others," I said, and we both laughed. I looked down at the table where he was still holding my hand.

"I like you a lot, Celeste." I met his dark eyes. "I was married for a time, back when I was playing basketball in Europe." When I did not say anything, he continued, "We were undergraduates together, and we got married right after we graduated. It only lasted two years."

"What happened?"

"We were young. She hated living in Europe, but mostly we discovered that when we left school, we had very little beyond sex in common." He sighed. "She was much more social than I am, and the road life of an athlete was definitely not a social whirl. She resented how hard I had to work, how many hours I had to put in. She was lonely living in Europe."

"Are you still in touch?"

"We exchange holiday greetings. She's married and has two kids. She seems happy."

We were both quiet for a moment until he asked, "What about you?"

"I lived with someone in graduate school and thought we would be together forever, but at the end of grad school, I got a job and he didn't. My first job wasn't even a great job—just a one-year replacement for someone on sabbatical. Mark came along and spent the year finishing his dissertation. We both looked for jobs. When I got this job. . . actually, things had been bad since the last semester of grad school when I had an article published in a good journal. He clearly resented my success and felt diminished by it. When I accepted this job, we ended it."

"Ended it"—mild words for the vicious argument that followed the phone call when I had accepted the job. I hated remembering how this man I had loved and whom I had believed loved me was so completely undone by my success. I hated remembering my sense of betrayal as I realized that the future he had been envisioning all along was one where my career would be a kind of recreational activity while my real job would be supporting his career. I hated remembering how stupid and naïve I had been, but I was sure that I would not have worked and fought so hard for tenure if I had not had the constant memory of Mark's sense of entitlement and belittling words to spur me on.

I withdrew my hand.

"We are no longer in touch."

"And since?" Marshall asked.

"I've dated a bit but nothing serious. I have a lot of women friends, and I'm a local from a huge, Catholic family. I work pretty hard. You?"

"I had someone in my life during graduate school. We were students together, but when we got jobs across the country from each other, the relationship didn't work out."

"The long-distance relationship is a hard thing to do. I think you have to want to live apart for it to work."

"I agree. In our case, we were both too domestic. We both wanted too much to be settled in our home place so the time between trips began to stretch out."

"I can understand that. It's also very expensive on an Assistant Professor salary."

"All too true. We thought about looking for jobs together or looking again and trying to get the other person a spousal hire, but," he paused and frowned, "We were both too pleased with our jobs to want to move so the energy just seemed to go out of the relationship."

"Was the end ugly?"

"No, actually we keep in touch and have a standing dinner date at one of the annual conferences in chemistry. She's married now, and I like her husband. They're thinking about starting a family. She's younger than I am."

"So she has time," I said and, feeling exposed, immediately wished I had not spoken.

The server cleared our dishes, and we ordered rose sherbet for dessert.

"I want to see you," he said.

"Well, here I am!"

"No, I mean it seriously. I want to spend time with you."

"I like you too," I said and thought how inadequately the words conveyed how much I already cared about him. "But I need to warn you that the next few weeks, maybe even the next month or two, are going to be very busy for me. Maureen's got some social stuff she wants me to do, and I've got to get a grip on the other stuff she has in mind as well as teach my classes."

"I understand."

"I just don't want you to think if I turn you down, it's because I don't want to see you."

"I appreciate the heads up. I've got this history paper I'm writing. It's a departure for me so I'm busy too."

"And I need to take things slowly," I said and felt a little embarrassed, but he nodded and stroked my hand reassuringly.

"Not a problem. Do you like classical guitar?"

"Yes, I do."

"There's a concert Saturday night at the School of Music. We could get dinner and go hear some music."

"Perfect."

"Shall we just be friends and see where it goes?" he asked gently as if he understood my anxiety perfectly.

"Thank you for saying that." I took his hand in mine. "It's nice to know that every date won't be a wrestling match."

"That's not the way I am!" he said, clearly offended.

"No. I didn't mean that at all." I smiled at him. "I meant that I'd be wrestling with myself. You're an attractive guy."

He laughed.

"I'll pick you up at six on Sunday."

The next morning, I was drinking my second cup of coffee and reading an article when my phone rang. I did not recognize the number.

"Hello, Celeste Brinkman speaking."

"This is Blake Hess. I'd like to come talk to you. Where are you?"

"Home."

"Are you busy now?" I looked at my ratty bathrobe and slippers.

"How about in half an hour? I have to be at the university by eleven."

"Okay. I'll be there in half an hour."

By the time the doorbell rang, I was dressed for the day. I ushered Hess into the living room, which I had cleaned up by hiding stacks of papers, journals, and books in the kitchen.

"Can I offer you something to drink? Coffee, tea, milk, or juice."

"I'd take a cup of black coffee."

"I drink espresso so I'll make you a lungo—it's more like American coffee."

"An Americano?"

"Yeah, actually."

"That's what I drink so it's fine."

A smile lit his features for the first time since I had met him, and I realized that he was quite good looking. I smiled back.

"You know your cousin thinks I should ask you out."

"What?" I stopped in the kitchen doorway and turned back.

"Harold. He wants me to ask you out. He's been singing your praises for the last two years, ever since I got my promotion, and we started working together. He thinks the world of you."

"Well, thank you. He was always like a big brother to me. He's a great guy."

"I agree."

I went into the kitchen and realized that Hess had followed me. So much for hiding the mess. I cleared a chair and said, "Sorry. You can sit here while I fix the coffee."

"I'm not hitting on you, Dr. Brinkman."

"Call me Celeste. Not Cece. That's my childhood nickname, and Harold's the only one who uses it."

"Sure. Call me Blake."

"Okay."

"I'm not hitting on you. I'd like to ask you out, but I won't until these murders are cleared up."

"Okay." I could not think of anything else to say.

"I don't mix business and pleasure."

"Business?"

I poured the boiling water into the cups that were about a third full of espresso. I handed Blake his cup.

"Cream or sugar?" He shook his head.

"Let's go in the living room."

He sat down on the couch and I took the easy chair. He blew on his coffee and took a sip.

"Wow! This is great!"

"Thanks. I love coffee."

"I do too. I have an espresso machine in my office, and the guys make fun of me, but everyone sure likes the coffee." He smiled and took another sip. I realized that he was having trouble getting to the point, and I was beginning to worry about being late for my class.

"How can I help you?" I asked.

He looked embarrassed, and I wondered if I had accidentally used my "teacher voice."

"Frankly, I'm having a terrible time getting any kind of grip on these murders." He leaned forward. "Harold acts as a mentor to the younger detectives, and he's been helping me, but he's as baffled as I am. He suggested that I talk with you and maybe use you as a kind of consultant on the case."

"What would that mean?"

"I'd ask you questions about the university, about the people involved, about how things are done. I've done some interviews, but honestly I feel like a Martian invader. Even when people are talking openly to me, I'm not always sure what they're telling me because I don't know the system. I went to college, but being a student shows you only a small part of what goes on at a university. So I'd like your help."

"I'm willing to help, of course."

"Great, but first I'm going to ask you to sign a confidentiality agreement."

He pulled a form from his inside pocket and handed it to me. I read through the dense, bureaucratic prose that informed me that anything the police told me was to be kept in absolute confidence or I could be prosecuted for interference with an on-going police investigation or obstruction of justice. I handed the triplicate form back to him.

"I'm willing to help you, and I'm willing to keep what we talk about in confidence, but I'm not willing to sign this form."

"Why?"

"My commitments elsewhere make me uncomfortable signing this form."

"What do you mean 'commitments elsewhere?'" He sounded irritated and suspicious.

"I am now working for the Provost. I think that she might see this form as creating a conflict of interest."

"But we wouldn't pay you," he protested. I restrained myself from engaging the topic of free labor from academics ("Oh, Dr. Brinkman, wouldn't you like to give a lecture at our library group/book club/community center for Women's History Month?") and shook my head.

"Whether I'm paid or not doesn't matter."

"If you're going to help me in good conscience, why should the form matter?"

"Because it's a legal, binding form. I shouldn't sign it without formal legal advice, and I'm not going to pay for that."

"Don't you have lawyers at the university?"

Again, I restrained myself from lecturing him on free labor from academics but also had to admit that law professors, better paid than I, could probably afford to give away some time.

"Let me talk to Dr. Shaughnessy," I finally conceded, taking back the form. "She may have a suggestion on how to handle this."

Blake looked so disappointed that I felt sorry for him and added, "I'll try to talk with her this morning. I'll call you as soon as I can."

He fished a card out of his wallet and wrote his cell phone number on the back.

"I'm sorry," I said, and to my surprise, he smiled.

"Your cousin warned me that you're the smartest person in his family. Actually, you're doing exactly what I would do in your place."

We then chatted about neighborhoods and coffee houses for another ten minutes while we finished our coffee.

The moment I closed the door behind Blake, I texted Maureen: "Must talk to you ASAP. Police matter." Ten minutes later, she called.

"What is it? I'm between meetings and only have a few minutes."

"Blake Hess, that detective, came by and asked me to sign a confidentiality agreement in exchange for helping the police."

"So sign it."

"This is a serious document that could get me in trouble if I do not keep all the police information confidential."

"Shit."

"And what if they ask me about withholding information? I'm not comfortable with this document at all."

"I understand. Give me some time to think about this."

"Sure. I'll scan it and e-mail it over so you can see it. I'm in class until 2:00."

64

"Okay. Why don't you stop by then, and we can talk for a minute?"

"I'd like more than a minute."

"Me too, but that's what I have. See you then."

I stood looking at my phone and feeling alone. Maureen was the only person I could talk to about the murders, and she could only give me "a minute."

After class, I dashed over to the Administration Building and ran up the stairs to Maureen's office.

"Dr. Brinkman. I'm here to see Dr. Shaughnessy," I told the receptionist breathlessly. She called Maureen and soon waved me into her office.

"Are you okay?" Maureen asked, studying my red face.

"I got out of class late and ran to catch you."

"Flattering."

"No, business," I quipped, and she chuckled.

"I talked to a lawyer, and he agrees that Hess is blowing smoke. The cops never prosecute on breach of confidentiality because needing help from other people would make them look incompetent. It's a scare tactic. My attorney said to sign it and not worry."

I studied Maureen carefully. Could I believe her? She wanted what she wanted and knew ways of getting it. What if I ended up in trouble?

"I've been thinking about it since this morning. In good conscience, I can't sign that form, and I'm not going to do it."

"What a good, little Catholic you are!" Maureen said sarcastically.

"It's not that," I began and then nodded. "You're right. I am. I will talk to Hess and try to get him to let me in without the form, but I won't sign it."

"Okay." Maureen shrugged. "You figure it out."

"Can we talk for a few minutes?" She glanced at her watch and nodded, motioning me over to the sofa.

"What's going on?" she asked.

"I need to talk to Frank O'Donnell."

"Frank? Why?"

"I'm following up something and need to talk with him."

"I'll come up with something."

"I also need to know where you were the weekend LouAnn Bond was killed."

Maureen sat silent, staring away from me.

"Maureen?"

"I was home in bed."

"With Sam?" The question slipped out, and Maureen greeted it with a hearty laugh.

"No. What an imagination you have!" she exclaimed and laughed again.

"It gives me hope for the future," I said, and she rolled her eyes.

"I was literally home in bed," she said emphatically.

"Were you sick?"

"No. Sick of."

I must have looked even more puzzled because she sighed and explained, "About once a month, this job, my life, all of it, just gets to me, and I spend the weekend in bed."

"Did you see anyone?"

"No."

"You didn't even order a pizza or Chinese?"

"No. When I collapse, I don't even cook. I eat chicken pot pies and ice cream or cheese and crackers."

"You didn't rent a movie or answer the phone?" She shook her head. "What about your cell? Did you talk to your daughters?"

"No. That's the point. I watched five old movies, read a couple of trashy books, ate, and slept a blissful twelve hours a day."

"There's no way to verify this? You didn't text someone about what you were watching?"

"No. The point is that when I do this, I don't answer any of the phones, I don't do e-mail, and I don't answer the door."

"You don't even answer a call from one of your daughters?"

"I would, of course, but they didn't call. They know about this. I've done it for years to decompress so I usually send them a text on Wednesday or Thursday that I'm taking the weekend off."

"When did you leave work on Friday?"

"Early. Two o'clock so yes, I could have gone to the library, killed LouAnn, chopped her up, put her in the retrieval system, and then returned home to eat chicken pot pies and watch movies."

"What about Sam?"

"He was out of town visiting his daughter."

"He didn't call."

"I e-mailed him to say I didn't want to talk until he got back."

"Why?"

"So he wouldn't worry, but he knows about my weekends off." Her tone told me that she thought it was a stupid question, but it also told me that she was worried.

"I think you need to talk to the police about LouAnn Bond and the stuff she did."

"I can't and I won't. If you tell them, I'll deny it all."

"That's why I'm not signing any agreement on your advice," I said angrily. "You might just hang me out to dry."

"I'm sorry, Celeste. You're smart and have good intentions. I know you're giving me good advice, but I can't do what you're asking me to do. There is always a leak."

66

"Did Bond actually blackmail you over Sam Jacoby? That story about the call in the middle of the night?"

"You may think lightning doesn't strike in the same place twice, but I was telling the truth. You can ask Sam." Maureen paused and then added, "I think she did it to let me know she was still watching me."

"Tell Mr. Jacoby that I'll be calling for an appointment." She nodded.

"So what are you going to do?" Maureen asked as I stood up.

"I'm going to talk to Hess again and see if I can come to an agreement with him without the form." She regarded me with a kind of watchfulness I found almost unnerving. "I'm not going to tell him about your experiences with Bond."

"So you're going on with this..."

"Investigation? 'Sleuthing,' as Nancy Drew would call it?" Maureen smiled. "Yes, I'm going on with it."

"There's a party for some big donors on Sunday evening. Very dressy with a sit-down dinner. All the trustees will be there. I'll put you next to Frank O'Donnell."

"No, just introduce me to him at the cocktail hour so I can actually talk with him."

"You're right. That's even better. I'll have Pat send you the details."

"Fine."

My tone was cold and angry, but I felt disheartened so half of my anger was at myself for having gotten hooked into this situation. She called to me as I reached for the doorknob, and I turned back.

"Thank you, Celeste." She sounded sincere, and I have manners.

"You're welcome."

I walked out into the late afternoon sun and turned back toward the department in search of Cass Britten. When I walked into her office, she was sitting with her long legs propped up on the desk, staring out the window.

"Hey, Cass."

"Hey, dear. What's up?"

I closed the office door behind me.

"I need to ask you a couple of questions, and I need you to promise that you won't ask any questions in return."

"That's weird," she said, frowning. "If this is about lesbian sex, can't I just buy you a manual or, better yet, give you a hands-on demonstration?"

I had to laugh.

"It isn't about sex. If it were, I'd definitely go for the demonstration, but I'm still shopping in the man market."

"Their gain, my loss," she said with mock resignation. "Ask away."

"Where were you the weekend of February 17?"

"Who knows?" She threw up her hands.

"I'm serious."

Cass studied me for a moment, and then picked up her cell phone.

"I keep my calendar on here so let's see." She manipulated the phone and finally said, "The Hot Biscuit Marathon in Memphis on Saturday. I went down on Friday and stayed until Sunday."

"Did you fly?"

"Of course not. It's too damned expensive. I drove."

"Did you go with someone?" She shook her head. "Did you stay with friends?" She shook her head again. "Did you see anyone you knew at the marathon?"

"No. What are you getting at? You sound like my dear, departed mother, or the police."

"I'm sorry. I can't explain, but it's important that you answer my questions."

She looked at me for a long time and then whistled.

"That was the weekend before they found LouAnn Bond, wasn't it?"

"Yes."

"So you're asking me if I killed her?" A flush spread across Cass's cheeks. "I can't fuckin' believe this! I thought we were friends."

"We are friends. That's why I'm asking." There was an uncomfortable silence while Cass continued to stare at me in disbelief. "Where did you stay?"

"Some dumpy hotel downtown."

"Which hotel?"

"I honestly don't remember."

"Did you use your credit card?"

"No. I paid cash." Cass was six feet tall and in great shape--she regularly ran, cycled, swam, and lifted weights. For her, moving LouAnn Bond's small body would have been, if not easy, possible. As for cutting her up...knowing what I did about Cass's home improvement projects.... I refused to go there.

"Why did you pay cash?"

"I've totally fucked up my credit card," Cass said, looking embarrassed. "I was up to the limit, and I don't have a debit card so I had to pay cash."

"And you can't remember the name of the hotel?" Cass leaned back in her chair and closed her eyes for a moment.

"It was the Swan, I think."

"Okay, call them and get a receipt faxed or e-mailed to you."

"You are kidding, aren't you?"

"I wish I were, but I'm not." I stood up and turned to leave.

"Celeste." I paused with my hand on the doorknob. "You don't believe I killed her, do you?"

"No, I don't believe that. I'm actually trying to protect you."

I was getting ready for bed when my phone rang that evening. It was Cass.

"Celeste, I can't fuckin' believe this!" She sounded desperate.

"What?"

"I called and faxed them my request with my signature, and they don't have me registered at their crappy hotel."

"What?"

"They don't. I'm almost positive it was that one."

"But you aren't 100% sure?"

"No."

"Google the area and look at the other hotels. Maybe you can spot another name that rings a bell."

"I've already done that—it looks like a fuckin' aviary."

"You need to find the hotel and get a receipt or..."

"Or what, Nancy Drew?"

"Or the police will be doing it for you."

"So you're reporting me?" Her tone was angry and accusing.

"No, but the university is full of people only too willing to gossip."

"Like I'd kill someone for a fuckin' committee appointment. Actually, it's more likely I'd kill someone for putting me on a committee." I chuckled and could feel some of the tension between us easing.

"Cass, you and I both know that Bond's blackmailing Maureen and your break up look like much bigger motives than any stupid committee appointment."

"Well, that's certainly comforting."

"I'm sorry. I shouldn't have said anything, but I'm your friend, and I don't want to see you get in trouble."

"I know." She sighed. "I'll see if I can find that damn hotel."

Chapter Nine

On Wednesday morning, I called Blake Hess and told him that I could not sign the confidentiality form.

"I'm a good Catholic girl, and you can trust my word that I will exercise discretion with regard to police secrets, but I'm not opening myself to any more legal wrangles. I've had enough to last a lifetime."

"I'm sorry you feel that way. I was hoping we could work together."

"Not unless you can forget about the form."

"I don't feel comfortable doing that."

"I understand."

"But no hard feelings. I will call you after this case is over."

"Sure."

When I hung up, I felt freer than I had since the paper had come out of Hess's coat pocket. I finished breakfast, graded a stack of quizzes, and began preparing my classes for the next day.

In the late afternoon, as I drove to campus, I turned on the local news and heard that an arrest had been made for the murder of Tareka James. The man with whom she had been living, the father of her two children, had been arrested for her murder. They interviewed his crying mother who kept saying, "Ray would never hurt Tareka. He spent the weekend searching for her. He loved her." Apparently this claim flew in the face of an earlier charge of domestic violence that had been dropped without prosecution. I now thought I knew what Emily Hartshorn's hesitation had meant.

As I walked to the President's office, my cell phone beeped and there was a text that the library would open as usual on Thursday morning.

Marilyn Wilhoyt was away from her desk when I came in. A clean-cut, preppy-looking student in an adjacent work area informed me that she would return in a few minutes. The student then excused herself, gathered up her backpack, and left. No one else seemed to be in the office.

"Hello, you must be Dr. Brinkman."

"And you must be Ms. Wilhoyt."

"Just call me Marilyn," she said. "I'm sorry, but we need to stay in here because everyone else has gone for the day." She was a forty-something, buxom, bottle-blonde who radiated worry.

"This is fine," I assured her, taking a seat in the waiting area. Wilhoyt perched on a nearby easy chair.

"So how can I help you?"

"My alma mater is interested in having President Truman speak at commencement."

"And what is your alma mater?"

"Beloit College," I said truthfully.

"That's very interesting."

"I'm surprised you've heard of Beloit."

"But, of course, I have! Wasn't it one of those 'schools that change lives?'" She put the quote marks around the phrase with her plump hands. I felt ashamed. Just because Wilhoyt was not faculty but staff, I had underestimated her knowledge of the academic world.

"Yes, it was in that book." I felt even more embarrassed.

"So how did you like it?"

"I got a wonderful education and made some life-long friends. It was the kind of college experience anyone who is a total nerd wants to have."

"Very different from here," she said softly as if her remark might be overheard.

"Yes, but I like teaching here. I like the diversity and challenges," I assured her and suddenly realized that I was losing control of the conversation. "But about President Truman…"

"So what would your alma mater be interested in hearing about from President Truman?"

"Since he himself is the graduate of a small, private college and served as vice president at one, they were thinking that he might want to talk about the differences between a large, public university like ours and a smaller, private institution. Many Beloit graduates will be going on to larger institutions and some, like me, will end up teaching in them. It would make for an interesting graduation speech."

I wanted to stand up and take a bow, but my increasing fluency as a liar gave me pause.

"That sounds very interesting, and, as you know, President Truman is always interested in reaching out to other institutions. When would they want him to speak?"

"Graduation is on May 18."

"Let me check the date before we go any farther." She walked over to the reception desk and sat down at the computer. I had already checked the President's online, public calendar and knew that the date was blocked.

71

"Oh, shoot, I thought so. That's when the President and his wife leave on the alumni trip to Norway."

"Norway? Wow!"

"Yes, every year a select group of alumni take a trip with the President and his wife." I translated "select group of alumni" to mean richer-than-God donors and shuddered. Sucking up in view of the fjords was probably better than sucking up in town, but on a boat, you would be trapped. I tuned back in to hear Marilyn telling me, "I'm so sorry that you waited so late to ask. Maybe he could speak next year."

"Perhaps, but they may already have someone. They had someone scheduled for this year who backed out due to a family emergency so a friend of mine in the administration sent out a general call for help."

"It's so nice of you to try to help." It was a big, fat pitch right over the plate.

"I do try to be helpful, and I will talk to them about next year or perhaps the year after. How are you doing? You've taken over LouAnn Bond's job, haven't you? I imagine that must be so difficult in addition to your own job."

Marilyn sank back wearily and sighed.

"It's just been hell, if you'll pardon my language."

"I was there when they found her body."

"So you saw it? How horrible!"

"No. I couldn't see anything, but the professor sitting next to me could, and he almost fainted."

"I can imagine!"

"Are you going to have her job permanently?"

Marilyn shifted in her seat uncomfortably, and I thought that I might have asked too personal a question.

"Definitely not!"

"Why?"

"I like being clear about what I'm doing and what I'm responsible for," she said, pursing her lips in a firm line.

"Weren't you LouAnn's assistant?"

"I was not!"

"I'm sorry, but…"

"She liked to make people think I was her assistant, but my title is Business Manager for the Office of the President. I work for the President and University. I did not work for LouAnn Bond."

"How very odd. I thought someone told me that she was your supervisor." I felt a little guilty throwing gasoline on the fire.

"LouAnn liked to pretend she was my boss and Dorothy Sizemore's boss, for that matter, but she wasn't."

"Who is Dorothy Sizemore?"

"She runs all the events for the Office of the President."

"So you're both glad Bond is gone."

"Good Heavens no! I would never wish anyone dead," she began sanctimoniously, "But after working with LouAnn for ten years…" She caught herself and did not finish the sentence.

"It's kind of scary, but around the university, I've heard nothing but bad things about her."

"And most people—not to speak ill of the dead—don't know the half of it."

"She wasn't dishonest, was she?" I asked in what I hoped was a naïve tone.

"Not so long as I was keeping the books!"

"I read her obituary, and she doesn't seem to have had much of a life," I said.

"She didn't have any life at all except for that crackpot church she belongs, I mean, belonged to."

"Which one?"

"That Episcopal church on Orchard Street. You know, the one that broke off and went independent when they made the gay guy a bishop."

"St. Luke's? I think I saw the name in her obituary." Marilyn nodded. "I didn't realize that was the church that left the denomination. I thought they had closed their doors years ago."

"No. It's still going and, if you ask me," she lowered her voice conspiratorially, "Not doing any part of the Lord's business."

"So this affected her job?" Marilyn nodded, opening her mouth to speak when she happened to glance at her watch.

"Heavens, it's almost five thirty! I'm so sorry, Dr. Brinkman, but I have to go. I have to pick up my daughter from basketball practice, and if I don't go right now, I'll be late."

"I'll let you know about next year." She nodded distractedly as she took her purse out of a desk drawer.

"I'm sorry if I spoke out of turn," she said, ushering me through the door which she locked behind us. "I don't mean to be uncharitable, but LouAnn Bond was the bane of my existence. I would never wish anyone dead, but I can't help being glad she's gone." Marilyn searched my face, checking my reaction to her confession.

"Don't worry," I said comfortingly. "I'm sure you're doing a great job, and I can't think of anyone who would blame you for how you feel. I just can't understand why the President kept LouAnn on if everyone found her so difficult." Marilyn shook her head.

"It beats me except she was very good at keeping the Trustees happy, and they are a real pain in the patootie, but don't quote me on that!"

Before I could ask her if she had actually used the word "patootie," an expression I had not heard since childhood, Marilyn had waved and was hurrying toward the parking lot next to the administration building. Trying not to consider issues of proximity as they reflected issues of hierarchy, I began the three-block walk to where my car was parked.

As soon as I got home, I sat down at the computer and found St. Luke's Church on Orchard Street. I went to their professional-looking website where the historic reasons for leaving the Episcopal Church were enumerated: the revision of the Book of Common Prayer, the ordination of women, and, the final blow, the installation of an openly gay bishop. The Most Reverend Joseph Potts shepherded the congregation. I checked the worship schedule and was thinking glumly about where I might be at 9:30 the next Sunday morning when it occurred to me that attending services might not be my best strategy.

The next morning, I called and left a message that I wished to meet with Reverend Potts about joining the congregation.

Within the hour, Reverend Potts' mellifluous voice was agreeing to visit with me later that day. I taught my classes and went home to change from my usual pants into a modestly long skirt, sensible shoes, and a dark sweater with a slight scoop neck. I dropped my arty earrings into the jewelry box and put on some plain pearls. I pulled my shoulder-length hair back into a small, tight knot, removed my eye make-up, and dug out my glasses from three years ago. My prescription had changed very little, but what had I been thinking when I got those round tortoise shell frames? I sighed and then knotted a bright green scarf around my neck.

The small, formerly Episcopal, now independent church on Orchard Street was in excellent repair as was the rectory next door. The website had informed me that the congregation was a "small, devoted community of faithful followers of the Lord." When Reverend Potts led me into the rectory, we passed picture after picture of church activities—meetings, retreats, potlucks, and picnics. The community was small enough that by the third or fourth picture, I realized that I was seeing the same people, some of whom looked familiar, but I could not stop to study the photos.

"Do you have a Sunday school?" I asked curiously.

Reverend Potts shook his head sadly.

"We are an older congregation so there is no need. Do you have children?"

"No. I'm not married and actually have no intention of ever marrying."

"But you're still young," he protested gallantly as we sat down in his office which was lined with cherry paneling and built-in bookcases. The windows that looked out over the well-kept back garden had small, stained-glass panels of Jesus as the Good Shepherd and His blessing of the loaves and fishes. I knew that any kinship I felt with this church probably ended with the subject matter of these windows.

"I'm very serious about my teaching."

"And what do you teach?"

"French." The lie was out before I thought about it.

"Where?"

"At the university."

74

"I see and what brings you here?"

He leaned back in his chair, away from the circle of light cast by the desk lamp. He was in his fifties and handsome in an anemic way as if he had made one too many blood donations. He studied me with his pale blue eyes, folding and re-folding his long fingers as he listened.

"I was raised Catholic but have been attending the Episcopal Church since college." I added a silent prayer that Mary, the Mother of God, and my own mother would forgive me for this lie. It was one thing to skip mass and quite another to change churches.

"I've been uncomfortable for a while, but since they made that homosexual a bishop, I haven't felt a part of things." He was nodding. "I feel like the time has come to explore making a change to a church where I'll feel more comfortable."

"And why do you think that might be here at St. Luke's?"

"I checked your website and read all the material there." I didn't add that most of it made me want to vomit.

"And you agreed with what you read?"

"It was like the answer to my prayers." I paused and looked down as if I were having difficulty speaking. "I know now that I may not have much time."

"Is there something wrong?" he asked with real concern. "Are you sick?"

"No, but since LouAnn Bond died, I've been thinking how none of us know when our hour might come. It's exactly what it says in the Bible. We can't know, and it might even come today for me like it did for LouAnn."

"So you knew LouAnn," he said softly, and a look of genuine sadness crossed his face.

Amazing. I had finally found someone who cared about her.

"She was a mainstay of this congregation. Of course, it would be inappropriate to have a woman serve on the altar or as Sacristan or in leadership, but in her capacity as a lay woman, she was an invaluable servant to this community and to me."

"I can't imagine who would do such a terrible thing to her."

"We can't either. The police came to talk with me because they knew she was a parishioner here, but I'm sorry to say that I could be of no help whatsoever. I could only tell them that no task was too humble for her and how very much she will be missed here at St. Luke's."

"Everyone at the university misses her too," I assured him.

"I am glad to hear that because she often said that at the university she felt like a missionary in a hostile land. She was a great reader of Paul and said that she felt almost as if she had been sent to convert the pagan. She was distressed by so much of what she saw happening."

"I know. Forcing students to study subjects like women's literature and women's history as if the ordinary courses don't include that information."

75

"Yes, that, of course, but LouAnn was even more deeply disturbed by the championing of," Reverend Potts curled his lip before he almost hissed, "Homosexuality."

"Ah, yes. There have been cases…"

"She told me about a faculty member in the English Department who is openly homosexual and flaunts her life style. This woman actually expected to be given an important committee appointment, but LouAnn told me she had found a way to fix things so that would not happen." I nodded in an enthusiastically approving manner. "She told me that she did what she could, using the cunning of the serpent and wisdom of the dove, to try and guide the university in the right path."

"It's very difficult to do anything without power."

"Yes, but she felt that her job in the President's office, as his trusted right-hand man, so to speak, gave her influence in the right places."

"I've heard that she was most helpful to the Board of Trustees."

"Yes, she was certainly of service there. She always said that she thought it was her special mission to keep them informed about issues and help them identify sympathetic allies. She was very pleased with how she had been able to help this recent group of trustees. They were so receptive and grateful."

"Do you have any idea what issues she was currently helping them with? I might be able to do something to further her work."

"I didn't understand it all since I've never been part of a university, but she was helping some of the trustees find a way to revisit the issue of partner benefits." He shook his head disapprovingly with a doleful air. "She also mentioned that there was some question of a totally unsuitable person getting tenure."

"Did she tell you this person's name or department?"

The good reverend looked shocked.

"That would be relaying confidential information. LouAnn was always discreet, so careful to keep the confidences entrusted to her, as she should be, I mean, should have been. She just said that the situation was so shocking and 'morally reprehensible'—those are the words she used—that she could not even bring herself to tell me the details. She was such a modest woman."

He sat lost in thought for a moment, and then said eagerly, "So you knew her well?"

"Not well, but when we met, we recognized that we had interests in common."

"She was always ready to reach out to others to help them find the right path."

"Of course."

"So you are interested in joining St. Luke's?"

"This is a first step really."

"Of course, one does not want to rush into such a commitment," he said sanctimoniously.

"How do you suggest I proceed?"

76

"Please join us at services on Sunday. We also have evensong daily. LouAnn often used to come on her way home after a busy day. Sometimes we would end up getting a bit of supper together."

"So you aren't married?"

"No." He suddenly shook his finger at me and said, "Young woman, you are doing more of the interviewing here than I am."

I laughed girlishly, something I did not even do as a girl. The easy lies were worrisome, but this newfound flair for disguise and drama was downright horrifying.

"I like to know about people," I assured him with a smile.

"LouAnn was like that—always getting to know about people, drawing them out," he said nostalgically. "She had an uncanny knack for finding things out."

I wondered exactly how she had used this gift in the parish.

"Do you know her family?"

"Her mother very occasionally came to church when she was able, but her heart was broken over LouAnn's brother. He got into trouble with the law, and LouAnn always said that her brother's going to jail, not cancer, was what killed her mother."

"And there was no other family?"

"Not here. Maybe back in West Virginia, but LouAnn always talked as if she were alone in the world except for her mother."

"She was not in touch with her brother?"

"I believe she sent him money and prayed that he would find the right path, but she said they had always had conflicting values."

"That's difficult, but, of course, she had friends."

"Here at St. Luke's we are all friends."

I nodded, remembering what Granny, a veteran of a thousand Altar Guild meetings, used to say, "If you want to see unchristian behavior, join a committee and go to a meeting at church."

"I was sorry to miss her funeral, but I had the flu."

"It was a very difficult service for me," he murmured, and I nodded sympathetically.

"Were there many people?"

"Very few, I'm afraid. The President of the university, of course, and his wife, a few parishioners, and Mary Smythe—she's our parish photographer and never misses an event—but only a few others from LouAnn's office. Of course, it's hard to get away on a work-day morning, and, as we know, a prophet often goes unhallowed in his own land."

I glanced at my watch.

"I'm so sorry, but it's getting late, and I have a dinner engagement," I said, rising from my seat. "Thank you so much for your time." I held out my hand.

"We should fill out the parish census form for you so you'll be on our mailing list," he said, seeming a bit flustered. "I've been so distracted by our conversation and thinking about LouAnn that I entirely forgot."

"I'm sorry, but I do need to go."

"At least, let me give you this brief history and guide to the parish. We could perhaps fill out your census form after church on Sunday."

"Of course," I said, taking the handsomely bound book from him.

"I can introduce you to some of our parishioners at the coffee hour following the service, and then we can fill out the form and talk about your course of instruction. Have you been confirmed?"

"Yes."

"Then this will be a course of instruction to learn about our church and its affiliates."

I must have slipped and looked skeptical because he quickly rushed to add, "Just so you'll feel more comfortable. We have an acceptance ceremony—a small public welcome--we do for new members who are already baptized and confirmed in another Christian church. I also need to tell you about the various activities we sponsor. There's a Bible study I lead every Sunday evening."

"Great. I look forward to hearing about all of it."

I picked up my purse, tucked the book inside, and turned to go. He walked me to the door where we shook hands again.

"My goodness, I am getting absent-minded," he said. "I apologize, but I don't think I asked your name."

"Susan Faludi."

"Interesting last name. You did say you were raised Catholic?"

"Yes, it's Italian." This time I lied just for the hell of it.

I said ten Hail Mary's on the way home, asking forgiveness for all the lies I had told and for taking Susan Faludi's name in vain. The only other name that had popped into my mind was Mary Daly, and I was afraid that he might, even out there on the fringe, have heard about the radical theological thinker. Susan Faludi was an appropriate choice. When I considered St. Luke's, I felt sure that I had never before encountered such an example of what Faludi called "backlash."

After taking a long, hot shower, I made a grilled cheese sandwich, poured a glass of milk, and sat down at my computer. It struck me as curious that Reverend Potts was not married. He seemed like the kind of high-maintenance guy who needed a live-in servant and what easier way to get one than by marrying a woman?

I went to the archives of the local paper and began reading about the acrimonious departure of St. Luke's from the Episcopal Diocese. The Diocese had held the deed on the property where St. Luke's was located so an anonymous benefactor had put up a cool million dollars to get the property and building free and clear for the newly-formed St Luke's Independent Church.

I pulled out the directory, went through the forty pictures, and counted. The church had about sixty members. I looked for familiar names or faces, finding evidence of a university connection on page three. Alexander and Millicent Popham. Big, old money. Alexander, notoriously conservative, was on the current Board of Trustees. As far as I knew, Millicent mainly served tea, but neither I, nor anyone else, would know much--the Pophams were so rich that their names were rarely in the news. I remembered a scandal about Bitsy Popham (Was that her real name? Money is no excuse for some things!) killing someone while driving drunk, but the news had been there one day and gone the next. It seemed to me that her sister Mary, known as "Poppy," had also been in the car, and there was some question about who had been driving. Mary Popham. Uncomfortably close to Mary Poppins. Honestly, did these people have no sense? I could hear Granny saying, "They have so many dollars, they don't need sense."

I went back to reading about the establishment of St. Luke's. Reverend Potts had been the Rector when the split came, but a split of another sort had happened when his wife of fifteen years came out publicly against leaving the diocese and then left her husband. Her letter to the editor articulated in painful detail her decision to leave her husband and pursue ministry on her own. She had been accepted to a prestigious, liberal seminary, and her goal was to work for women to have equal opportunities to serve in all aspects of ministry. I was stunned by her letter and wondered if she had told the good Reverend in advance or just propped the editorial page by his place at breakfast.

I went back and printed all the articles and her letter to the editor. I put them in a file that I labeled "St. Luke's," thinking that someday I would find her and ask if I could write something about her struggles.

When I got to bed, I lay awake for a long time trying to sort things out. I finally turned on the light and got a spiral notebook from my desk. I sat staring at the blank page not knowing how to organize my notes. I finally put Harold's name on one page and wrote down everything he had told me. Then I wrote Marilyn Wilhoyt's name at the top of one page and Reverend Joseph Potts' on the next. I then listed everything each one had told me. Surveying my notes at the end, I again realized that only the pastor had expressed fondness for LouAnn Bond. I felt a moment of intense pity, unmitigated by Potts' claim that they were all "friends" at St. Luke's.

I decided that I would call Maureen the next day and see if she could find a pretext for me to talk to Dorothy Sizemore, the woman who ran events for the President's office. Sunday was coming and at that dinner I would get to meet the Board of Trustees. They all had official university biographies as well as public profiles, and I needed to study whatever I could find. I also needed to call Emily Hartshorn and schedule my tour of the library. I made a neat list.

As I turned out the light, I sighed. Trying to make sense of all this information and see the path before me excited the researcher in me but never before had I felt so uneasy about the potential impact of my findings.

Chapter Ten

Thursday I made an appointment with Emily Hartshorn. When I expressed my sympathy over Tareka James' death, she sounded overwhelmed and forlorn. At three-thirty, I walked through the door of Hartshorn's second-floor office to find one of my former students seated at the desk that had once been Tareka James'.

"Briana, what are you doing here?"

"Don't sound so shocked!" she said cheekily. "I'm temping until I find out whether I got accepted to the teacher certification program."

"Really? You're going to teach?" I tried to keep the surprise out of my voice. Clearly bright, Briana had been visibly bored in my class and resentful of the interest I had shown in her.

"I know it's a shock, but I've been working at a pre-school and discovered I'm good with kids. I'm a lot more serious now than back when I was in your class," she assured me.

"I'm relieved to know that. You were so bright that it frustrated me to no end that you seemed to care so little for your studies."

Briana looked down and frowned. Feeling I might have overstepped the boundaries of politeness, I said, "I'm sorry."

"Not at all. You actually took an interest in me, which annoyed me at the time, but I appreciate it now. I'm sorry I was such a jerk."

"No, you weren't. You were just young."

"And very stupid. But I'm on my way now."

"I couldn't be happier about this! If you need a recommendation, I'd be glad to write one," I offered.

"That's all done for now, but I'm going to put you on my list for the future."

"Great! Actually, I have an appointment to see Ms. Hartshorn."

While Briana was letting Hartshorn know I had arrived, I noticed the framed photo on her desk.

"Is that your daughter?"

"Yes." Briana gave me a big smile. "She's just three and the light of my life."

"A great motivator toward maturity."

"That and living with my mother," she laughed, and then added, "My baby's father left town when he found out I was pregnant."

"I'm sorry to hear that."

"Actually I'm glad. He was total bad news. It's not a good excuse, but being with him is part of why I was such a terrible student when I had you."

"Hello, Dr. Brinkman," said Hartshorn as she came in. "Briana, can I have the key to LORETTA. I'm sure Dr. Brinkman wants to see the system up close."

Briana opened the left door of her desk to reveal a row of hooks on which hung neatly tagged keys.

"Here it is." She handed the key to Hartshorn as she made a note on the clipboard from the space next to the keys.

"Thanks. I'll put it back if you aren't here when we finish," said Hartshorn and turned to usher me out the door.

"Good seeing you, Briana," I said and reached over the desk to shake her hand, "And good luck!"

"You'll be hearing from me," she promised.

"I hope so."

"So you know Briana," said Hartshorn when we were out of earshot.

"She was in one of my classes several years ago. Smart but not terribly serious. She would write a brilliant paper and get it in late, and then bomb the exam. She'd miss class and then come in and say something so smart it would take my breath away. I tried to talk with her, but she was unreachable at that point. I'm so glad to know that she made it."

"I can hardly believe what you say because she's been a godsend! Totally responsible, and, as you say, she's very smart."

"She said that she's going back to school to get her teacher certification."

"I know. I was hoping to convince her to stay on, but teaching offers her a much better career."

"Will Tareka James be hard to replace?" Hartshorn shot me a keen look. "I didn't mean personally. God knows we are none of us replaceable. I meant hard to replace in terms of her work."

"She was my close friend and right hand for seven years," Hartshorn said sadly.

"So you knew about the problems with her boyfriend."

Hartshorn had guided me into the elevator and now gazed resolutely at the buttons.

"Here we are," she announced when we arrived at the basement level. "I'll bet you've never been down here," she added as she led me down a hallway.

"Right. I never even knew there were staff stairs."

"Yes. It's in case of fire so the people in this part of the library are closer to an escape route."

82

She opened the door to the cataloging department, saying, "I assumed that you wanted a full tour of the library and some information about the status of our various projects."

Although her tone was polite, I sensed an underlying current of wariness or disapproval.

"I don't want to waste your time, but that seems to be what Dr. Shaughnessy wanted me to do in order to get up to speed for my new position on the Library Advisory Committee. I gather that being her liaison and being a department rep are two different tasks."

"Of course."

She gave me a quick overview of cataloging including information about which books came automatically from which presses with their complete information uploaded into the system. Although the days of meticulously cataloging each book on site were gone, some books, acquired by donation, ordered at the request of librarians, faculty, or other patrons, still required cataloging.

"We used to have three full-time catalogers, and now we have one, and she's part-time," she said softly.

We walked further into the large open area that held desks, boxes stacked against one wall, and many trucks of books in various stages of processing.

"Hello, Pamela," I said, stopping by the desk of a stocky brunette who was putting labels on the spines of books. She jumped and looked up.

"I'm sorry. I didn't mean to startle you," I said in a friendly tone, and she blinked her large, brown eyes.

"Oh, hi, Celeste."

"How are you?" She was pale and had dark circles under her eyes.

"I'm okay."

"I hope you aren't worrying about Steven. I'm sure he'll get tenure. We all think he's just great." Instead of reassuring her, I seemed to have hit a nerve. She stood up and murmured something about her stomach as she headed for the ladies' room just outside the department door.

"I hope she's okay," I said, turning to Hartshorn.

"Probably just the stomach thing that's going around," she replied as we made our way back to the only enclosed office in the large room.

"Carl, can we come in?" she asked, rapping on the open door. A harried, balding man in his sixties motioned for us to enter.

"Okay," he was saying into the phone, "As long as we don't get billed until the books ship, we should be okay. I'll talk to you soon. Thanks for the help." He hung up the phone and smiled at Hartshorn.

"Emily, this is a rare pleasure!"

"Carl Smarinsky, this is Dr. Celeste Brinkman from the English Department."

"Nice to meet you, Dr. Brinkman." He came around the desk to shake my hand. "To what do we owe the honor of this visit?"

"Dr. Brinkman is now the Provost's liaison to the Library Advisory Committee. I'm giving her a tour of the library and decided to start here."

"Good idea since all items, including the virtual ones, pass through here."

"I wanted to mention that I think one of your employees might need to go home."

"Oh, really?"

"Yes, Pamela Rykker seems to be sick," said Hartshorn.

"She hasn't been herself for the past few weeks, but none of us have been, and there's that stomach bug that's been going around. I will talk with her and see about giving her the rest of the day off."

"How long have you worked here?" I asked curiously.

"Since they built this library. I was hired the year it opened--thirty-five years ago this spring. I started here right out of school as a reference librarian."

"You've certainly seen a lot of changes."

"Yes. Some for the better, some for the worse, but there is always change," he said with a smile.

"So you handle acquisitions?" I gestured to what looked like invoices covering his desk.

"Yes. The materials and the bills both go through me. I have an assistant who handles the payables and another assistant who does the ordering, but I oversee the whole operation."

"Was it always this way?"

"No. Back before databases and digitized materials, when everything had to be cataloged, acquisitions was a separate department, but when automation came and the demand for on-site cataloging diminished, it became cost-effective to merge the two departments. When Caroline Harrow retired eight years ago, I inherited her job." He smiled ruefully.

"So you're the one I complain to when the book I requested that the library buy two years ago never shows up?"

Irritation crossed his face, quickly covered by a smile.

"The buck does stop here, and communication is sometimes not our forte, but do feel free to let me know if anything like that happens." His smile seemed forced this time.

"I'll keep that in mind," I assured him, smiling back.

"I know that you are, as always, swamped so we'll say good-bye," Emily said.

I shook hands again with Carl Smarinsky who struck me as the not entirely benign product of a by-gone age, and we walked back to the elevator.

"I can't imagine how difficult all these changes have been for him," I said, and Emily studied me for a moment before nodding. "Do you think library science has hanged more or faster than other professions?" I asked as we rode up to the first floor.

"I don't know about other professions, but I do know that in the last twenty years libraries have undergone rapid and pervasive change. Carl's bright and figured out which way the wind was blowing earlier than most people." She did not mask her hostility.

"What do you mean?" I asked, and Hartshorn shifted uncomfortably. "Please. Tell me what you mean. I can be trusted to be discreet, and I need to understand how things operate here. Not just how the books or databases get to us but also how the operation runs."

Hartshorn said nothing and held the elevator door for me. I did not enter but stood facing her. I decided to go for broke.

"I know that you run this library, and that the Director does virtually nothing but glad-hand and fund-raise. Dr. Shaughnessy is putting me on the Library Advisory Committee because she cares about the library and wants to do what she can to help it improve. I am here as her eyes and ears so, as the most knowledgeable person in this operation, it behooves you to be honest with me. I'm not just another stand-in ribbon-cutter. And if you don't believe me, I'll get Maureen on my cell phone right now and have her tell you that what I'm saying is true."

"That won't be necessary, Dr. Brinkman," said Hartshorn, flushing.

"Let's start with your calling me Celeste. May I call you Emily?" She nodded. "So did Carl push out the Head of Acquisitions?" Emily nodded again.

"I can't prove it, but I believe he did. It was the year we had the first big state budget cut. Carl figured out that he could survive and keep most of his department intact if he figured out a way to merge Cataloging with Acquisitions so that's what he did."

"Are the in-house politics here always so territorial? I asked, and Emily smiled her first genuine smile since we had met.

"You are a quick study."

"Keep in mind that the English Department includes a huge composition program that both is and is not a part of its self-definition. Within the English faculty, every member has a special area. Whether an English department is like the United States on a good day or the Balkans on a bad day depends entirely on the faculty members. It's a matter of personalities and chemistry. But enough about me."

She laughed with me as we walked up to the circulation area where LORETTA's shelves and boxes loomed in the background behind the large windows.

"So what about LORETTA? Whose baby is she?"

"The Director and Head of Circulation along with the Head of Technical Services got together on this one."

"You don't approve?" She looked uncomfortable. "Come on, tell me."

"I'm an old-fashioned librarian. I hate the idea of storing books so that users cannot browse the shelves."

"Me too. The times chance has favored my under-prepared mind are beyond counting!"

"That's exactly what I mean. So often in research, the book you need is not the one whose title you have found but the one next to it or on the next shelf. That's the wonder of cataloging books the way we do. We no longer have paper card catalogs to offer those opportunities for chance discovery, and now you can't even walk to the shelf and browse." She stopped. "I could go on at length, but the truth is that we can't afford the bricks and mortar any longer and users want access and convenience so increasingly creatures like LORETTA will house our books. The ones, that is, that aren't 'digitized.'"

"Now, that is a whole other argument," I interjected, and she nodded.

We stood quietly looking through the windows at the storage ranges that extended down to the basement level and up to the second floor.

"Boys and toys," I muttered. "Does it make you nervous?" I asked, noticing that Emily was shivering as we approached the entrance.

"I don't go in here alone now, since the...." She stumbled over what to call Bond's murder and simply abandoned the sentence. Instead she gestured me over to a set of metal stairs by which we descended to the floor below and stood looking up at the huge ranges of shelves that held the hopper boxes I would forever think of as coffin-shaped.

"How many books can LORETTA store?"

"Depending on the size of the books, 250,000 in the space you could shelve about 50,000 on conventional shelves. To get to capacity, we will have to buy two more robots, and they cost the earth. However, most of our acquisitions these days are databases or access to digitized collections so that may not be a problem for years, if ever."

"Can we walk around?" She nodded. "The robot won't get us and put us in a box?"

She did not laugh at my tasteless joke.

I walked to the end of the range of shelves and found a large open space with a freight elevator at the back.

"Where does the elevator go?"

"It opens onto every floor plus the loading dock. It has a back door."

"So almost anyone could use that elevator to access this space."

"Not without a special key."

"Where is the key kept?"

Emily shot me a quizzical glance and seemed about to protest my nosiness but instead shrugged her shoulders.

"The director has one. The supervisor of the loading dock has one, there is one kept in cataloging, security has one, and there's one in my office."

"On the key board in Briana's desk?"

Emily nodded.

"Where exactly are we?" I asked, trying to sound casual. "Are we above cataloging?"

"Yes, right over their space."

"What is supposed to happen in this area?"

The open space was about thirty feet long and twenty feet deep.

"Eventually there are supposed to be more ranges of shelves, serviced by more robots, but right now this is just a temporary work area until they finish the archives upstairs in the new wing."

She gestured to the piles of lumber, saws, and other equipment, some covered by drop cloths, others uncovered and hooked up by extension cords for use.

"Shoot!" she suddenly said, and I must have looked puzzled because she pointed to two empty book trucks sitting by the elevators. "Those are supposed to be taken to Circulation or Cataloging as soon as they are emptied. We're always running short of trucks," she said in the exasperated voice of a manager who is reluctant but forced to micro-manage.

"So this is where…?" I did not need to finish the question.

"Yes, the police took the saw that was used and still have it, I think." She looked pale.

"Let's get out of here," I said, and we started back toward the stairs when I noticed there was a second computer work-station.

"Is that computer connected?"

"Yes, it's how items from cataloging get stored in LORETTA."

I suddenly felt queasy--obviously more than books had gotten into LORETTA from this lower workstation.

We left LORETTA's lair, walked through Circulation, and climbed an elegant wood staircase to the second floor where the new wing smelled of carpet and fresh paint. As I thought of the monetary and political capital that had gone into making this elegant "Smythe Center for the Study of Government," I felt almost as queasy as I had in LORETTA's lair.

"Our tax dollars at work doing things we are probably best off not knowing about," I murmured, and Emily nodded grimly.

"But it's beautiful, isn't it?" she said, and I had to agree.

The large reading area sought to mimic an early twentieth-century gentleman's club with leather sofas and easy chairs, cherry tables, and dark carpet. Discreet signage pointed the way to the Samuel Hornback Smythe Archives and Center for the Study of Government. Given Smythe's conservative politics, I shuddered to think what would be housed in the archives and, worse yet, what might pass for the study of government, not to mention what sort of student they were recruiting and what sort of "opportunities" they were providing as part of the Smythe Fellowship Program.

"Do you want to see the archives or center?" Emily asked in a low voice.

"I think that I might have to be taken in restraints from the building," I whispered and she laughed. "How in the hell could we be so stupid as to sell ourselves to the right wing?" I made no effort to keep the anger out of my voice.

"That's a question for your boss," Emily replied, arching her thin eyebrows. "I'd be interested to know how she answers it."

"Since she is my boss, if I ask it, you can be sure, I'll do so tactfully." Emily chuckled. "But I'm sure it's all about the millions of dollars this little piggy is bringing into the university."

"And I guess we don't care what comes with it," Emily muttered.

"Either we don't care or we don't yet understand."

"And when we do, it will be too late."

"I couldn't have put it better myself."

We exchanged grimly knowing looks as we crossed through a hallway, now a student art gallery, into the older part of the library. The rest of the tour took in public areas with which I was already familiar although I noted how the reference librarians' offices were below the administrative offices and had access to the staff stairs. When we returned to Emily's office, Briana was gone for the day so Emily unlocked the office door. Once we were inside, she walked to the desk and opened the door that held the keys.

"Where are the other keys to LORETTA kept?" I asked.

"Denitra Wilson, the Head of Circulation, has two. She keeps one with her and the other locked in her desk in her office, which is also kept locked. The head of Technical Services has one, which he keeps on his key ring, and then there's this one. Security also has one."

"That desk compartment has a lock." I gestured to the door that she still held open. "Is it ever locked?"

"No, because whenever we leave, we always lock the office door."

"What's that room?" I asked and pointed to a closed door to the left of the desk.

"It's the mailroom and supply area."

"Do people come in here to get their mail?"

"No. It's a system of boxes that lock on both sides. The mail carrier sorts the mail on this side. It's like in apartment buildings-- the individual access is by key from the outside corridor."

"That's odd," I said, more to myself than to Emily as I thought of my own department's open pigeonholes in the main office.

"It is, but we had a lot of trouble when someone took a confidential memo out of someone else's box and copied it for all the employees. In fact, that's how Caroline Harrow found out that she might be taking early retirement."

"Ugly. Did your friend Carl do it?"

"He's not my friend, and I couldn't prove it, but he's my favorite suspect."

"Why? If the decision was coming anyway, why did he do it?"

"The decision wasn't final—it was still being discussed, but Caroline was so furious about not being included in the discussion that she went in and retired on the spot."

"So he forced the decision."

"Yes, and it was a horrible way for a decent person's career to end," she said angrily.

"Someone didn't want to wait, and Carl was the only one who benefitted," I summed up, and Emily nodded. "I hate that kind of stuff," I said sincerely. "So enough about the mail system. What about supplies? Does everyone have free access?"

"Not in these lean times. Tareka…Briana, I mean, my assistant controls the supplies. People send her an e-mail or just come in and ask for what they need."

"And she gets it for them."

"Yes. They sign for it, and she enters it on a database," Emily said, and I could tell that she was wondering about all my questions.

"So if you could make one big change in the library, what would you do?"

"Make me the director, and my first act would be to fire Carl Smarinsky."

I must have looked shocked because she added, with a grim smile, "Well, you asked!"

When I got back to my office, I found Harold standing in the hallway outside.

"You could have called," I said, hugging him.

"I did, and you didn't pick up."

I pulled my phone out and realized that I had turned the ringer off for class and forgotten to turn it back on.

"Can I buy you dinner?"

"Jeanette's at her book club so I was hoping you'd ask," he said, grinning like the mischievous boy he had once been. "Let's go to that Mexican place down the road, and don't tell Jeannette. You know she's always riding my ass about cholesterol."

"You know I'm on her side."

"Okay, but just for dinner, be on my side."

I looked at his wise-ass grin and had to smile. Although you are far removed from childhood, when your big brother/cousin, asks you to cover his tracks, you do it because it is a sign that he thinks you are cool, and you spent your entire childhood trying to make him think you were cool. There was still that little burst of pride that he was trusting me.

"Just this once," I said sternly, and, laughing, he nodded.

He drove me to my car, and we parked side-by-side outside Manny's Mexican Diner. It was a dive. I had absolutely no doubt that someone named Manuel, but known as "Manny," had opened its greasy doors and hung the then-new sombreros and velvet paintings many years ago. The health department consistently wrote it up for violations, and the immigration officers visited once a year to round up as many undocumented workers as possible, but after closing temporarily, Manny's always re-opened, offering authentic food at cheap prices. Unlike the more modern Mexican restaurants in town, Manny's still had spacious booths. The host led us to a comfortably dim back corner. We ordered margaritas and a large queso and both dug into the basket of chips.

"Jesus, I love Mexican food," murmured Harold.

"Me too."

"It's good to know I can count on you for a sneaky meal."

"Only this once! Jeanette might kill me," I replied sternly, and he laughed.

"Look out, missy, this cholesterol thing seems to be hereditary!"

"All too true so I have to get my Mexican while I can."

The server brought our drinks and queso. Harold and I might share the cholesterol gene, but we also shared the love-to-eat gene. We indulged for several moments before I finally asked, "What are we doing here?"

"You mean that you are not delighted to have dinner with your favorite cousin especially when he's bought you a margarita and plans to pick up the tab."

"Hey, I invited you," I protested.

"I'm the guy," he replied, and then waited. I crossed my eyes at him and did not take the bait.

"You know, smart ass, my favorite cousin—I mean favorite as far as a guy cousin can be a favorite-- is a cop and although he might bring me an ice cream at the family picnic, he usually lets his wife fix me my free dinner."

Harold laughed, saying, "Too true."

"So what's up?"

"I want to talk about these murders...."

"I'm not signing any form," I interrupted bluntly, and Harold held up his hands.

"Brent is a by-the-book sort of guy, and he's young. He's smart and good at what he does, but he worries a lot. He should never have put that form in front of you."

"Why?"

"We use that form for expert advice. If we need to bring in an accountant to look at some books—that kind of thing."

"So you don't think I'm an expert?" I spoke with mock hurt.

"I think you're the smartest person I know, Cece, but what you have to offer us is not exactly professional advice." Harold sighed. "I wish Brent had asked me."

"Okay. So the form's not something in my future. It wasn't anyway. What do you want to know?"

Our server came back, and we focused on the menu for a few moments, both ordering large combination plates with both beans and rice.

"These murders are like being handed a case in a small town where you don't know anyone. It's almost like we don't know the language. Know what I mean?"

"I do. A long time ago I took an anthropology course, and the professor used educational institutions, especially universities, to introduce us to the idea of sub-cultures." Harold looked puzzled. "Stay with me and you'll see my point," I promised. "The prof showed us how large universities set up systems parallel to the larger culture. For example, they provide a wide range of services to satisfy basic needs, do business in their own way, and even have their own police force. He talked about the specialized language and customs that rule different academic disciplines as setting the university further apart from the main culture. He argued that all this makes for a sub-culture that operates within but is very different from the main culture. There is an interesting argument about the margin where the university and main culture overlap, for example, in policing, but I won't bore you with my speculations." Harold snorted. "Although I understood his argument at the time, I remember thinking how weird this idea was, but the more time I've spent in higher education, the more truth I've found in his analysis. The university is a sub-culture. This is the source of your problem."

"Your professor was right, but it's also like a," Harold frowned, searching for a word, "Like a tribe. And cops aren't in the tribe at all. In fact, a lot of the tribe members hate us or, at the very least, don't much trust us."

"Often too true, but rest assured, dear, I don't hate you." I smiled with exaggerated sweetness, and Harold snorted. "So, as a member of this hostile tribe, how can I help you?"

He took some folded papers out of his jacket pocket and handed them to me.

"This is a printout of everyone who used the library on the Friday Bond was killed. I want you to look at it and see if anything jumps out at you."

"Like what?"

"Hey, if I knew what, would I be asking you?"

"Even though I'm an expert?"

Harold rolled his eyes.

The printout was pages long in order by time. It showed if anything had been checked in or out or both, but it did not, of course, reveal titles.

"My eyes are crossing. Can I take this home? I'll either return it to you or shred it."

"Okay, but try to look over it tonight, okay? It's taken us forever to get it. Some kid with pink hair had to write a program or something to get the information out of the system."

"His name's Nathan Ramirez, and he's a genius."

"I know, and I'm not sure any of this is going to be helpful. I mean, how many murderers think, 'Gee, before I off this lady and cut her up, I think I'll just check out a book.'"

I chuckled in agreement, slipping the papers into my purse. Harold took an appreciative sip of his margarita.

"Here's how I see this case. There are only four building pass-keys. President Truman (Boy, that feels weird to say!), Provost Shaughnessy, Charlie Crawford—Head of Security, and what's-his-name Head of Physical Plant each have one."

"Stan Kranitz."

"What?"

"He's the Director of Physical Plant."

"Okay. As far as we can figure, they all keep their keys with them. They had to re-key the buildings about ten years ago when all those computers were stolen on a weekend, and the university realized that way too many people had pass-keys. When the buildings were re-keyed, it was made clear that the passkeys were only for emergencies, and very few people would have them. Other building keys would be tracked and distributed strictly on an as-needed basis." I nodded as if this were all news to me. "So that's one way a person could get access to the library." I nodded. "Or the person could already have access to the building by working there or could have just walked in during business hours and hidden somewhere—God knows it would be easy enough to do."

"Sounds logical but not helpful."

"Too true. The real problem is that we cannot find any connection between LouAnn Bond and Tareka James."

"From the news reports, I thought you had already made an arrest in Tareka James' death."

"It doesn't feel right to me."

"Why?"

"There was one domestic incident about two years ago. He slapped her, and she called the cops. They went to mediation and have been going to counseling regularly since then. There have been no further incidents."

"The problem is there may have been more violence, but that one incident was the only one that she reported."

"I know. We talked to the counselor and got nowhere, but both her mother and his mother swear that they were doing well. His brother and her two sisters also swear things were on an even keel."

"You should talk some more to Emily Hartshorn, her boss."

"Why?"

"The night Tareka's body was found, she hesitated when she was asked if anyone had anything against Tareka. She was close to her and might have something to tell you."

"Good idea. I'll stop by and chat with her."

"Don't mention my name, okay?"

"I wouldn't, but why are you worried?"

"I just saw Emily for a tour of the library, and Provost Shaughnessy has made me her liaison to the Library Advisory Committee so I don't want to get off to a bad start with the person who actually runs the library."

"Okay. I guess my question is whether you see any connection between these two murders. We've asked everyone we can think of both on and off campus, we've read e-mails, and we've looked at phone records. We have to conclude that they clearly didn't know each other. They had absolutely no dealings with each other that we can trace, and there's no third party to connect them except some library staff, but not one of them seems to have a motive and all of them have alibis."

"The university's a big place, and they may not have known each other."

"So what's the connection?"

"Coincidence maybe?"

"That's a last resort. We've also been trying to figure out who had access to that retrieval system."

"LORETTA?"

"Yeah. There are a couple of ways in." Harold started to laugh and choked on a chip. He finally wiped his eyes and said, "Who in the hell thinks up these names? I almost said, 'There are two ways into LORETTA."

I had to laugh too.

"It's an acronym for Library Retrieval, Tracking and Technology Assistant."

"I know," Harold said with a smirk, "But I couldn't resist."

He paused as the server set our hot plates before us. The tamales lay in a sea of rice and beans. I took the final sip of my margarita and dug in. Harold was already in the middle of a taco. We ate in contented silence for a few moments.

"Man, these are good!" he finally said, wiping his mouth on his napkin.

"Delicious! Want a bite of tamale?"

"Sure. Want some taco?"

I nodded, and he cut one of his pork tacos in half and took half of one of my tamales.

"I'm glad you're retiring," I said suddenly.

"Why?"

"I've lived my whole life worrying that you would be shot by some drugged-up maniac."

"In those situations, you better believe that I wear my Kevlar vest," he said with a smile.

"You know what I mean!" He stopped smiling and nodded.

"Jeanette never said anything, but when I got promoted to a desk job, she cried like a baby and told me how worried she had been. I think she's worn out the Virgin Mary praying for me when I was on duty. When I finally understood how hard it was for her, I decided to retire as soon as I could."

"You're still young enough to have another career."

"Actually I've already got another career lined up," he said, dropping his voice. "I plan to tell Jeanette on retirement day."

"Landscaping?"

"No, something better. I've got a job doing security analyses and selling security systems for one of the best companies. They interviewed me a while back, and I just found out that I've got the job."

"That's wonderful!"

"I'm sure I'll miss the guys and being a part of things in the city, but I like the idea of helping people make their businesses more secure."

"You'll be out and about, and you'll like that."

"I think I will, but don't say a word to anyone in the family."

"Of course not. What a wonderful surprise for Jeanette!"

"Yeah, and the money's good so maybe we can travel like she's always wanted. But let's get back to LORETTA."

"Okay."

"There are two ways in, and the doors are keyed alike."

"So who has keys?" I asked innocently.

"The head of Circulation has two keys--she keeps one on her person at all times during the work day and the other key locked in her desk. She also locks her office when she isn't in it."

"That's Denitra Wilson—the head of Circulation."

"Yeah. She apparently never turns loose of her keys and personally lets people into the retrieval system. They sign in, she admits them, they do their work, and the door locks behind them."

"Kind of cumbersome."

"She told us that they wanted strict control over who was using the system and storing things or working in there so they would know who to talk with if something went wrong. They also wanted to be sure anyone who used the system was completely trained."

"Is there any way to prop the door or block the lock mechanism?"

"No. If you prop the door or interfere with the lock, it has a very annoying, continuous alarm."

"What about the workers?"

94

"Workers?"

"Those people who are working on the second floor and have the saws and stuff down behind LORETTA."

"Wilson lets them in every morning, but they go up and down in the freight elevator which requires a key, but they leave the key in while they're working. We've interviewed them all and done background checks. None of them knew either victim except two guys remember seeing James around and one remembered seeing Bond in the new wing."

"Bond upstairs?" I asked, and Harold nodded. "What was she doing?"

"He said she was looking around with Hartshorn and another woman." I made a silent note to ask Emily about this.

"So someone could have ridden in the freight elevator?"

"You have to know to turn the key. The workers all swear that no one rode with them, but who knows? Now, the Director has an elevator key. It's on his keychain, and he's never used it. The head of Cataloging and the head of Circulation also have keys. Security has a key in order to do the building check. Emily Hartshorn has a key, and she keeps it in her assistant's desk."

Harold and I shared a moment of complete telepathy: keys to LORETTA and the freight elevator were both kept in Tareka's unlocked desk. He pulled out his cell phone and punched in a number.

"Hey, Brent, someone needs to go over the stuff from Tareka James' desk. It just occurred to me that she had a key to the freight elevator and a key to LORETTA-- maybe there are prints. She may also have had a sign-out list for the keys. I'm not sure we checked this carefully enough." He listened for a moment. "I know there may not be any prints, but we could get lucky. This connects her to the Bond murder and makes a lot more sense than the boyfriend."

He listened for a few more minutes, rolled his eyes, and then said good-bye.

"Brent thinks it's a wild goose chase. He said that they went over the desk the night we found her body and didn't find anything. The keys were all there, according to Hartshorn. They lifted prints. He's going to check to see if there were any on either key, but he thinks they were clean."

"Borrowing keys makes a lot more sense than riding in the elevator and hiding."

Harold nodded. Something had been nagging at me since I had visited LORETTA's lair, and I suddenly realized what it was.

"You could use a book truck to move the body." Harold dialed his phone again and, looking grim, asked Hess about the book trucks.

"You may be right," he said, after hanging up. "All the book trucks in Cataloging were there and accounted for, but there were very few prints. They had recently been wiped clean as a whistle. We asked the head of the department about it, and he said it was unusual, but occasionally, usually between semesters, the maintenance crew wipes down the trucks. We asked maintenance, but they hadn't wiped down the trucks in a couple of months."

We ate in thoughtful silence for a few moments.

"That office is so damn isolated," Harold finally said in an irritated tone. "People could go in and out all day and not be seen."

"The administrative offices were designed to be off the beaten path."

"I think we're going to have to talk with everyone on the library staff again. No one from outside would know about the keys."

"Actually that's not true."

"How so?"

"I knew where the key to LORETTA is kept, and I knew the desk was unlocked because today Emily got the key from her assistant to take me to see the system."

"We still need to talk with the staff and find out who went to that office on Friday. At least we know it was locked at seven o'clock on Friday when the security officer made his rounds."

"Did he check the freight elevator?"

"No, he checks the public elevators, stairwells, and walks around all of the stacks and carrel areas. It is assumed that the freight elevator is off limits because it requires a key."

"If the murderer hid Bond's body in the freight elevator, then he or she would have had from seven on Friday until the library opened at one o'clock on Saturday to saw her up, hide her parts in LORETTA, and clean up. That's the longest period of closure for the library all week," I said.

Harold studied me for a long, uncomfortable moment before saying, "You've done some thinking about this."

"You know I've always loved murder mysteries," I replied innocently.

"Just be sure to let me know if you have any other ideas," he said. "I'm serious, Cece."

"Of course. Will you tell me what you find out about the keys?"

He eyed me suspiciously.

"Why?"

"Because you owe me, and I'm curious. I've never really understood what you do. I love mysteries and here's a chance to follow a real investigation."

I must have overdone my enthusiasm because Harold's eyes narrowed.

"You are such a liar, Cece. Tell me the truth. Why do you want to know?"

"I'm working for Provost Shaughnessy now, and she's very worried. This mess needs to get cleared up as quickly as possible. The university has been making scholarship offers to high-end students—excellent students who have many choices about where to go—and their responses are due soon. The idea that a serial killer is running amok in the university library does not play well."

"So not getting these students has implications for the Provost," he murmured thoughtfully.

"Not just her—the whole university. Universities have what is called an academic profile." Harold looked puzzled. "It's like ranking for a sports team. The better the students we get—judging mainly by test scores—the better the profile. You can see why the Provost is worried. So I want to help in any way I can to get this solved." I could tell from Harold's expression that he did not entirely buy my explanation.

"I've also been thinking that I'd like to go into administration. Around here, it's the only way to make decent money, and this might give me a way in."

"I thought you loved teaching."

"I do, but if I do administration part time, I can keep teaching and make more money," I explained, trying to sound mildly bitter which was not hard since I was telling the ugly truth about the situation. But I was lying about my goal: I had no intention of becoming even a part-time administrator.

"I'll keep it in mind," he said with a non-committal grin that told me he was not entirely convinced. I let the subject go knowing that I did not want to be on the receiving end of the third-degree from Harold.

"So let me ask you one more question." I tried to sound casual.

"What?"

"Have you found anyone who actually liked LouAnn Bond?"

"Have you?"

"I asked first." Harold snorted.

"Okay. We interviewed some crackpot preacher who seemed fond of her."

"Did you talk to anyone else at St. Luke's?"

"How did you know it was St. Luke's?" he demanded.

"Her obituary plus I heard around the university that she was active there."

"We talked to a few parishioners and the pastor. We didn't get much except the sense that, although the pastor liked her, she was not popular."

I thought fleetingly of going to the Sunday service or Bible study, but the danger of crossing paths with the Pophams or someone else I might meet later seemed too great.

"You might ask more questions," I encouraged Harold.

"Why?" He eyed me suspiciously.

"Maybe she shared some of her attitude toward the university with her fellow parishioners"

"What attitude?"

"Let's put it this way. I've heard she thought the university was located next door to Sodom and Gomorrah. St. Luke's is an archconservative church. At least one member is also on the university's Board of Trustees. Bond was also active in the Smith-Jones Family Fund."

"How do you know that?" he demanded.

"Someone mentioned it."

"Who?"

"I forget. I just heard it around when everyone was talking about her death."

"So what are you getting at? Come on. Just tell me."

"She worked in the President's office at the university, an institution that tends to be liberal, and her politics were clearly very conservative." Harold studied me thoughtfully as I continued, "If I were you, I would find out exactly what her relationship with the Family Fund was."

"Why?"

"Money and information." Harold looked puzzled. "Over the last couple of years, the Family Fund has bankrolled some reactionary counter activities to events on campus such as the Celebration of Human Rights and Coming Out Week. Lately it seems like every time you go to an event, the Smith-Jones Family Fund has some kind of information table."

"The university calendar is public—it's on the website."

"It is, but it isn't always up to date. When that organization shows up for Campus Visit Day, you have to wonder. It's an event with a very specific audience. Most outsiders have no clue what that event is or when it takes place unless their kid receives a personal letter of invitation, but this year, the Fund for the Family was present. They even had a table the entire week of auditions for the Music School."

"You've given this a lot of thought." I nodded. "Why?"

"I told you…," I began.

"Yeah, yeah, yeah. Come on. I want to know the real reason why you are so interested."

"The truth is," I said, meeting Harold's eyes, "I've never encountered anyone at the university or anywhere else as thoroughly disliked as LouAnn Bond."

When I got home, my second margarita had put me beyond doing any of my own work, but I did not feel sleepy so I got ready for bed and then sat down with the computer printout of names. There must have been five hundred, and that seemed a small number, but it was for Friday, a lightly scheduled class day, and many, if not most, students went to the library to dock their computers and use online resources or check social media sites and play games. I used a ruler to isolate each name. I found ten colleagues in the humanities who had used the library, probably twenty-five students I knew, and another fifteen acquaintances from various parts of the university. I had no thoughts about any of these people until I turned to the last page and found both Maureen and Cass's names. Late that Friday afternoon, Cass had returned something and checked something out while Maureen had simply checked something out. They were both at the library within a half hour of closing time.

I hoped it was a coincidence. The thought of reporting to Harold made me realize how badly suited I was to the job at hand. I was incapable of suspecting people I liked, but I also could not quiet the fear that I might be wrong.

Chapter Eleven

The next morning, I awoke with a nagging headache, less from the margaritas than from my night of anxious indecision. When I got to school, I found an envelope in my mailbox with a receipt from The Eagle's Nest Hotel in downtown Memphis. The attached note read, "I found this in the car. Hope it will satisfy your suspicious mind! Cass." As I studied the crumpled, slightly soiled receipt, the idea that anyone with a computer could have designed and printed it occurred to me.

When I got to my office, I flipped on the computer and Googled "Hot Biscuit Marathon." There had been a race, just as Cass had told me. There was a mini-marathon as well that accepted same-day entries. Runners and times for the marathon were posted, but I could only find a list of the top ten finishers in the mini. I dialed the information number, but it had been disconnected. I tried the e-mail address, and my note bounced back. After studying the receipt for another long moment, I called the number on it.

"Hello, my name is Cass Britten, and I requested that you fax a duplicate of my room receipt from a couple weekends ago. I haven't gotten it yet." Very apologetic and helpful, the desk person took my name, fax number, phone number as well as the dates of my stay. She promised to fax the receipt immediately. I assuaged my guilt by going over my notes an extra time before I went to give a guest lecture on women's diaries and letters in a friend's "Introduction to Women's History."

When I returned to my office, the message light was flashing. It was the very helpful desk clerk saying, "This message is for Ms. Cass Britten. She gave me this number. I'm so sorry, but I've checked the register and called all three managers, and we cannot find any record of your stay, Ms. Britten. Perhaps you have misremembered the name of the hotel where you stayed. Please call me back if I can be of any further help."

I went to Cass's office and walked in without bothering to knock, closing the door behind me. I threw the receipt on her desk, saying, "This is completely bogus, but I do appreciate the artful crumpling and soiling of the paper."

"I don't have to answer your questions. You aren't the police!" Cass retorted, yet when I met her eyes, I saw not anger but fear.

"I'm trying to help, Cass. I can't help if you won't be honest with me. Where were you?"

"You just have to trust me that I wasn't in the library cutting up LouAnn Bond."

"Maybe you weren't cutting up Bond, but you were in the library on Friday."

Cass paled.

"I returned a couple books and checked out some movies for the weekend," she said, "As if it's any of your business."

"What movies?"

"*Silkwood, Elephant Man, Mermaids*, and *The Witches of Eastwick.*"

"Sounds like a Cher film festival."

"Exactly. Don't you wish you had been there?"

"And where was that?"

"I repeat—none of your business. None of this is any of your business."

"Fine, but I'm warning you: the police won't have to dig deep to find out about the Committee on Women, not to mention you and Maureen. They already have the list that shows you were both in the library the day they know Bond was killed. They will not think twice about doing the kind of check that I've just done so don't try to run this stupid story about the mini-marathon again."

I paused for a second and decided to change tactics.

"Look, I've always thought we were friends, and if there is any way I can help with whatever's going on, you just have to ask."

"Thanks, but I don't think there's anything that can be done."

She turned away and began typing on her computer. I waited. Turning back, she said flatly, "I think you'd better go now."

"Okay. I'm not mad at you. I'm just sorry."

Cass nodded but did not meet my eyes.

I left feeling that Cass was telling the truth about what she had checked out. Of course, I had to admit that I desperately wanted to believe that all she had done was check out some movies.

When I got to my office, I texted Maureen to call me. When I did not hear from her in half an hour, I picked up the phone and called Sam Jacoby's office. I assumed Maureen had talked with him, but at this point, I was so frustrated that I did not care.

"This is Dr. Celeste Brinkman. May I please speak to Mr. Jacoby?"

"I'm sorry, but he's in a meeting. Can I give him a message?"

"I'd like to talk with him for about half an hour this afternoon. I'm free so whatever time works for him is fine."

"May I ask the nature of your business?"

"It's a private matter."

Maureen must have talked to him because a half hour later, the phone rang, and I had an appointment for two o'clock. I went to the Student Center to get something to eat and was just sitting down with my sandwich when I looked up to find Emily Hartshorn standing at my table with her tray.

"May I join you?"

"Of course. Sit down." I moved my book and purse off the table. "How are you?"

"Getting used to talking to the police on a daily basis."

"What now?"

"I got the third degree about the keys we keep in our office and whether we lock the desk, whether we lock the door, whether we keep a list of who takes keys and on and on and on!"

"This must be incredibly hard for you."

Her eyes filled with tears which she quickly wiped away.

"I feel so awful about Tareka. It's my fault she went upstairs. My God, her kids are so small, and now they've put their father in jail." I wanted to assure her that he would not stay there but did not dare say anything.

"Is he a good guy?" I settled for asking the question I had been wanting to ask since reading about him in the paper. Emily studied me for a moment and began to eat her sandwich so I began to eat mine.

"They had problems. He came from a home where there was a lot of violence, and he joined a gang when he was in high school, but he loved Tareka and the kids. He had gotten out of the gang and was going to school to be an auto mechanic, and they were seeing a counselor regularly."

"Was there more violence after her original complaint?"

"I don't think so because Tareka made it clear that she would disappear with the kids if anything else happened."

"Strong woman."

"Tougher than most of us can ever dream of being." We ate in silence for a moment before she continued, "What I miss most is Tareka's sense of humor. She always saw the funny side of things, and there were days in the library when if it hadn't been for her, I would have found a window that opened and jumped."

"Is Briana still set on leaving?"

"Yes, and she needs to."

"I think that I may have someone to recommend to you," I said tentatively. "She works in an academic unit so she's already in the university system and could bid on this job. She's very smart and deserves a better job than the one she has."

"Who?"

"Let me talk to her first, and then I'll tell you." We ate in silence for a few moments, and then I said, "Can I ask you a library question?"

"Sure."

"Is there any way of finding out what someone has checked out in the past? I know there is a current list of what's out on someone's account, but what about past checkouts?"

"This isn't a question, it's a legal quagmire."

"I thought so."

"I am sure there is a way of eliciting that information from the computer system, but no librarian would do that or authorize the doing of that. We are pretty much united in believing the First Amendment covers not just freedom of speech but private access to information. It's nobody's business what books you read."

"What about information pertinent to a criminal investigation?"

"The rubber has hit that road, and librarians do not give up their patrons, period."

"That's the way I remembered the issue," I said with a rueful smile, knowing there was no way to check Cass Britton's story.

When I got back from lunch, I went by the department office and found Dari McAllister running the copier in the small room off the main office.

"Can I talk to you for a moment?"

She paused the copier and looked at me expectantly. She had taken my course on women's autobiography and had written her autobiography for one assignment so I knew that her given name was Darlene and that she had changed it legally to Dari, her nickname, ten years previously when she had come out. After high school, she had gotten a scholarship to NYU but lost it in the emotional turmoil of her identity crisis. As a consequence, she was now in her third year of working full time and taking two classes each semester toward a degree in Women's Studies. From our casual conversations, I also knew her partner was a social worker who was unlikely to move elsewhere.

"There is someone who is going to be looking for an Administrative Assistant here at the university. I'm not sure what the exact title of the job is or what the pay grade will be, but I'm sure it will pay more than your job here. I think you'd like the person you'd be working for."

"A man?"

"No, a woman, and she's smart and capable. You wouldn't have to do her job for her."

"Now that would be refreshing!" Dari laughed, and I had to join her.

Although occupying the lowest staff position in the office, Dari was a technology whiz. Her skills were constantly in demand so she provided many services to faculty and staff for which she was never compensated. When I had talked with her about this, she had shrugged and said, "I'm getting my degree, and then I'll move on. Or maybe not. I like working at the university." She had considered jobs in technology at the university, but she did not want to have men supervising her, and although she got along well with the guys who worked tech, she did not, as she put it, "want to live with them."

"So you're interested?"

"Of course."

"I'll let you know what develops," I said and turned to go, but Dari called me back.

"Thanks for thinking of me."

"I like this woman you'd be working for, and I like you so it was a no-brainer," I assured her, and she smiled. "I'm just sorry it's taken so long for this to happen."

"Most professors have no idea how this place runs," Dari said quietly. "I appreciate it that you pay attention."

"Thanks for saying that."

I told her good-bye and had to walk briskly to make my appointment with Sam Jacoby, the only Vice President not housed in the administration building. For once was grateful to be kept waiting. The twenty minutes I spent sitting outside his office gave me time to think about how I wanted to approach him, but it turned out that I did not need to worry. He came out, shook my hand warmly, apologized for keeping me waiting, and offered me coffee or tea. We sat down with our coffee, facing each other across his desk.

"Someday I'm going to have a usable conference room," he laughed, "But most of the time it's convenient to keep this desk between me and what's happening."

I laughed with him, thinking what a nice man he seemed to be.

"So how do you like working for Maureen?"

"She's incredible."

"I would have to agree."

"I appreciate your recommending me although I am not sure about my ability to do what she wants."

"A frequent state of mind in those around Maureen."

"Do you mind if I ask you some questions?"

"Not at all. Maureen said that you would have some very personal questions for me, but she assured me that all answers would be kept in confidence. I know you're trustworthy from the other problem you brought to my attention. Actually, I owe you so ask away."

"Where were you the weekend of February 17?"

He pulled out his phone and checked.

"I was in Toledo with my daughter's family. I left at noon on Friday and got into Toledo late that evening. I left around two on Sunday and got back late."

"From something Maureen said, I assume you make this trip frequently."

"Yes, I try to spend the weekend with them once a month, but sometimes it stretches to once every six weeks. Occasionally they come here, but my wife has Alzheimer's and no longer recognizes any of us. With the grandkids' activities, it helps my daughter if I go there."

"I'm sorry about your wife."

104

A look of grief and pain crossed his face, but then he shrugged.

"One of life's little ironies."

There was a long silence, and I decided my best strategy was to plunge ahead.

"When did you meet Maureen?"

"During her on-campus interview. Of course, after she came, we saw each other at various events and were in meetings together."

"When did you begin seeing each other outside of work?"

"You mean, as we might say, although it sounds ridiculous at our age, 'dating?'"

"Hey, I'm unmarried but live in hope so it doesn't sound ridiculous to me."

He chuckled.

"I guess it was spring of her first year here. We were in a meeting late one Friday afternoon, and she seemed kind of down so I asked her out for a drink. I took her downtown to Snake Eyes. She had never been there, and we ended up talking until late in the evening, and that was the beginning."

"Do you ever take Maureen with you to visit your daughter?"

"God no!"

"I'm sorry."

"No, I'm sorry. It's just," he choked and looked out the window by his desk, "It would be disrespectful to my wife." He cleared his throat. "My daughter knows that I see Maureen occasionally, and she's met her, but there is no way I would bring Maureen...," he paused again.

"I understand," I murmured with genuine sympathy.

"My wife is still the love of my life," he said simply. "Maureen knows this."

It occurred to me that this statement, in fact, the whole tone of the conversation did not fit with Sam's "wanting to marry" Maureen. I decided to change direction and said, "Tell me about LouAnn Bond."

"What about her?" He sounded wary for the first time.

"Actually, Maureen told me about the night Bond called you, but you've been here and have known, or rather, knew her longer than Maureen has. Just talk to me about her. I'm probably over-estimating my powers of deduction, but I keep thinking something someone tells me about her will suddenly be the key to finding out who killed her."

"I don't know where to begin," he said uncomfortably.

"Okay, here's how you can help me. Everyone seems to have disliked or hated her. Right?" Sam nodded reluctantly. "Why did the President keep her in his office?"

"I don't really know why. I've always assumed the President didn't know what she was doing. As you well know, we in the upper administration can be very cut off from what goes on in daily operations even right under our noses."

"Do you think she knew something damaging about him?"

"That might have been true about President Carson, the former President, but Kenneth, President Truman, has always been a pretty straight arrow."

"What was your relationship to her like?"

Sam smiled grimly.

"I'm sure Maureen or someone has told you that LouAnn liked men far better than women so when she was around me, butter wouldn't melt in her mouth. It was rather off-putting."

"So she never did anything to interfere with your relationship with the President or to influence you to do something."

Sam thought for a moment.

"I see where you're going. I know the kind of tricks she pulled on Maureen with her calendar and stuff, but the only time she ever tried to interfere with something I did was over a personal matter."

"What?"

"Last fall I gave the kids who ran Coming Out Week $1000 to print t-shirts."

"Out of your budget?"

"Of course not! I wrote them a personal check. On their website, they thanked various donors. They had asked me if I could be listed, and I didn't hesitate for a second. I support equal rights for everyone, LGBTQ people included, and I'm very willing to say that in public."

"So what happened?"

"A week or two after the event, I went over to meet with the President. After the meeting, LouAnn and I were alone in the conference room. She told me that she had been shocked to see my name on the Coming Out Week website and hoped it was a mistake."

"What did you say?"

"I said that I supported equal rights. I'll never forget the look on her face. She was usually very reserved, but she looked not just shocked but disgusted. She said in this very ugly tone, 'Even for those people?' and I said, 'Most of all for anyone you might consider one of 'those people.' Remember, I'm a Jew.'"

"What did she do?"

"She didn't say another word but left the room. It's the only time I ever saw her do anything overtly rude."

"And she didn't threaten you?"

He shook his head.

"She didn't retaliate in any way?"

"Of course not." Sam was quiet for a moment and then said thoughtfully, "I told you that she had never done anything to me personally, but from that time on, my seats at sporting events and my on-the-road accommodations were never quite as good as they had been. It wasn't anything to complain about, and I didn't much care but she pretty consistently seated me away from Kenneth—the President--at athletic events and dinners."

"You're sure she did the arranging?"

"Absolutely. She liked controlling access to the President."

"How do you know that?"

"Someone came to me about a personnel matter. Long story, but a relative of a trustee got a job." I raised an eyebrow. "Okay, it stinks, but this trustee was a bigwig at the time. It's a while back. Then, down the road, this relative got moved to another position. It was complicated, and I don't remember all the details now, but it involved a program that got a new director who did not want this person so the person got transferred to another job."

"Lucky to have a job, I'd say."

"Me, too, but the employee was not happy about the move so the former trustee, who was a friend of sorts, got the runaround from LouAnn when he tried to talk to the President so he asked me to look into the situation. I sent a note to Kenneth. Apparently he passed the note on to LouAnn, and she wrote me—I still remember her exact words: 'The President's office no longer has an interest in this situation.'"

I thought back to the e-mail Miranda had received.

"Did the President always have her do his dirty work?"

"I don't know, but I've heard over the years that if the answer from the President's office is yes, you get a note from Kenneth, and if it is no, you hear from LouAnn."

"So maybe she was just doing her job."

"Sometimes, of course, but when I saw her a few days later, she asked if I had gotten the note. I said that I had. She was clearly looking for some kind of reaction, but I didn't give her the satisfaction."

"Good for you."

"I suppose, but I hate that kind of game."

"I know what you mean. That night in the hotel room, did you realize it was her on the phone?"

"I had a vague feeling that I knew the voice, but I didn't recognize it right away."

"It's late to call. Are you a night owl?" It was the most innocuous way I could think of to ask what they were doing.

"Not usually, but I had been agonizing over what to do about Judith's care. I had caregivers at home, but she needed more skilled nursing care. Anyway, I was having trouble sleeping so Maureen was keeping me company. We were just sitting there having a drink and playing cards."

Maureen had led me to believe that she and Sam were lovers, but he seemed to indicate at every turn that they were just good friends. Someone was lying, and I suspected Maureen.

"Do you see Maureen often outside of work?"

"We usually have dinner and maybe see a movie or play or go hear a concert about once a week—usually on Friday night. We have opera and symphony tickets together. We occasionally see each during the week, but not usually. She's so busy, and I've got my responsibilities. We spend a lot of time together when we go to games on the road. It's been a blessing to have her company because Judith and I..." He stopped. "It's just hard."

"My folks have been married forever so I think I can probably imagine what you mean."

He glanced at his watch, and I realized that we had been talking for an hour.

"I'm sorry to take so much of your time. Can I ask you just one more question?"

"Sure, and then I do have to run. I have a meeting in ten minutes across campus."

"What does Maureen do when you're out of town?"

"I could say that I have no idea, but she's actually told me," he replied with a grin.

"What?"

"She takes the weekend and does nothing whatsoever. She says it's her own version of out of town. I've tried to get her to go visit her girls more often, but I think there may be some problems, especially with Carlotta. Anyway, she works like a maniac so if she wants two days of down time, I'm all for it."

"You don't call her?"

"No. We usually talk early Monday morning, and she tells me how many movies she watched, how many books she read, and which ones I might enjoy." He chuckled, adding, "If only LouAnn had known how very unromantic we actually are!"

I was driving home when Maureen finally called me back.

"Do you have time for a drink?" I asked.

"How about dinner?"

"What time?"

"Seven."

"Can I bring the salad?"

"Sure. It'll be something pasta."

As I drove home, I thought how this seemed less like a meeting and more like a typical "girlfriend" meal. I took my mind off Maureen's lies by making an elaborate salad with dried cranberries, pine nuts, shredded carrots, and a nice mix of greens including arugula and baby spinach. Then I made a simple oil and vinegar dressing.

As I worked, I could not help thinking about Cass. Physically she was capable of killing Bond and moving the body. She clearly blamed Bond for the end of her relationship with Maureen. Although she had ample reason to hate Bond, I still could not imagine Cass killing anyone except to defend herself or another. I considered another possibility: what if Cass had been defending someone? Maureen was the logical "someone," but while they had both assured me their relationship wa

108

over, they had both shown signs of continuing attachment. Where did Sam fit in? Why had Maureen wanted me to believe they were romantically involved? What if I were completely gullible because my fondness for them both reduced me to a complete idiot? This thought infuriated me because I have always considered myself a good judge of character and astute observer of other people.

A bit after seven, I stood watching Maureen sautéing shrimp in garlic and olive oil to mix with parsley, olives and feta cheese to make her version of Pasta à la Grec. She quickly threw sliced bread from a baguette into a basket, we sat down, and then we ate in silence for a moment.

"This is wonderful!"

"Quick and easy," replied Maureen. "I'm an expert at that kind of cooking." She wound more pasta, using her fork and spoon, and asked, "So what's up?"

"Why did you first contact me?"

"What do you mean?"

She busied herself serving salad so I could not see her eyes.

"Why me? How did you find me?" I did not bother to keep the edge out of my voice.

"Sam recommended you."

"That's what you said when we first talked."

"It's the truth."

I served myself some salad. Something about her answer struck me as either incomplete or false, but I could not figure out what.

"I had dinner with my cousin, and we think we know where the key to LORETTA came from. It might explain why someone killed Tareka James."

"What?"

"There are very few keys to the area where LORETTA is located. To get in you would have had to hide yourself and the body in the freight elevator which you would also need a key to operate. Or, if you hid elsewhere or came back later, you would have needed a key to the area in order to, uh, take care of Bond's body. We don't know where she was killed. We do know the murderer had to access LORETTA."

"I see."

"Tareka kept keys to LORETTA and the freight elevator in her desk which was left unlocked. The murderer must have borrowed the keys."

"How did you figure this out?"

"Serendipity. My library tour with Emily Hartshorn. She got the key to LORETTA out of the desk, and when I talked to my cousin Harold--the cop you met Sunday night--the penny dropped."

"So you decided to sign that form?"

"No, actually Harold said it was unnecessary. He just wanted to talk to me off the record."

"So you told him you were working for me?"

I could tell that her calm voice did not reflect her feelings and decided to lie.

"Yes, but I told him that I was interested in going into administration to make some real money." Maureen laughed, clearly relieved. "You asked me to keep things confidential, and I will unless my silence becomes a danger to someone. Also, if I figure out who the killer is, I go to the police, end of discussion."

I watched Maureen carefully as I said this, but she did not react.

"Of course. You think it was someone in the library?"

"You mean someone who works in the library?" She nodded. "I don't know. What I need is a way to talk to Dorothy Sizemore. She worked closely with Bond, and I'd like to find out what she thought about her."

"There is a banquet in two weeks for the Harrigan Scholars. Each new scholar needs a community mentor. There are now sixty scholars in the program. I will have Betsy send you the profile material for both the scholars and the mentors. Read over it, do the matches, and meet with Dorothy. I'll make sure I introduce you to her Sunday evening."

"Thanks."

"I suspect that Dorothy knows where all the bodies are buried."

"Why?"

"She's been running events for the President's office for twenty-five years." Maureen sipped her wine thoughtfully. "She's an extraordinary person. In fact, she's probably the smartest person in the upper administration."

"Including you and the President?"

Maureen laughed.

"Including the President." She chewed reflectively for a few moments. "Yes, and maybe me. Dorothy has a mind like the proverbial steel trap, and I sometimes suspect that she has something akin to a photographic memory. She can describe every venue in this city which will hold over fifty people, and if you ask her about an event, even an event years ago--where it was held, who attended, what was served, how the food was presented, who sat with whom, or who prepared it--she can tell you. Right off the top of her head."

"Weird."

"Yes, weird and invaluable. She is discreet--doesn't gossip. We have always had a good working relationship because I recognize how smart she is and always show her respect and express appreciation for the incredible way she does her job."

"Will the Pophams be there Sunday night?"

"I think so."

"I'd like to meet them."

"They are part of a very conservative circle of friends. The women have a book club of some sort that they invited me to join. I begged off because I could not imagine the kind of books they would be reading."

110

"Were they all friends before they got on the Board?"

"Dumb question, Celeste. Actually, it's the first dumb question you've asked." Maureen's teasing tone took the sting out of her words. "In this town, rich people, especially the ones with old money, all know each other. In fact, many of them are related from way back. They sit on the same boards, they join the same country clubs, they winter in the same part of Florida, their children attend the same private schools, and they support the arts so they see each other at the ballet, opera, theatre and symphony. Google a couple of the trustees, check the bank or corporate boards and arts boards, not to mention foundation and private school boards, and you'll see what I mean. It will not take you five minutes to begin to see the connections."

"I'm sorry. It was a dumb question. And to think I'm from here."

"Not dumb. Naïve, but how would you know? These people are rarely in the news."

We had finished dinner, and Maureen looked tired.

"One last thing."

"What?"

"Can you talk to the President? Can you talk to him about LouAnn Bond and get him to tell you how she kept her job? I'm convinced there's some dirt there."

"I can't do it," Maureen said flatly. "I wish I could, but our relationship is very formal. All business. There is no room for personal stuff."

"But you told him about Sam Jacoby and you," I protested.

"I did, but he had had a fair amount of holiday cheer, it took two seconds, and there was no further discussion. The most personal discussion we've ever had was about the politics of this current Board of Trustees and what this particular group of religious conservatives would mean for the university."

"The President's liberal?"

"How would I know? Our conversation was focused on the university, but he saw clearly how these trustees could spell trouble for our development and also for our reputation as an institution of higher learning. He was worried that they would block anything even remotely progressive. At the first informal gathering of the year, they asked how they could revisit partner benefits and review some of our 'controversial' programs."

"What programs?"

"They had a list. Women's Studies was at the top. The new Latino Studies major next, but they were also interested in some specific courses like 'Political Dynamics of Social Change' and any other course that had 'revolution,' 'change,' 'race,' or 'gender' in the title. They had done their homework, or someone had done it for them. The President and I were both disturbed to discover how organized they were from the beginning to start forcing their opinions on the university."

"What about the president's wife?"

"Eleanor? I like her. She's very nice to me, but she's nice to everyone. We've gotten into a deep discussion of the weather once or twice, but otherwise, I have no idea what she's like and have had no opening to find out. The only thing I can say is that she did not join the book club when invited. Millicent Popham asked us at a party where we were standing together and chatting. Eleanor softened the blow by saying that she was in a book club that had been together ever since she and Kenneth moved here." Maureen paused for a moment and looked thoughtful. "I always think of Kenneth's wife as Eleanor the Elegant. I don't mean to make fun of her—she is a very poised, very classy lady."

I glanced at my watch.

"I need to go now, but one more question." Maureen raised her eyebrows. "What were you doing in the library the Friday Bond was killed?"

"How did you find out I was there?"

"A little bird told me. What were you doing?"

"I checked out a couple movies for the weekend."

"What movies?"

"Two French films actually: *Umbrellas of Cherbourg* and *Potiche*. The library has a large collection of foreign films."

"Why didn't you send someone from your office?"

"I was done for the day and wanted to browse a bit."

"Why those films?"

"This is beginning to feel like the third degree," Maureen murmured with a smile. I did not smile back so she continued with a sigh, "If you must know, I saw *Potiche* in the theatre and thought it was very funny. I thought there were references to *Umbrellas of Cherbourg,* which I hadn't seen for over fifty years, so I wanted to check. For the record, I love French films and adore Catherine Deneuve."

"You and Cass were both in the library late in the afternoon the Friday Bond was killed."

"It's a free country," Maureen said flippantly and then added with real irritation, "So you think I stopped off to pick up a couple of French films before murdering someone. For God's sake, Celeste, get a grip."

I felt angry and embarrassed, especially when she added abruptly, "I'd ask you to stay for an after-dinner drink, but I have things to read tonight."

"I do too and probably much less expertly written," I muttered huffily.

"Oh, you'd be surprised," laughed Maureen, taking a sip of her wine. Her tone was friendly again as she asked, "Anything else?"

"I need to ask you something personal, and I don't want you to get angry."

"You mean, any angrier than I am already? Okay. What now?"

She was looking at her wine glass, not at me. She was using it as a prop. She might be worried about the incoming crop of first-year students, but I was now sure that this was not her real motive for hiring me.

"Tell me about your relationship to Sam Jacoby."

"I've already told you. Why are you asking?"

"I talked to Sam today."

"And?"

"He led me to believe that you are just friends. Good friends. Close friends. But just friends."

"Sam is such a gentleman of the old school," she began in an amused tone.

"You told me that he wanted to marry you."

"He did."

"He told me he still loves his wife and indicated clearly that you are just friends."

"Maybe he's embarrassed because I turned him down."

I was sure that she was lying, and I was sure that she knew that I knew, but instead of continuing the Jamesian charade, I stood up, and she walked me to the door.

"You know I have no idea what I'm doing," I admitted as I slipped into my coat. "I feel like I'm adrift and clutching at straws and that mixed metaphor sums things up all too aptly."

"But you're smart and observant, and you know so much more about the university than the police do. If you stumble across a lead, you'll recognize it. I'm willing to pay for chance favoring your prepared mind."

"Thanks for the vote of confidence, but this would be so much easier if everyone would just tell me the truth the first time around."

"That could be said about life in general," Maureen replied.

My diminishing trust in Maureen and Cass was playing like the bass line of a song as I spent the drive home berating myself for not forcing Maureen to tell me what she was lying about and why. I wondered if I should have gotten angry and threatened to quit in order to get information out of her, but I suspected that this strategy would have backfired. I also had to admit that I held back because I wanted to go to the party on Sunday night. My curiosity was not idle. If I were ever to get anywhere in solving this mystery, I needed to know as much as possible about the environment in which LouAnn Bond had lived and worked. Only by entering that environment would I learn anything of value.

I began to consider what to wear.

Chapter Twelve

When I awoke around ten on Saturday morning, my first thought was that I needed to re-read LouAnn Bond's obituary. I had no idea why until I googled her birthplace--Holloway Springs, West Virginia—and discovered that it was about ten miles, as the crow flies, from Fanger Wells, Stephen Hope's hometown. Thinking that he might help me understand where LouAnn Bond was from, I sent him an e-mail to ask if he could have lunch on Monday and got an immediate yes. Although I felt a little guilty about the lunch, I justified it to myself by arguing that people socialize more easily over food.

For dinner on Saturday night, Marshall took me to a small Senegalese restaurant where he knew everyone. He spoke Wolof and joked with the proprietors, as we ate delicious *cheb ou djen*, although "fish and rice" does not begin to convey the tasty goodness of Senegal's national dish. We were so busy talking and eating that we barely got to the concert on time. Afterwards, because I wanted to reciprocate, I treated us to ice cream, and we argued amiably about the jazz we had heard. I was glad to avoid talking about the murders because, as my sense of confusion and isolation increased, I felt even more tempted to confide in Marshall.

When I got home, I could not sleep, and it was not just my response to Marshall's good-night kiss. I got up and began making lists of who had keys to what, who had possibly known LouAnn Bond, and who I needed to interview.

I believed that Tareka James had been killed because of the keys to LORETTA and the freight elevator. There was nothing else to connect her to Bond's murder. It had to be the keys, but what about them? Only one fact seemed pertinent: they were the only keys not kept in a person's pocket or locked up. So what had Tareka seen? Not the taking of the keys, or surely she would have intervened, demanding a proper sign out, but no one had signed the keys out on Friday afternoon. The keys were in the desk so they had been used and returned. Why return the keys?

In the midst of my note making, which had begun to look more than a bit obsessive, I began to wonder how spies functioned in an environment where they could trust no one and write nothing down.

What made me most uncomfortable was how the investigation seemed to be changing me: I had begun to assume that nothing was exactly what it seemed. I forced myself to write notes about Maureen and Cass. They had the motive, Maureen could have summoned Bond, Cass was capable of moving the body, and she also knew how to operate the saw. Whoever had gotten Bond to the library had told her something to entice her. What? Knowing the President's office was involved in the Smythe Center for the Study of Governments, I needed to ask Emily Hartshorn if this meant that Bond herself was involved in the project. Feeling that I should have asked this question earlier, I threw my pen down in frustration and went to bed where I tossed and turned for another hour.

Sunday evening at six, I rang the doorbell to the President's house. An older black man in white serving attire took my coat and drink order. I then stepped through the foyer to be greeted by Maureen, flanked by the President and his wife.

"President Truman, this is Dr. Celeste Brinkman. She's the English professor who has agreed to help me with some special projects."

I had shaken the President's hand on a few other occasions, but his full attention had never been turned on me. His gaze was not unfriendly, but cool and appraising.

"Dr. Brinkman, I'd like you to meet my wife Eleanor."

"How nice to meet you," I murmured as Eleanor smiled and we shook hands.

Before I could attempt further conversation, more people arrived, and Maureen took me by the elbow, saying, "Excuse me, but there are some people I'd like Dr. Brinkman to meet."

I turned and almost collided with another older black man in white who delivered my drink on a small tray . Maureen guided me through the crush toward the back of the house where she opened the kitchen door and said something I could not hear. Soon a woman of medium height who easily weighed two hundred fifty pounds came through the door.

"Dr. Shaughnessy, what can I do for you?"

"I know you're busy, Dorothy, but I wanted you to meet Dr. Celeste Brinkman." Maureen turned to me, saying, "Dr. Brinkman, this is Dorothy Sizemore who handles all the events for the upper administration so admirably."

We shook hands, and I was almost speechless because beneath all the flesh was a stunningly beautiful woman. Sizemore, the name itself forced one to reflect on God's little ironies, had wide dark eyes with long lashes, a beautiful smile with even white teeth a movie star would kill for, and the kind of olive skin that begs to be touched and rarely wrinkles with age. Her hair was dark, probably with a little help, but the short, loose curls looked natural.

"I've heard that you are an absolute wizard," I finally managed to say, and she laughed. Her voice was a low, husky contralto that made me wonder if she sang.

"Yes, Dorothy, I told her all about you," chuckled Maureen. "Dr. Brinkman will be working with you on the Harrigan banquet. I've sent her the files so she can match the community members with the new students, but I want the two of you to go over the seating."

"Of course. Call me whenever you get the matches figured out, and we'll sit down," she said to me with a smile.

"Hopefully this week."

"Great!" she said touching my arm lightly. "Now, if you don't mind, I need to go check the table."

"Thanks a lot," said Maureen.

"Nice meeting you, and I will call soon."

"Good. I'll look forward to it, Dr. Brinkman." She sounded like she meant it.

When Dorothy had gone off toward the dining room, Maureen turned to me with an amused smile.

"You didn't tell me she was beautiful," I said in a vaguely accusatory tone.

"There's no possible preparation for Dorothy. None at all. I think she is a mystery to all of us. A wonder and a mystery."

"Not married?"

"Never that I know of, but no one knows much about Dorothy except the obvious fact that she's brilliant at her job. Many people and places have tried to hire her away from the university."

"And she hasn't gone?"

"No. Actually, I do know something about Dorothy: she attends a lot of the lectures and music events on campus. She also takes classes. That's probably why we've been able to keep her, along with a pretty good paycheck."

"How old is she?"

"Probably somewhere in her fifties. She's worked at the university forever."

"So she knew LouAnn Bond for many years."

"And worked closely with her." Maureen touched my elbow. "Walk with me toward the solarium, and I'll introduce you to Frank O'Donnell."

We threaded our way through the growing crowd of people until we came to a sunroom. The furniture was covered in a bright African print, the interior wall adorned with African paintings on glass and a few ebony masks. The room was filled with potted plants kept happy by glass on three sides.

"Frank, this is Dr. Celeste Brinkman from English. She's my new Assistant for Special Projects." O'Donnell shook my hand.

"Welcome to the jungle," he said, and I laughed.

"I need to get back to the President," said Maureen. "Can I leave Celeste with you, Frank? She doesn't know anyone so will you look out for her?"

"Of course. My pleasure."

We watched Maureen move back toward the reception area.

"So how do you like working for Maureen?"

"I haven't been doing it long, but she's amazing."

"Yes, she is."

"How long have you been at the university?" I asked, hoping to get the conversation on more informative ground.

"Almost forty years." He laughed at my surprise. "I was an undergraduate here, and then went to grad school back east and took a job out west. The Chair of the History Department back then—David Mitchell—had been my mentor and always wanted me to come back here so when I published my first book, he found a way to offer me a job."

"Just like that?" Incredulity filled my voice.

"Pretty much. Back in the day, this kind of thing happened. Someone knew you and got the department to hire you because you were promising. It was all pretty much done over drinks with a handshake. I won't romanticize or defend it because it led to a totally discriminatory way of doing business. As we know, people hire people who look and think like them."

"Did you like teaching?"

"Did and still do. I teach a course every spring semester."

"What?"

"My specialty—history of the American West."

"Now, there's a field that's changed over the years."

"Yes, and to answer your unasked question, I've changed with it," he said sharply. When I looked surprised, he added, "Your areas of expertise are not unknown to me."

"I was pretty sure that I detected a flash of recognition when Maureen introduced us."

"I could not ever say this on the record, but I'm sorry about the mess surrounding your tenure decision. I'm glad to meet you if only to have a chance to say that. Your scholarly record clearly speaks for itself, or would have spoken for itself, had anyone been listening."

I was speechless with shock. I had never expected to receive anything resembling an apology from the university, which seemed to operate consistently on legal advice that said, "Fix it, pay for it, keep it confidential, but don't ever admit to making a mistake."

I swallowed hard.

"Thank you for saying that. It's very good of you."

"And I'll deny it to the death if accused." He laughed bitterly.

A server came in, and O'Donnell ordered another Scotch, and I another tonic water.

"So if you like teaching, how did you end up in administration?"

"Beware, Celeste—you don't mind if I call you Celeste, do you?"

"Of course not. May I call you Frank?" He nodded. "So what should I beware of?"

"Getting sucked into administration. The money is good, but the sense that you might be able to change things, make them better, is even more seductive."

Our drinks were delivered by yet another older black man in white. It crossed my mind that Central Casting at the university had a pipeline to Tara.

"From what I've heard, you have made some great changes. The faculty all seem to think well of you." Frank shrugged modestly. "If you could make two changes by fiat, what would they be?" I was genuinely curious.

"Keep my answer in confidence?" he asked, and I nodded. "We would become a totally undergraduate institution and ditch our athletic programs except for intramural sports."

"Any chance of either change ever happening? And, for the record, I agree with both ideas."

"Well, let's put it this way," he said philosophically, "These changes versus snowball rolling through hell—I'd put my money on the snowball."

We both laughed, and I realized that he was a bit drunk.

"Can I ask you something else in confidence?"

"Sure."

"What did you think of LouAnn Bond?"

"Why do you ask?" He sounded wary.

"I know what Maureen says about her, and I've heard all kinds of talk on campus. I cannot believe how universally she was disliked."

"Actually, if she were still alive, getting rid of her might have been one of my two university reforms," he said grimly.

"That bad?"

"Yes, and in so many ways."

"Can you give me an example?"

"I'd prefer not to speak any more ill of the dead than I already have," he said flatly.

"Sorry."

"No, no, not at all."

"It was tactless of me to indulge my idle curiosity."

"You aren't the only one who's curious. We all want to know who did it, but most of us want to give the person a medal."

Before I could respond to this remark, we were called to gather for dinner where I found myself seated next to Millicent Popham who had her husband Alexander on her other side. On my other side was Martin Speary, the Vice Provost for Personnel, a relative newcomer to the job. We were seated across from Louise and Griswold Gattner, a couple in their late sixties. Griswold was on the Board of Trustees, and I recognized them as people who gave generously to conservative causes. Next to them sat Matt Dingle, the current chair of the Board of Trustees, and his wife Cindy. They were both around fifty—he looked it, and she was making efforts not to. I

118

knew they were both close friends and political supporters of the current conservative governor. I was out on the right wing, seated in the middle of the most conservative trustees.

We introduced ourselves, and after Matt Dingle had announced, to predictable laughter, that his "worst subject had always been English" and Cindy had pertly added, "We had all better watch our grammar," they began chitchatting about the past winter in Florida, sports, travel, and upcoming political fundraisers, in other words, their common social life. Millicent, however, had old-fashioned manners and felt moved to engage me in polite conversation. While I listened with half an ear to the table talk, I answered her questions about how long I had been at the university and what schools I had attended. After a bit of silence, I said quietly, "I understand LouAnn Bond worked closely with the Board. You must miss her greatly." I was surprised that Millicent shot me an ambivalent glance before saying, "Oh, yes, such a loss. She was also a member of our church."

"St. Luke's?" She nodded. "Is the congregation large?"

"Oh, no. Quite small."

"Was LouAnn very active?"

"Yes. Our pastor especially will miss her."

Was it my imagination, or was there hostility in Millicent's well-bred voice?

"Isn't he married?" Millicent shook her head. "Being a pastor is a hard job to do alone."

"Our pastor and LouAnn were very close friends."

"It can be difficult when the pastor listens to one member of the congregation more than another."

"Well, things do change," she said and quickly added, "LouAnn was always a wonderful help to the Board of Trustees, and Alexander will miss her advice."

"I didn't think she was directly responsible for the Board. Isn't there someone assigned to takes care of the agendas and documents?" I asked innocently.

"Yes. Sandy Minton handles all that, but LouAnn was always willing to provide special help and counsel. You know, background on important issues."

"Interesting. What sorts of issues did she help the Board with?" For a moment, I thought Millicent had recognized my unusual interest, but actually she was staring into space thinking.

"Well, last semester, there was that business about, you know," she dropped her voice and her lip curled, "Coming Out Week. It was scandalous."

"The speakers?" I asked innocently, and she nodded.

"Totally inappropriate." Before I could answer, she added lightly, "But what do I know about any of this?" and joined the general conversation.

I let her go and turned to Martin Speary who was quietly eating his dinner.

"How did you come to join the administration?"

"I was in Sociology," he said, shooting me an appraising look to see what I would make of this odd answer.

"How long have you been working for the Provost?"

"A little over a year."

"So what made you go into administration?" I asked again, keeping my voice low, but the general conversation had become so animated over various places in Florida as winter homes that no one was paying any attention to us.

"Five kids."

"As a sociologist, you must find the administrative culture interesting," I offered, and he rolled his eyes.

"Most of what I find interesting, you can't write down."

"From experience, I think I understand what you mean," I said softly.

"I bet you do." Martin Speary had not been in charge when my tenure decision was made so I had no hard feelings. He gave me a small, grim smile and then continued, "The biggest part of my job is cleaning up the mess when people don't follow the written policies. I will never figure out how academics who are in the business of imparting knowledge so often..." He stopped himself, realizing that Matt Dingle had tuned into our conversation. He looked across the table and said amiably, "Did you go to Tennessee for the game last weekend?"

"Yeah, we should have won, and if we had a better basketball coach, we would have," replied Matt, sounding aggressive and aggrieved.

"I thought this new coach was supposed to be the answer to our problems," I interjected, and Matt snorted while Martin just shook his head.

We spent the rest of dinner talking sports, a discussion that only increased my dislike of Matt Dingle who proved to be a conversational bully and clearly thought of sports discussion as men's work. As we were leaving the table, Dingle came around to Martin. I dropped my napkin and bent to pick it up.

"Before she died (God rest her soul!), LouAnn Bond told me there's a real prize coming up for tenure."

"What do you mean?" Martin asked and then added quickly, "Matt, you know I can't discuss personnel decisions."

"I know that." Dingle patted Martin's shoulder patronizingly. "I just want you to know that we know what's going on and this Board is serious about its mission to the community."

"The Board usually is serious about its mission," Martin said in a neutral tone.

"Maybe not entirely in the past," said Dingle contemptuously, "But this Board believes the university should uphold moral standards in the community and not mock them or teach students to mock them."

I could not crawl around under the table forever so I stood up.

"I had not heard that 'moral standards' were a litmus test for tenure," replied Martin evenly.

120

"Well, in certain situations, they need to be," replied Dingle sharply.

"We'll just have to see," said Martin with forced amiability.

As Dingle walked away, Martin looked at me and shrugged, muttering, "I have no idea what he was talking about."

"Me neither," I assured him, but the remark made me remember Reverend Potts' remark about Bond's concern over an upcoming tenure case. It suddenly seemed urgent that I find out what Bond could have told Matt Dingle.

As I was waiting for my coat, I had a moment alone with Maureen.

"Can you get me a list of people coming up for tenure this year?" I asked her quietly.

"Why?"

"Something I heard tonight. Matt Dingle has some bee in his bonnet about a tenure decision and someone's morals. Can you ask the President if he's heard anything?"

"I can get you the list."

"And the President?"

"I'll see what I can do."

Maureen looked upset. Trustees, especially this group, micromanaging the university clearly gave both of us the creeps.

When I got home, I tried to summarize what I had discovered. Frank O'Donnell had hated LouAnn Bond, St. Luke's was not the happy community its pastor presented, Bond had probably tipped off the conservatives about Coming Out Week, Martin Speary was not enthralled with his job, and Matt Dingle thought the Board of Trustees should intervene in a tenure decision on "moral grounds." I went to sleep hoping that there were no more of these high-level social events in my future unless I felt free to drink to excess.

Monday morning, I went to see Emily Hartshorn at eight, her only free time. I asked for a tour of her office which she reluctantly gave me. There were only three rooms so it did not take long.

"The police have already looked at everything, Nancy Drew" she said, clearly not believing a word of my invented story about looking at all aspects of library operations.

"I can't share any details, but I'm not just on a fool's errand," I told her.

"Okay. Ask me whatever you want."

"I want you to explain how this office works. Who goes in and out and why. Explain this operation to me as if I were coming to work here with no idea how the library is run."

I listened carefully for the next few minutes and finally said, "Okay, so someone could be left alone at this desk. Say I needed something from the store room. Tareka opens the door, and then I can't find the paper or printer cartridge or whatever that I'm supposed to get. She comes into the storeroom to help me. The office door is open, her desk is sitting here unattended, and that board with all the keys is unlocked."

"Is that how the murderer got the keys?" Emily looked horrified.

"Maybe so." I did not add that I thought the real problem came up when the keys had to be returned. Why not throw them down the sewer? Something about the keys being returned nagged at me, but I could not figure out what.

"It couldn't happen now," Emily assured me. "Now we are now keeping the board with the keys locked at all times. My assistant and I now both have keys to the desk that we carry with us."

"Okay, but before, this could have happened." She nodded reluctantly.

I went out into the hall to walk up and down. The placement of the windows and doors, particularly in the conference room, could have allowed someone to lurk in the hallway and observe when Tareka left her desk unattended. If caught, that person could pass off being behind Tareka's desk by pretending to throw something in the wastepaper basket and then asking for supplies.

"What department comes in most frequently for supplies?" I asked.

"Cataloging," Emily replied without hesitation. "One of my biggest fights with Carl Smarinsky has been over supplies. When we centralized supplies, he tried to insist on keeping his own supplies, but the whole goal of centralizing was to get a grip on spending, and Cataloging was a big spender."

"And has centralizing helped?"

"It's cut the supply budget line by twenty percent because now you have to sign for what you get and we charge it back to your department. A lot less stuff is walking out the door or sitting unused in closets. For a while, I was the Wicked Witch, but now most people don't remember we used to do things differently."

"I have another question."

"What?" Emily's "What now" tone made us both laugh.

"Was Bond directly involved with the Smythe project?"

"Of course. She was the liaison with the President's office for the new wing."

"Isn't that a little unusual?"

"Not when you consider who provided the funding."

"So she was the person who kept the Congressman happy?"

"More or less."

"How big of a pain was she?"

"On a scale of one to ten, she's been a ten ever since we got to the stage of interior finishes and furniture. She was driving both me and the university design team nuts." She suddenly stopped, realizing how angry she sounded. "Of course, none of us would ever...."

"It's okay, Emily. It's a big leap from annoyance to murder."

When I left Emily, I went to my office and called Harold. I told him what I had found out as well as what I suspected about someone lurking to take advantage of

122

Tareka's momentary absence. Once in the supply closet, actually a small room, she would not have been able to see her desk without turning around and looking out the door.

"Okay," said Harold. "I'm going to go back and talk to everyone who got supplies that day and everyone who works at a desk that looks out over the corridor."

"Will you let me know?"

"Sure."

"Oh, my God! I just realized something."

"What?"

"Why the murderer returned the keys. I've been asking myself over and over: why take the risk of returning the keys? Why not just dispose of them? Why did they have to be put back in place?"

"Okay, Miss Marple, speak."

"We'll talk about your taste in detective fiction later, but I think I have the answer. Whoever killed Bond didn't expect the body to be found for days or even weeks. That area of the library has good climate control so it could have been a while before..."

"I get it, and it sounds logical. Who would have expected a bingo on LORETTA's first public performance?"

"Exactly."

"So maybe when the body turned up so soon, the murderer was worried that Tareka James might remember something or maybe James even made a comment or asked the wrong person a question. Maybe she missed the keys and started asking around, and the murderer knew she'd made the connection." He paused for a moment. "I'll run it by Blake."

"I have one more question. Did you find blood in the staff stairwell?"

"Yeah, but not much. Just a little like someone had stepped in blood and wiped it off. A tiny smear, no footprints—the forensic people say the perpetrator was probably wearing booties. You can buy them at any building or medical supply just like gloves."

"So where do you think she was killed?"

"Maybe in the work area behind that storage system. Absolutely nothing anywhere else except a touch of blood in the freight elevator and a touch on the stairs. Nothing at all helpful except the drop cloths were the same brand as they use but all new. And we got that tiny bit of flesh and fabric out of the saw guard."

"A lot of planning went into this"

"Not just planning. The guy who did this was smart and knew the library inside out."

I shuddered and said, "One more thing."

"What?"

"I think I know how the murderer got her over to the library."

"Okay, how?"

"She was the President's liaison for the new wing. She probably got a call to look at some furniture or finishes, something for the interior. According to Hartshorn, she was pretty obsessed with the project. I bet if you check her calendar, you'll find some kind of note about an appointment."

Half an hour later, Harold called back.

"I talked to Brent to be sure I remembered this right. Bond's desk calendar has a pencil note to meet Susan Lauter from Design at 4:55 in the library. It says 'government--finishes' next to it. They talked to Lauter at the beginning of the investigation, and she knew nothing about the appointment. In fact, she was out of town for the day, and someone checked—she's telling the truth."

"Have you checked the university phone records?"

"Dear," he said wearily, "We are the police. Even we know that voice over internet phone systems create immediate records."

"So?"

"Not a university phone. Pay phone."

"One of the two left in the city?"

"Yeah. It came from downtown. When we tried to get a lead on who might have called—we do know the time of the call—the homeless guys in the area didn't remember a thing. It's a very busy pay phone on the street outside a convenience store. In fact, the same phone was used to report the family emergency that covered Bond's absence from work so no one missed her."

"I can't believe I didn't ask about this before."

"Live and learn, Nancy Drew."

I ignored his teasing.

"Who did the person call about Bond's absence?"

"That other woman who works in the President's office."

"Marilyn Wilhoyt?"

"Yes."

"Was it a man or woman on the phone?"

"Impossible to tell because the voice was very low and kind of hoarse."

"What was the message?"

"Bond had asked the person to call because she had been forced to leave town suddenly on a family emergency. She said that she could not be reached but would call back early the following week."

"So by the time anyone thought of her as missing…"

"She wasn't at church so the Reverend Potts called to check on her. He got no answer at her apartment so he called her direct line and then the main office number Monday morning. Wilhoyt told him about the message. He said that it probably concerned her brother."

"So the caller didn't know her well enough to use the brother in the message."

124

"Could be or maybe chose not to, but we know it was someone who used that pay phone. In other words, someone who knew that the university phone system would record all the information about the call."

"But, as you pointed out, that's about every person over twelve in the universe at this point." I paused and added, "I have this strange feeling that I'm looking at something but not seeing it."

"Cece…"

"What?"

"Be careful. Okay? If you think you've got something, come to me. Don't go off on your own."

"Of course."

"Promise?"

"Yes. I promise."

Stephen and I met for lunch at Farouk's, a small Middle Eastern restaurant on the perimeter of campus. I had gotten my first administrative pay so I felt no guilt over eating out.

"How're you doing?" I asked as we sat down.

"I got the Dean's letter today so I'm walking on air—all very positive so far."

"The Provost never overturns the college, especially if the department's recommendation is also positive."

"The letter was great. Did I tell you how good my outside reviews were?" Stephen looked at the menu for a moment. "I hope I don't sound like I'm bragging."

"No, you just sound like the rest of us—relieved! And you've worked hard so you have a right to be proud." He smiled. "How's Pamela?" I asked, when we had ordered.

"She's had a stomach bug and been completely undone by this library stuff." He sounded worried.

"I can understand, especially if she knew Tareka James."

"It's that, but I think any violence brings up the past, and that's very hard for her."

"How so?"

"Her father was a mean drunk, and Pammy, uh, Pam was his main target." Stephen paused, almost as if he were startled at having made the revelation. "Please keep that in confidence."

"Of course." The server brought our gyros, and we both poured tziki sauce over the savory lamb. I took a bite and exclaimed, "I love this place!"

"Pam doesn't much like Middle Eastern food, but I love it!" He bit happily into his sandwich.

"Just out of curiosity, where did you and Pamela meet?" He looked at me uncomfortably. "I'm sorry. It's okay if you don't want to talk about personal stuff."

"No, it's not that," he assured me. "I just never talk about the past with anyone. Part of my upbringing or 'raisin,' as we would say back home," he said, sliding into a mountain accent. "Actually, Pam and I grew up together in Fanger's Well. There were only about five families in our area, and Pam's folks lived right down the road from mine. Somewhere back a generation or two we're actually related.

"Fanger's Well was too small to have a school so we were bussed into Mountain Valley. Pam and I were always close because of where we lived and we were both smart." He paused. "The town kids made fun of us--they shunned all us kids from the hollers."

Stephen's eyes got a faraway look, and I realized my own ignorance. We ate in silence for a few moments. I had no idea what to ask him because I had no clue what his life might have been like. I went for a familiar question.

"So how did you end up studying literature?"

"I loved books. So does Pam. That was another bond between us. There was a small library in Mountain Valley. Just a big room full of books, but the woman who ran it was educated. She told me once that she had come to the mountains on some kind of mission trip when she was young and ended up coming back later to stay for the rest of her life. I have no idea why she did this, but the few of us who got out were quite literally rescued by Miss Priddy."

"Is she still alive?"

"No, she died a while back," he said sadly. "We kept in touch. She was the closest thing I have to family, besides Pammy, and I miss her a lot."

"Did you go back for the funeral?"

"No, I couldn't. There was a memorial service, but I couldn't take the time mid-semester to go, and afterwards her body was sent back to her family in New England."

"You know LouAnn Bond was from Holloway Springs."

"I think you told me that the other day."

"Would she have also gone to school in Mountain Valley?"

"Yeah, Holloway Springs is about as big as Fanger's Well. It's the opposite way from town."

"Do you think that she might have known your Miss Priddy?"

"Probably. Anyone who got out was probably one of her friends. She knew more about how the world worked and how to find scholarships than the high school counselors or teachers, most of whom did a piss poor job and would never lift a finger for kids like me and Pammy." I noticed the slightly lilting accent had come back again into Stephen's voice.

"So she helped you go to college after high school?"

"No. Pam and I took a bus to Charleston the day after graduation. Miss Priddy had a friend there who ran a diner, and he gave us jobs and actually let us live over the diner for free. Pam learned to be a short-order cook, and I waited tables. When

126

we had saved for a year or so, we moved to Atlanta where I got my undergraduate degree. Once I had done my first year, I got a scholarship so I didn't have to work so much. I did well, and one of my professors suggested that I consider applying to graduate schools. The best offer came from UC Berkley."

"Ah, California!"

"Pam and I were both convinced that it was Paradise," he laughed. "And in many ways, it was although I worked awfully hard out there."

"Didn't Pamela want to go to school?"

"She wasn't sure what she wanted to do so we decided that it would make more sense for me to get through, and then we'd figure out her education." Stephen seemed to read my mind. "I know it seems sexist, but I had a clear goal—I've always wanted to teach literature--and Pam wasn't sure she even wanted to go to school."

"So you've been married forever?"

"No. We've been together forever but only married seven years." He smiled disarmingly. "We just didn't get around to it. We were always too busy making ends meet, and no one wants to marry someone who's writing a dissertation or facing the job market. We got married when I got the job."

I laughed with him.

"So what do you think about this first-year composition business?" he asked, and we spent the rest of lunch talking about the department.

When I got back to my office, I went online and found that Mountain Valley, West Virginia, had a newspaper. The website gave only basic information so I called the office and asked if I could talk with someone about obtaining a copy of an obituary. I was told that I had to call back the next morning after nine-thirty which was when Joseph came in. I was also advised to talk loudly and distinctly as his hearing was no longer the best.

Tuesday morning, I got ready for class and dialed the number I had been given.

"Joseph Saling, Mountain Valley News." His voice sounded old. Careful to speak clearly, I told him that I had met someone who knew Miss Priddy, and I wanted to know more about her as well as when she had died. Joseph had known Miss Priddy "from a boy." He would send me the obituary if I would promise to send him a money order for copying and postage. I promised to do so and took all the necessary information.

"You've been so kind, and I've taken so much of your time, could I please ask you another question?"

"Sure enough," he said gruffly, "Always glad to oblige."

"Did you ever know someone named LouAnn Bond?"

"From a boy, of course. We were at school together," he said, and I realized that he could not be as old as he sounded.

"I'm so sorry."

"About what?"

"She died a few weeks ago. I teach at the university where she worked."

"Last time I saw her was when they had the service for Miss Priddy before they shipped her body home. LouAnn had charge of her will."

"Really?"

"They were great friends from the time LouAnn was a girl. LouAnn always did have a way of finding those who could do her the most good, if you know what I mean—not to speak ill of the dead," he added.

"I think I know what you mean." I thought for a moment. "What did Miss Priddy's estate include?"

"Letters. Most of which were probably from LouAnn, but she acted like they were god almighty important. She boxed 'em up and toted 'em off to some archive."

"Where?"

"I'd have to look back, but somewhere here in West Virginia. Also there was a bunch of papers. She boxed up all the old library records—just bills and such like although most of the books were donated. I don't know what all, but she packed it up and got some young guys to load it all into a van, and she toted it off."

"What's happened to the library?"

"Miss Priddy left some money in a trust at the bank, and one of the local gals has taken it over, but I must say it just ain't the same."

"Did you know LouAnn Bond's brother?"

"Eustis? He's doing hard time. Bad lot. Actually all them Bonds was a bad lot, not to speak ill of the dead, and all of 'em, except Eustis, are dead and gone now."

"In what way were they a 'bad lot?'"

"Always lookin' to their own advantage, but LouAnn's the only one who ever got ahead." There was an awkward pause and when he did not continue, I tried another question.

"Do you know if LouAnn Bond ever did anything dishonest?"

"It depends on what you mean by 'dishonest.'" He cleared his throat. "But it's all a long time ago, and I got no call to speak ill of the dead. I've said more than I ought as it is."

"I'm sorry for being so nosy. Would you like me to send LouAnn Bond's obituary?" I asked in a conciliatory tone.

"If it's online, I could look it up if you'll tell me where it appeared." I got over my momentary shock and gave him the website address of the local paper along with the date of Bond's death. His mountain accent had tricked me into thinking he was ignorant. I felt foolish and tried to make up for my prejudice by thanking him profusely for his help before I hung up.

I opened my e-mail account and found that Maureen had forwarded me a list of professors coming up for tenure. Looking down the list of thirty names, I was completely baffled. I knew several of the people on the list from different departments on the main campus, but, even allowing that my definition of "morally objectionable" might not match the conservative trustee definition, nothing I knew about any of them suggested any great moral deviance. The other twenty-five people I had never even heard of before seeing this list. I tried to think of a way to find out who might have been on LouAnn's radar and of interest to the Board of Trustees.

I texted Maureen to call me after my class ended, and then went to the post office to buy a money order.

Chapter Thirteen

At four o'clock, as I was shutting down my computer to go home, my phone rang.

"What's up?" asked Maureen.

"I've looked at the list from Speary. I only know a few people, and nothing about them rings any moral bells."

"Your morals may not have the same bells as LouAnn's and the Board's," Maureen replied drily.

"Right. I'm trying to think of a way to get a handle on this without asking the police to start questioning everyone from Dingle to the department secretaries."

"Police?"

"I know. Will you talk to Speary? He was there when it came up and refused to talk about it."

"Of course he did." Maureen sighed audibly. "I'll see if I can catch him now."

Twenty minutes later, as I was unlocking my car, my phone rang.

"I talked to Martin. He was very concerned about Dingle's remark at the party. As you know, we can't ask Dingle anything directly without creating grounds for a grievance or lawsuit so Martin's been wracking his brain, going over the list, and looking at files. There is one guy down at the Med School who was dating an intern his first year on the job. She filed a harassment complaint, and it got messy, but she is long gone, and the Dean got him sorted out. Martin actually doesn't think heterosexual harassment would even cross the Board's mind as objectionable."

"He's probably right, but I was hoping he would have some idea."

"Me too, but he doesn't so far. Why don't you come over for a drink so we can talk?"

All I wanted was to forget this nonsense, go home, and climb into bed with a good book, but I also needed to talk, and who else did I have to talk to? It was either Harold or Maureen although the person I wanted to talk to was Marshall. I wondered when he would call again and sighed in resignation.

"What time?"

"I'll be home around seven."

"Okay. Shall I pick up a pizza?"

"Sounds good."

When I got home, I called an order into Pizza Napolitana so that I could pick it up on my way to Maureen's. While I made a salad, I called Harold.

"My favorite cousin!" he said when he picked up.

"And my favorite cousin! But don't tell Janey I said that!"

"So have you solved it yet?" he asked.

"Nowhere near, but I do have a question."

"Ask away."

"What did you find in Bond's apartment?"

"Not much personal stuff actually. Some papers. She didn't even have a computer."

"What kind of papers?"

"Typical personal stuff like bills and bank statements, cancelled checks. A few letters, but nothing seemed relevant."

"No tell-all diary?"

He snorted.

"In your dreams and in the movies, Miss Marple."

"Could I look at the papers?"

"Let me talk with Blake, and I'll see if I can take you over. The apartment is sealed. Since the next of kin is in jail, he isn't available to go through everything so no pressure. We've left it until we get this thing solved."

"Will you ask Blake soon?"

"Yeah, I'll see if I can get him now," promised Harold.

He called me back just as I was paying for the pizza and proudly using my debit card without worry.

"Meet me at Bond's apartment tomorrow morning at nine."

"Good, but I don't have the address. Hang on a minute."

I grabbed a pen off the counter and hauled my paid-for pizza over to a nearby chair where I sat down feeling the heat of the pizza on my legs and hoping I would not get burned.

"Okay. Give it to me."

I wrote the address on the pizza box.

"It's that weird little cul de sac off Sycamore."

"I'll use my phone to find it. Don't worry. I need to go now. See you tomorrow," I said, hurriedly standing up to hold the hot box away from me. I returned the pen to the frowning cashier and apologized. She gave me the typical teen-age, "Okay, nut-job" smile as I left.

Maureen opened the front door as soon as I rang and greeted me warmly, but I had the feeling she was more excited about the pizza than my company.

"Great! Napolitana—it's my favorite pizza place. What did you get?"

"The veggie special with extra cheese and artichoke hearts."

"I'm in Heaven."

We went into the kitchen where I set the pizza and salad on the counter. Maureen handed me a wad of bills, saying, "My invitation, my treat." She silenced my protest with a look as she expertly pulled the cork on a bottle of chianti and poured the wine. We took our wine and loaded plates to the table which was already set. Maureen put the salad in a bowl and brought it over. She sat down and raised her glass, saying, "To solutions!"

"Amen," I replied. We touched glasses and then ate in silence for a few moments, enjoying the fresh zest of the pizza toppings and the crunch of the thin, crisp crust.

"Tell me about what happened at the party."

I told her as much as I could remember.

"Dingle is a real son of a bitch," she finally said. "He's the one who wanted to revisit partner benefits so we know that he's got gays and lesbians on what passes for his mind."

"What did Speary have to say about that list of tenure candidates?"

"Nothing new. He agreed to call the chairs he knows well and kind of feel them out about any issues there might be."

"Now there's a delicate and complicated task."

"Yes and bordering on the unprofessional if not downright illegal. He's only doing it because I told him that he had to, and I'm his boss. If this mess involves a faculty member, it's even more important that we figure it out before it becomes public."

"Knowing what we know about Bond's and some of the trustees' connection to For the Family, I'd say public is just where this is headed."

"Great. Just what the university needs. Anything else?"

I told her briefly about my lunch with Stephen Hope and in more detail about my conversation with the archivist at Mountain Valley News, adding that I was going to Bond's apartment the next morning with Harold.

"There may be something in Bond's apartment that would be helpful, but I can't imagine her killer coming out of the holler to get her after all these years," Maureen teased making me feel self-conscious, and slightly irritated.

"I don't know where else to look unless I start looking very close to home."

"What do you mean?"

"You don't have an alibi for the time in question. Bond would have answered a summons from you, and you knew very well that she was obsessed with the new library wing. You also had good reasons to hate her."

"You can't be serious," Maureen began, and I was suddenly furious with her.

"Cass also lied to me about where she was that weekend."

"So?" Maureen kept her voice carefully neutral, but I could sense her wariness.

132

"Why would she do that if she didn't have something to hide?"

"How in the hell would I know? Maybe she does, but what does that have to do with me?"

The tone was slightly off—Maureen's first bad dramatic performance for me.

"You don't have an alibi. I can't check with the bedbugs to make sure you were lazing about that weekend."

"So?"

The small crack in her armor had now disappeared.

"I think that LouAnn Bond believed you were having a relationship with Sam Jacoby. I think that she liked the idea that she could control you. She didn't like women who step out of traditional roles plus she knew that you had had a lesbian relationship. She hated the idea of anyone having any kind of non-marital sexual relationship, but most of all, she loved controlling people. That's why she tried to blackmail you a second time over Sam Jacoby." Suddenly clarity overtook anger. "So what happened?"

"I told you already. I told the President about our relationship, and he was rather pleased."

"That's not what I mean."

I ate my second slice of pizza in silence and let Maureen stew. She gave herself time by filling her plate with salad and dressing it.

"I understand now," I finally said, speaking the truth.

"What do you mean?"

"I understand why you hired me."

"I told you that Sam…," she began.

"I know what you told me, but the real reason you hired me was not Sam's recommendation." She looked at me questioningly, and I continued with growing conviction, "You and Sam are friends, not lovers. He's a 'beard.' There's a nice literalness to that conceit in this situation since he's a convenient cover for the fact that you and Cass are still lovers."

"What?"

"Unless she was off killing Bond, why would Cass have lied to me about where she was the same weekend that you so conveniently took to your bed?"

"It's not true," began Maureen, but now I was sure that she was lying.

"So you wanted me to find out who killed LouAnn because you knew if that barista who heard you threaten Bond talked or if someone at the restaurant remembered that Bond came in the night you and Cass were there, the police were going to be very interested in you but even more interested in Cass who happens to be a big, strapping, athletic woman who knows how to run a table saw."

"This is nonsense."

A flush appeared along Maureen's cheekbones, and her eyes were electric with anger and fear.

"No, this is sense. I feel ashamed it took me so long to see it."

"You have no proof. It's just a theory."

"I don't have proof. You're right. But the police could probably dig up some neighbor who would either remember when you drove away on Friday and came home on Sunday or who would remember the tall woman who walked into your house on Friday and didn't leave until Sunday. Then there's Cass's history of home improvement. She did most of the work on her addition, didn't she?"

Maureen stared at me with fear and a new respect but also calculation.

"So what are you going to do?" she finally asked in a quiet voice.

"The only thing keeping me from going to the police right now is that I don't believe either of you capable of killing, not Bond, but Tareka James."

"Thank you."

"Don't thank me. I'm furious with both of you."

"I told you the truth."

"Excuse me, but which version was that?"

"Sam did recommend you, and I impulsively followed his recommendation. I knew that you and Cass were in the same department, but it's a fairly large department, and I never realized that you were friends. By the time I talked to Cass and found out how well she knew you, I had already hired you."

We finished dinner, and Maureen poured us each another glass of wine, saying, "Let's go sit in the den."

I followed her silently, wondering what else we could find to say. It suddenly occurred to me that I might be in danger. What if I had misjudged her? Had I made a mistake in voicing my suspicions? I mentally rolled my eyes and thought that only in murder mysteries did the killer turn out to be the person you least suspected, but I still felt uneasy. I shivered. It was not quite spring and the evenings were chilly. Maureen turned on the gas log in the fireplace.

"You know the best thing that's come out of this?" she asked, and I shook my head. "I met you." I rolled my eyes. "I mean it. In my position, it's hard to meet people within the university and just be friends. There is always stuff that I can't talk about or shouldn't talk about. I spend a lot of time with people I don't have much in common with, and I have to be careful even with people I do have things in common with."

"So it is true that you can 'win the whole world and lose your soul?'"

I had meant the remark to be ironic and perhaps sarcastic, but it came out sounding serious.

"You certainly can," Maureen replied grimly. "Having been married to a real politician, I should have known this."

"I have another question."

"Ask away."

"Who is Lila Daniliov?"

"Where, on earth, did you hear that name?"

"I actually overheard it and need to know who she is."

"Not 'is.' Was." Maureen suddenly realized the implication of what she had said and added, "She isn't dead, that I know of, but she's long gone from the university. That mess was, thankfully, before my time—about fifteen years ago when Kenneth first became president."

"Was she on the faculty?"

"No, she was a graduate student in Biology."

"So what happened?"

"She went to the university ombudsman with a complaint about her graduate advisor." Maureen stopped. "I'm not sure what this has to do with anything."

"Trust me—it's relevant. What kind of complaint?"

"She had had an affair with a faculty member, she had ended it, and he was not happy. The problem was complicated by the fact that he was her thesis advisor. She worked in his lab, and her thesis depended on the research she did there. Besides physically harassing her up on the job, he told her if she didn't keep sleeping with him, he would not put her name on the main research article when it was published plus he'd make sure that her thesis never got approved. He refused to schedule her thesis defense."

"That was before the university had a sex harassment policy?"

"Afraid so, but this case had a lot to do with finally getting a written policy."

"How did she end up talking to Frank O'Donnell?"

"How do you know she talked to Frank?"

"Little bird."

I waited for her to continue.

"The university ombudsman could not get any traction in the matter. He talked to the professor--a hotshot researcher with lots of big grants. The prof didn't even bother denying the claim and totally blew the ombudsman off. He then followed the chain of command and met with the department chair who apparently had trouble seeing what the problem was. He then talked to the Dean of Sciences who waxed eloquent on the professor's consummate grantsmanship as well as how prone women in the sciences are to misunderstand a little male attention. He then talked to university counsel who pointed out that there was no written basis for either a grievance or lawsuit. Finally, the ombudsman went to his boss. That was Frank, who, to his credit, listened. He talked to Daniliov and everyone else involved, got the same run-around, and then took matters into his own hands."

"How long had he been Vice-Provost for Academic Affairs at that point?"

"I don't know exactly, but a while, and he had done an outstanding job. So when he did not get anywhere with the case, he went to the President who, under pressure from the department chair and dean, declined to intervene. At that point, Frank threatened to go to the local television station and tell Daniliov's story on Live

Action News at 6. You can imagine how this threat played with Kenneth who had not been president very long. At the least, the situation showed how far behind the university was on developing a sex harassment policy. The professor had a wife and children so he was pretty quick to come to the party, especially since Daniliov had located two other women who were willing to talk about him publicly."

"So all's well that ends well?"

"Not exactly. The university began to work on a sex harassment policy with clear advice to faculty to leave students, even grad students, especially one's own grad students, alone."

"But it isn't a rule."

"No, and, frankly, although it's better than nothing, the harassment policy is a mess."

"So Frank O'Donnell is a hero," I offered, and Maureen shook her head.

"Only in some quarters. He barely kept his job, and almost the first thing Kenneth told me when I came was 'You cannot trust Frank O'Donnell.' He also said if I wanted to fire him, I could."

"Do you trust him?"

"I trust Frank to do what's right, but I'm clear that what's right may not always be in the university's best interest, and that's where my best interest lies. He and I have a clear understanding and good working relationship. He also knows that the minute he threatens the university or me, I'll fire his ass."

"So you would have let him go to the media with Daniliov's story?"

"Probably not. I might have found a different way to force the professor's hand, probably using or not using institutional support for his grants. Thank God I was not in charge, but I know my predecessor made a stupid mistake in blowing Frank off. If you aren't going to listen to the people who work for you, you need to get new people."

"I doubt you would make a mistake like that."

"No, but I make a lot of other mistakes on a daily basis, and sometimes it's only in hindsight that I know I've made them. This job requires constant decision-making, often without adequate time for reflection."

She leaned back and sighed.

"What happened to the professor?"

"He retired to great fanfare a few years back."

"You're kidding."

"I wish I were, but the university had no grounds for either disciplining or firing him, and he did bring in a lot of grant money."

She smiled grimly.

"So the bad, old days were just as awful as second-wave feminists tell us," I said.

"Actually, they were worse, and in many ways, they're not over yet."

The next morning, I met Harold in front of LouAnn Bond's. The six-unit building was an architectural mistake in an older, otherwise elegant, downtown neighborhood. Harold led me to the second floor where crime-scene tape marked a nondescript door. He punched numbers into the fancy security lock and led me into a small, one-bedroom apartment. Bond's mother had lived with her until she went to a nursing home, but I found it difficult to imagine how two adults had shared this space.

The small kitchen looked well used with a toaster oven and microwave crowding the counter. The breakfast dishes from the day Bond died were still sitting in the drainer—a plain white cereal bowl, a spoon, and a mug with the university logo on it. The dishes, left to dry, in the routine of going to work, waiting to be put away in the evening, suddenly made LouAnn Bond human to me. She had eaten cereal and drunk tea—the kettle was still sitting on the stove—and gone to work, never suspecting that she had embarked on the last day of her life. Although she was guilty of many things, there was an innocence to the beginning of her final day, a common humanity that touched me. Harold came up behind me as I stood in the doorway and put his arm around me.

"How, on earth, do you do this job?" I asked him, wiping away my tears.

"Somebody has to do it. You okay?"

"Yeah, I'm okay now. I want to look around the apartment and then look at the papers."

"They're all in the desk by the window," he said, gesturing across the living room. "I'm going to make some calls. You look at whatever you want to look at."

I nodded, walking toward the bedroom. The bed, jumbled in the police search, had a plain, cream-colored duvet and matching sheets of good quality. The towels in the bathroom, also good quality, were the same neutral color. There were no pictures on the walls and only two pictures on the dresser. One must have been her mother at around fifty. She looked into the camera and smiled hesitantly, radiating the ingrained distrust of someone whose life has always been hard. The other picture was of Bond and Reverend Potts talking together at what looked like a dinner. His look was attentive as he leaned toward her, and Bond was smiling, looking softer than she had in the other pictures I had seen of her.

I took both pictures out of their frames and looked at the backs. The first said "Mama, probably 40." I looked at the woman again. How hard her life must have been that she could have looked so old at forty. I hoped she had enjoyed what must have seemed like luxury in her later years. The second photo had a sticky note attached, "I thought you'd enjoy this picture. It's so good of you both. Mary." Probably Mary Smythe. I suddenly wondered if she were related to Congressman Samuel Smythe, the power behind the new library wing. I went back to the living room just as Harold finished his call.

"Did you interview Mary Smythe?"

"The photographer?" I nodded. "Blake talked to her."

"Is she related to Samuel Smythe?"

"They're cousins."

"Was she friends with Bond?"

"They went to the same church and occasionally had lunch. Smythe said that they weren't close friends because she always felt like Bond was pumping her for information. Blake said Smythe is a very nice woman, and he had to push hard to get her to tell him that."

"Okay. Thanks."

I returned to the bedroom and looked through the dresser and into the closet finding only the plain clothes of an older woman whose job required her to dress professionally. There were no jeans or pants of any sort, no sneakers. A fleece bathrobe and two sensible flannel nightgowns hung in the closet over seven pairs of neatly arranged, sensible heels in dark colors. Nothing flashy. It was like discovering that the Queen slept with her purse.

I walked back into the living room and noticed the modest, old television with a cable hookup. Bond had watched television, or perhaps she had bought the television for her mother's pleasure. I surveyed the contents of the small bookcase. It was filled with inspirational religious writing. I opened A Woman's Glory by Frank Hall and discovered exactly the kind of church-kitchen-children, do-whatever-your-husband-says, women-need-authority, keep-your-man-happy-no-matter-what advice that I had expected. There were anti-abortion books and one book called The Homosexual Choice whose author claimed to have "saved" hundreds of young men from their "disordered" desires through prayer and strenuous "mind-programming." I was certain that I could find most of the books in one of the "inspirational" or "Christian" bookstores in town. A stack of pamphlets from For the Family offered information on many subjects, including not just homosexuality but transgender issues, or, what they called "sex changes," apparently a hot, new topic for the foundation. I noted how their anti-gay marriage campaign had widened to suggest a conspiratorial army of transgender people behind the LBGTQ movement. Even touching the pamphlets made me want to take a bath, but I took my time looking through them. If LouAnn Bond had lived as simply as it appeared, she had possessed a fair amount of disposable income to contribute to For the Family.

"How much money did Bond give For the Family each year?"

"Since her mother died several years ago, she's given them about $10,000 a year. She also gave St. Luke's $12,000 a year."

"Wow."

"She was making over a $100,000 a year."

"I know."

I thought how if I ever made full professor and if the university did not have budget cuts every year, I might conceivably, when I was close to retirement, make that much money. Maybe. I sighed.

"That salary figure doesn't include the bonus the Foundation gave her each Christmas. Another $15,000. We went through all her finances with a fine-toothed comb, but they were very straightforward. Those big donations and contributions to a bunch of right-wing politicians. She also made a sizable donation to the university each year."

"Sizable?"

"$5,000. Sometimes more. She also gave money to that Christian school out on Montgomery."

I nodded. The school covered kindergarten through twelfth grade and provided a "conservative Christian education." Their billboard advertisements guaranteed "a thorough knowledge of the Bible and Creationism." The girls wore dresses, and the boys wore ties. I had read somewhere that the boys had after-school sports programs while the girls had classes in cooking, childcare, and sewing—what the school called "Home Arts." Just thinking about this school made my jaw clench.

I sat down at the desk and gazed out the window, which overlooked the neighbor's backyard and picture windows. A small pair of opera glasses sat on the window ledge. I shuddered, seriously doubting that Bond had engaged in bird watching.

"Did you interview the people in the house behind?" I asked Frank.

"Someone did. They didn't know her at all."

Maybe she had just watched them instead of television. It gave me the creeps.

I began to go through the desk drawers. The bottom file drawer contained alphabetical files mostly bearing the neatly lettered labels one might expect: Bank, CD, Rental Agreement, Retirement, Taxes, and Visa. The only file of obvious interest was labeled "Correspondence." I opened it to find that it contained only ten letters, two of them pleas from her brother, dated about six months apart, to send money to his prison account so that he could buy toothpaste and other small necessities. Bond had scribbled a date, check number, and "$50" on each letter.

I was surprised to find a note, dated February 14 of the previous year, written on St. Luke's stationery from the Reverend Joseph Potts. He had neat, fussily ornamented handwriting whose even march across the page suggested that he formed his letters against a straight edge. It was the sort of handwriting that seeks to make its recipient say, "Oh, I have received a work of art!" rather than "What does so-and-so have to say?"

Dear LouAnn,

I thought that I would take this day, usually reserved for lovers, to express my deepest gratitude for the varied, always thoughtful, ways in which you serve both me and the parish of St. Luke.

Please rest assured that your devotion does not go either unnoticed or unappreciated.

Sincerely Yours in Christ,

~~Rev. Joseph Potts, D.D.~~

Joe

Wondering if she had saved this note so that she could occasionally read it in order to feel, if not loved, special, I felt sad.

The rest of the letters were from Miss Leonora Priddy. With one exception, they were thank-you notes for gifts of either books or cash that Bond had sent to the Mountain Valley Library. They contained small amounts of local news. The one exceptional letter read:

My Dear LouAnn,

Dallas Traherne, the young woman about whom I wrote you, has gotten into the University of South Florida and will be leaving at the end of the summer. She will have some pocket money from her job here in the library. Again, thank you for helping me to fund this small, private charity. As you well know, college makes all the difference for these young people.

Thank you again for agreeing to be my executor. I hope that it will be many years before you are called upon to undertake this task, but I promise to keep my affairs, modest as they are, in good order so that settling my estate will be easy when the time comes.

A copy of my will should reach you in the next few days from Raymond Betts' office. He will retain the original on file.

As the first student from Mountain Valley that I helped to attend college, know that you hold a special place in my esteem.

As ever,

Lenora Priddy

The restraint and formality of this letter gave me pause, but perhaps Miss Priddy was simply undemonstrative.

At the back of the drawer were several boxes of check carbons. I picked up the one with the most recent date and began to look through its contents. Month after month the same checks were written—a check for cash at the beginning of the month and checks for rent, utilities, cable service, St. Luke's, For the Family, Christian School Development, and groceries. No car payment. She would have her health insurance premium and parking fee deducted from her pay. She had no need of life insurance because she had no dependents, but the university had automatically insured her in any case. She also wrote occasional checks to right-wing political figures or Miss Priddy's library.

"Who is Bond's beneficiary?" I asked Harold.

"Her brother."

"Thanks."

I went back to the check carbons. There was a quarterly check for automobile and renter's insurance. There was the single large donation in January to the university. Suddenly I stopped. There was a $1000 check made out to The Matthew Agency and dated November 20 of the previous year. It was the only carbon I had found out of order.

"Harold, did you see this check made out to The Matthew Agency?"

Harold came over and looked at the carbon.

"I don't remember this name from the accountant's report. I think I would have—the rest of it was so routine." He was already on his phone. "Brent, do you have the accounting report on LouAnn Bond? Pull it, will you? Is there a payment to The Matthew Agency?" There was a pause. Harold reached over and took the carbon from me. "The check number would be 8317. November 20 last year." Another pause. "Will you call the bank and have them look? Okay. Yeah, call me back. We're still here. Cece's looking through the carbons from her checks. Okay. Later."

"So?"

"No record from the bank on that check. Brent's double-checking. I can't believe we didn't look at those carbons, but I wasn't here."

I went through the other two boxes of carbons and found nothing else out of the ordinary in what seemed a very limited life.

"Does she have a storage locker in the basement?" I asked.

"Yeah. Let's go take a look."

We went down to the basement and easily spotted the locker with the yellow warning tape. It also had a fancy police lock. We stepped into the six by eight space, and Harold pulled on the overhead light. There was a cheap wardrobe at one end. I opened the door, and saw Bond's summer clothes, which were no more exciting than her clothes upstairs. In the bottom of the wardrobe were some lighter-colored purses and pumps, but no sandals. Needless to say, the two plastic totes held modest lightweight sweaters, not bathing suits or shorts. There were also two lightweight cotton nightgowns, a lightweight robe, and a pair of slippers. In an archival cardboard box full of papers, I found nothing more personal than her tax returns and supporting paperwork, going back the required seven years. No other check carbons. No more letters. No tell-all diary. Not even a stray shopping list.

"Was there a safety deposit box?"

"At her bank. It contains her birth certificate, her social security card, the title to her car, a note about her will, and her mother's birth certificate, social security card, and death certificate. Nothing else."

"And you didn't find another key or something?"

"No. She's banked at the credit union since she went to work for the university. Her only credit card was through them. No debit card."

"And her phone records?"

"Just the landline. She talked pretty often to Reverend Potts and occasionally to a few other people from that church, but nothing else. No long-distance calls at all."

"No cell phone?'

"No. Not even a sign that she had a pay-as-you-go cell. None."

I stood thinking, marveling at how figuring this out was like trying to find a toe hold on a smooth rock face. I finally said, "I think she was pathologically private."

"No shit, Sherlock," replied Harold. "I've never had a case where someone was so totally without personal connections. Brent said that he's talked to everyone he could think of, including the neighbors, and not found any friends except that Reverend Potts fellow." His phone rang. "Hey, Brent. So tell me. Okay. Talk to you later."

"What is it?"

"You may have hit pay dirt. The bank has no record of that check which means it was never processed. Brent googled The Matthew Agency and got a bunch of hits. He's making calls to see if he can find anything out."

"What sort of hits did he get?"

"Several religious organizations, but he also got a literary agency in New York and a private detective agency in San Francisco."

"Damn. It's probably just a donation that hasn't gotten processed yet."

"Maybe, but that's a big check not to process."

I looked at my watch. If I did not hurry, I was going to be late for class.

"I need to go. Will you call me when you find out about the check?"

"Sure thing. Thanks for the lead."

"If it is that!"

I could hear Harold laughing as I ran up the basement stairs.

Chapter Fourteen

Although I ran in the door on the hour, my class went remarkably well so I was in a good mood to meet with Dorothy Sizemore. I had never set foot in the older building where she and her assistant worked, but I finally located a glass door and walked into the nicest office suite I had ever seen at the university. In the reception area, the furniture looked comfortable, the walls were decorated with colorful, interesting artwork, and the live plants looked healthy. I realized that the room's non-institutional charm came from large windows providing natural light. No one was seated at the desk, but before I could begin exploring, Dorothy's ample body filled the doorway to her office.

"Come in, Dr. Brinkman. My assistant leaves early to get her kids from school so I'm here alone."

Her low voice was so warm that it made me remember coming inside on a snowy day to find hot cocoa and cookies waiting.

"I love your office, especially the windows. What beautiful orchids!" I said, gesturing toward the five orchids, all in bloom, on the window sill to the left of her desk.

"It's not me but Mother Nature," chuckled Dorothy. "You better believe that I fought for this space. Natural light makes people so much happier."

"I couldn't agree more."

I noticed an engineering textbook lying on her desk.

"Are you an engineer?" I gestured toward the book, and then apologized, "I have book fetish and always notice them wherever I am."

"I have it too," she admitted, smiling. "I'm flattered that you think I might be an engineer, but no." She sighed. "I came to my education too late to do anything so demanding. I only took my first engineering class two years ago.

"Why study engineering?"

"Actually I take an eight o'clock class every semester. I finished my undergraduate degree years ago, and my job is too busy for me to take graduate courses which are mostly in the late afternoon or evening so I take a course before work in the mornings."

"So what all have you taken?"

"A whole mess of courses, but I like math. One of the profs in math suggested that I talk with the Dean of the Engineering School to see if they'd let me into some of their early morning classes. They offer a lot of classes so people with jobs can pursue degrees. Anyway, I got permission and now I've taken four courses. I love it!"

"I wish my students had half your enthusiasm."

Dorothy laughed.

"I was almost forty when I realized that I needed to do this to keep my brain alive. I don't have the stimulation of a family—you know how raising kids puts you in touch with so many things."

"Not all of them pleasant," I said, and she chuckled. "But I do understand. Talking to you makes me think that I need to start those Spanish courses I've been meaning to take."

"I wish the language courses were on a better schedule for me," she sighed. "I just can't be gone during the day, and after the first level, none of the offerings are at eight. I also would like to take more art courses, but the studio courses are three hours, and I can't commit to late afternoons or evenings. I never know what the event schedule will turn out to be."

"That's too bad."

"It's just the way it is," she said, flashing her lovely smile. "Maybe when I retire, if I'm not too old and decrepit...," her voice trailed off.

"I don't want to take up more of your time than I have to."

"Don't worry."

"Well, I've gone over the information about the community mentors and students and made the matches. I don't think this should take all that long."

"I don't think so either. Hang on a minute." She went to a file cabinet and came back with a floor plan she unfolded, saying, "This is the set up in the room we're using." She took up a pad of small sticky notes. "Let's just start seating people." I noticed that she had already put the names of the dignitaries on the chart. "It's a lot easier if you can see where you're putting people. Then I'll have my assistant print name tags with table numbers on them which the guests can pick up at the reception table on their way in."

"You're so organized," I said.

"It's my job." She smiled, and I realized that she was the warmest person I had ever met. From the moment I set foot in her office, I had felt welcome and with each passing moment I felt an increasing, albeit irrational, trust that all would be well.

"This is excellent, Dr. Brinkman," she said as she reviewed the list of people I had matched up. "I'd just like to suggest putting Christina Penn with Donald Rowan

144

rom the Bank Corp office since she's majoring in finance, and he is much nicer to
⁄oung women than young men, but you couldn't be expected to know that." She
aughed. "Patrick Heintz will do fine with Don Maynard."

She studied the list for another moment and suggested two other changes. We
hen worked companionably on the seating. When we finished, she stood looking
lown at the chart and said, "If you have any second thoughts, just call or send me an
⁊-mail, and we'll figure it out."

"Actually, I feel like we've nailed it, and I, thank God, won't have to think about
ı any more."

"Until next year," she laughed, "But we'll keep the seating chart on file. Send me
ı note after the event if you see something either not working or working very well.
'll put it in the file for next year." She caught my look of admiration and said,
ʹRemember--I've done about half a million events in my time. I know that I can't
ɾemember everything so I always make notes and file them away for the next time."

"Provost Shaughnessy thinks you have a photographic memory," I replied, and
Ɔorothy laughed heartily.

"I wish I did. This," she gestured toward the engineering text, "Would be much
ɾasier if I did! Actually I've just learned to pay attention and take notes."

"And stay organized," I said, and she nodded. After a small silence, I said, "I'd
ıke to talk with you about something else, but I feel very awkward bringing it up."

Dorothy looked concerned, and I wondered how many people, drawn by her
varmth, had confided in her.

"Would you like a cup of tea?" she asked.

I nodded and followed her into the small break room down the hall. When we
vere seated back in her office with our steaming mugs of tea, she opened her desk
Irawer and brought out a canister. She placed small, shortbread cookies on the plate
he had brought from the break room and passed them to me. I bit into one.

"Delicious!" I reached for another.

"Thanks. I made them." Dorothy smiled, ate one slowly, sipped her tea, and
inally said, "So what is it you need to ask about?"

"I need to have your promise of confidentiality."

"You have it." She sipped her tea. "Is this about LouAnn Bond?"

"How did you know?"

"Marilyn Wilhoyt in the President's office told me that you had been in to talk
vith her about some commencement speech, and you ended up talking about
ʟouAnn. We're pretty good friends, and she was afraid that she had said too much,
hat what she said might get back to the President. She asked me what to do, and I
old her to sit tight and just not talk any more."

"Good advice," I said with a small smile, "But you can also assure her that I
ιaven't told anyone what she said."

"So why are you interested in LouAnn Bond?" Dorothy asked, eying me speculatively.

"I've never met anyone quite so disliked as she seems to have been."

"And?"

"I wonder how she kept her job."

"That's easy—not everyone disliked her."

"Did you?"

"Dislike is a pretty neutral term for what I felt about her, but I had to work with her, and I did. Don't misunderstand--I'm not glad she's dead, but her demise has certainly reduced the stress in my job."

For the first time since I'd met her, Dorothy did not look cordial.

"How did she make your job difficult?"

"She was meddlesome and controlling and often took credit for the work of others."

"You said that not everyone disliked her..."

"She was a first-class suck-up. When she wanted to please, butter would not melt in that fake ladylike mouth of hers. She used that routine on the Trustees, especially the men, and also on President Truman. She made it clear at every turn that she only had their interests at heart. She was always slipping the Trustees information."

"How did she do that?"

"I don't know how she did it in the past, but I suspect that she picked up the phone and called. Actually, I know that for a fact. One day I walked into her office and got to observe her at work. She was on the phone about some athletic tickets but went on to say, 'While I've got you on the phone, Alexander, there's something else that you might be interested in. A group of faculty has been in to see the President about the partner benefits package...' I'll never forget the look on her face when she swiveled around and realized that I had been listening. She knew that I knew 'Alexander' was Alexander Popham, a trustee, and she also knew that I knew she was giving out confidential information—a private secretary is supposed to keep your business private. She should not have been telling anyone who was meeting with the President, much less what they were meeting about."

"How did she react?"

Dorothy laughed grimly.

"She read me a lecture on the virtues of knocking on doors, and I told her that if she wanted people to knock, she had better close her door all the way. We left it at that."

"So no one ever complained about what she was doing?"

Dorothy studied her tea for a long moment.

"Dr. Brinkman, I need to know why you're asking these questions. I'm not comfortable telling tales out of school, and I've already been questioned by the police."

"Do you mind if I make a phone call?"

"Sure. I assume it's private so I'll take this opportunity to visit the ladies' room.

After Dorothy left, I called Maureen and prayed she'd pick up which she did not. I texted her that I needed to talk to her immediately and waited. Dorothy came back just as my phone rang. Without a word, she turned and left, shutting the door behind her.

"What's going on?" asked Maureen in a hushed voice.

"I need your permission to tell Dorothy Sizemore the truth."

"What will you tell her?"

"That I'm working for you and cooperating with the cops because you're concerned about the impact of these murders on the university's recruitment of first-year students."

"Do you have to tell her anything?"

"She won't talk otherwise. She already knows there is something fishy about my questions—she's friends with Marilyn Wilhoyt who told her that I had asked about Bond."

"Tell her what you've just told me but nothing more. Is that clear?"

"Yes, ma'am."

"Don't be a smartass. I have to get back to this meeting."

I opened the door and found Dorothy seated at the reception desk talking on the phone. She signaled with her hand that she needed a few minutes, and I went in search of the ladies' room. When I came back, she was in the break room boiling more water for tea.

"I have permission to tell you the truth."

"Okay."

"Provost Shaughnessy hired me to try and find out who killed LouAnn Bond because the police don't have a clue how the university works and she's worried that if these murders aren't solved soon, they will have a huge impact on whether high-achieving, first-year students choose to come here to study."

Dorothy poured the water, we dunked our teabags in silence, and then we carried our mugs back into her office.

"So why did she pick you?"

"Good question," I replied with a chuckle. "I had actually been involved in something else that required discretion, and someone in the upper administration recommended me. Beyond that…" I shrugged.

"Beyond that, the Provost knows you're smart and easy to talk to. She's a good judge of character." Dorothy studied me thoughtfully. "There are probably only a few of us still here that know this." She paused to sip her tea, and I waited her out. "President Carson—the one before President Truman—was president for thirty years." I nodded. "Did you ever meet him?"

"No. Didn't he die shortly after he retired?"

"Yes." She sipped her tea and remained quiet for a few moments. "He was the most charming man I have ever met. When you were with him, it was like you were the only person in the world, as if he had just been waiting for you to show up and make his day." Dorothy shook her head with a small smile. "Different times, different mores, as they say. He liked women, and one of the women he selected for his attentions was LouAnn Bond."

"Bond?" I could not keep the astonishment out of my voice.

"No one is born old," laughed Dorothy. "LouAnn was not unattractive. When she was young, she had about fifteen yards of thick, wavy, brown hair that she usually wore down. Men just love that." I nodded encouragingly. "She was working in the controller's office and ended up in charge of auditing some expenses in the President's office. She wasn't bad looking, but President Carson was not all about looks--he liked smart. I think LouAnn was a real challenge for him, but he finally got her into bed. When an assistant secretary in his office left, he brought LouAnn over. I knew Barbara Greenwood, his secretary, well. We had worked together, and she was very good at her job, but within six months, Barbara had retired, and LouAnn had her job. Barbara wouldn't say much about what had happened, but from the little she did say, I got the feeling that LouAnn had looked at the books or maybe even fixed the books and threatened Barbara with a more-than-routine audit. It was sad. I hadn't been working in this office very long, and although people talked, there was nothing anyone could do."

"And LouAnn was still involved with the President?"

Dorothy smiled at my question.

"That's kind of interesting. President Carson didn't stick with any woman too long. Anyone who was around the university administration in his day could easily provide a list of five or six women who had slept with him, but he had never reckoned with the likes of LouAnn Bond. Now I'm going to tell you something that I have never told anyone. One night, after an alumni award banquet, when everyone had left, President Carson came back to get his overcoat. I was in the kitchen, and the first thing I knew he had his arms around me." I must have looked surprised because Dorothy added tartly, "I wasn't always this fat."

"Dorothy, you're beautiful. I'm just amazed that anyone in his position would have done that even though I believe what you're telling me and know times were different. I'm always just a little stunned."

I thought of Lila Daniliov—not a little stunned, shocked actually.

"He was pretty drunk, and I offered him some coffee and told him that I would drive him home. I was scared he'd kill someone if he drove himself. He waited for me, but he didn't sober up much. When we got in the car, he started talking about how LouAnn Bond was ruining his life. I asked him why he didn't fire her, and he said that if he ever let her go, she had threatened to go to the papers with stuff about his personal life and how he used the university's money. He said, 'I'm paying for all my sins, Dot. I'm stuck with her.'"

"And was he still sleeping with her?"

Dorothy laughed heartily.

"There's a kind of poetic justice here. He told me that she was worse in bed than—and I am quoting here—his 'goddamn wife.'"

"But all this still doesn't explain why President Truman kept her on?"

"The President is a gentleman and doesn't, to my knowledge, mess around. I've thought about this quite a lot over the years, and I think when President Carson left, he told President Truman that he could keep or not keep Bond. If President Truman ever tried to get rid of her, I'm sure that LouAnn would have threatened to go public with something compromising about the university if she didn't have anything personal on him. Given the on-going budget crisis of the last fifteen or twenty years and given our current president's aversion to conflict, I think he decided to turn a blind eye to LouAnn's shortcomings, and, let's not forget, she does, or did rather, her job."

"I can't believe it."

"Yes, you can. Think about it. The President is very busy. Access to him is limited, and LouAnn was very good at two things: doing her job as watchdog and keeping the President and the Trustees happy. If I didn't like her in my business, what was I going to do? Call her to get an appointment to see the President and discuss it? That's not the way it works if you want to keep working here, and I decided a long time ago that I like my job. Lots of other people have come to that same conclusion."

"The President must have known that she was feeding information to the conservative trustees."

"I'm sure that he suspected as much. I don't think anyone has relished having a front row seat for the political awakening of LouAnn Bond," Dorothy said drily.

"Did she ever threaten you?"

Dorothy cocked an eyebrow at me and smiled.

"Threaten? In what way do you mean?"

"Some kind of blackmail?"

"Dr. Brinkman…"

"Call me Celeste."

"And you call me Dorothy. So, Celeste, I carry my sins in my flesh—I love to cook and I love to eat--it's there for everyone to see."

"So you never had any confrontation with Bond."

"Nothing that isn't so far back in history that it doesn't count."

"So there was something?"

"Yes. Way back. Like I said, too far back to count."

"Please tell me. I'm trying to understand who she was, and your experience might help."

"Keep in mind that this was years ago before the comptroller's office got a real grip on purchasing and everything got computerized. LouAnn came to me with a list of suppliers—catering, flowers, audiovisual equipment—stuff I would order in the normal course of arranging special events. She told me that President Carson had approved the list and would appreciate my doing business with these vendors. I was suspicious and told her that I had been doing business for several years without problems and had established relationships with companies that gave good service, but she insisted that the President had approved the list and wanted me to use it. So I told her fine and took the list."

"So you used the vendors?"

"Not exactly." Dorothy smiled slyly. "There were ten vendors on the list, and I decided to visit each one. Two of them told me they would kick back a percentage to me personally for any university business I sent them. When I innocently expressed dismay at their reduced profits, they laughed and said not to worry, they would jack up their price to cover my cut."

"What?"

"This kind of scam was very common before some state laws changed and financial procedures got both codified and computerized."

I thought of the supplies that had recently been going out the back door of Building and Grounds. There were still ways to game the system.

"So why did Bond do this? She must have gone to a lot of trouble."

"She was setting me up. If I'd fallen for it and used those vendors—I think some of the others knew what was going on but didn't want to talk about it--once I'd used them, I would have just gotten a check in the mail. Eventually she would have had one of them report me, or she might have dropped a dime and called anonymously. Reporters are pretty good at ferreting out this kind of fraud. God knows, the system of bidding on, or rather fixing, state contracts has given them plenty of practice. In the end, no one would have cared where I had gotten my list, and my university career would have been over."

"So what did you do?"

"I chatted with the Director of Purchasing and gave him the list without saying where I had gotten it. He personally visited each vendor to outline how the university does business and what was forbidden under university purchasing procedures. Actually, Purchasing had to write the policy manual he took with him to these meetings."

"What a diabolical plot! Did she want your job?"

"I don't think so. She knew what a diverse group of people I work with, and she was such a snob that I'm sure she knew that she wouldn't like my job."

"So why did she do it?"

150

"She never liked it that President Carson thought well of my work and was fond of me, but I've come to the conclusion over the years that it wasn't hatred or jealousy as much as a perverse kind of intellectual curiosity. She wanted to see if her plan would work."

I nodded, thinking how Dorothy's insight fit with what I knew of Bond's fondness for wielding power over people.

"Did she do anything else?"

"No, except for taking credit for my work anytime she could. Recently, she settled for turning every encounter we had, public or private, into a discussion of the latest findings on obesity and weight loss."

I shook my head.

"Did Bond ever bring her mother to anything? You know her mother lived with her for the last years of her life."

Dorothy laughed heartily for some minutes.

"I met her with her mother at the supermarket once. They were way out of their neighborhood so I'm sure LouAnn didn't expect to see anyone she knew. I was on my way back into town and just happened to stop at that market. LouAnn tried to pretend not to have seen me, but I went right up to them. LouAnn was clearly embarrassed, but good manners triumphed, and she introduced me to her mother."

"What was she like?"

"I don't think she was anywhere near as old as she looked, but she had lost her teeth. You could tell she was wearing dentures. She was very thin. She shook my hand and was very polite."

"Why did you laugh at my question?"

"Not at the question but at my own mean little joke. After I met her mother, I made sure that she was invited to any event where she could conceivably be included. I'd always include a note about how I looked forward to seeing her again."

This pettiness seemed out of character, but Bond had a knack for making decent people do ugly things.

"Did she ever bring her?"

"Are you kidding? Her mother would have been living proof of where LouAnn was from, and LouAnn was a snob in the way upper echelon servants often are."

When I got home, I found the envelope from the Mountain Valley News. The front page of the paper was completely filled with an obituary tribute to Leonora Priddy who had died peacefully in her sleep, at the age of 76, still going to work each day at the library she had founded. The reporter had contacted some of the many students Priddy had helped over the years. LouAnn Bond had been the first student Priddy had aided to go to college, and the article duly noted that she would serve as executor. Priddy's private papers, along with the library papers, were to go to the Lawrence Priddy History Archive. It was located at Carruthers College, a small Presbyterian college, outside of Wheeling, West Virginia. The archive had apparently been established by Priddy's family at the death of her older brother ten years earlier. It turned out that Priddy's grandfather, Leroy Carruthers, had founded the college with a group of like-minded Presbyterians who all had roots in the mountains and had done well in the world. The article did not explain what had led Leonora, at the relatively young age of thirty, to found a library in Mountain Valley. She had apparently helped anyone who came to her with a desire for learning. Approximately one hundred students over the years had gone on to college, not to mention the countless ones she had helped to finish high school.

She had also started an adult literacy program in the library, which had now expanded to a separate center that taught literacy and also helped high-school dropouts complete their degrees. The center also offered various courses on budget and health and teamed with the agricultural service to teach farming and animal husbandry courses. Priddy had written the grants that renovated the building and funded the center.

Bond was quoted in the article: "I met Miss Priddy when I was sixteen, and she had just opened the library. She let me work in the library so my family had some income after my father died, and she helped me apply to colleges. She has remained my best and closest friend all these years." I remembered the letters I had seen from Priddy—they did not sound like letters from a close friend.

I googled the Priddy family of Albany, New York, and found out that the family fortune had been made in timber. Miss Priddy's great-grandfather had gone north and found work in the forests of upstate New York where he began buying land as soon as he had a few dollars set aside. He had invested as far south as the Carolinas. The family had apparently become Presbyterian when one of his three sons had become a Presbyterian minister who felt called to missionary work in the mountains of West Virginia where his father had been born and raised.

I sat staring at the computer screen as I thought about LouAnn Bond's friendship with Leonora Priddy, how many letters they must have written, and how few I had found. Had Bond put her side of the correspondence into the archive as well? Joseph Salinger had hinted at this possibility. Since I had no clue where else to turn for information, it might be worth visiting the archive to look at the letters. Just as I located the homepage for the Priddy Archive, my phone rang.

"Marshall, how are you?"

"Missing you. Have you eaten dinner?"

"Not yet. I'm planning a trip to West Virginia."

"When?"

"Today's Tuesday, isn't it?"

"Last time I checked."

"I'm thinking about going later this week."

"Can we talk about this over dinner?"

"Hungry?"

152

"Always, but I just taught a seminar, and I'm starved. Come have dinner with me. My treat!"

"We'll see about that, but thanks. I'd love to. Where shall we go?"

"I'd suggest tapas again, but I don't want you to get bored."

"Never," I assured him. "Tapas sounds great."

"I'll pick you up in ten minutes."

"I'll be outside."

I printed the archive's contact information and set it aside to call in the morning. I ran a comb through my hair, put on a bit of perfume, threw on a coat, and was waiting outside when Marshall pulled up in a Camry that matched mine except for being about ten years younger.

"Nice ride," I said, sliding into the passenger seat. Marshall laughed.

"Great minds thinking alike!"

"I love Toyotas!"

"So how are you?" he asked, taking my hand as we sat at the first red light. "I've been missing you."

"And I've missed you. Honestly, my life isn't always this complicated." He let go of my hand to drive.

"Mine either. I don't always find dead bodies. Do you think the cops will ever find out who did it?" Marshall sounded anxious.

"Why ask me?"

"You know this town better than anyone else I know, and your cousin's a cop."

"That he is."

We arrived at the restaurant so I did not need to say more, but when we were seated, Marshall brought the subject up again.

"Has your cousin told you anything? I've been watching the papers, and there hasn't been anything except that they let Tareka James' boyfriend go for lack of evidence."

"Cops aren't supposed to talk about investigations so Harold is pretty closed mouth, but he did tell me that this is one of the more difficult cases he's been involved in."

"Why?"

"He said that for a cop, having something happen at the university is like being handed your badge in a new, small town where you have no connections and barely speak the language."

"But he has campus security and you," Marshall said, smiling.

I choked on my water, unclear as to whether campus security or I were the bigger joke.

"Why are you worried?" I asked when I had recovered.

"You aren't?"

We watched the server uncork and pour Malbec into large-bottom glasses. She then took our order.

As we sat sipping our wine, Marshall said, "I am worried."

"Why? Don't you think the police will figure this out?"

"I suppose so, but, in the meantime, I feel like a freak. I try not to go anywhere where I'll be alone because, God knows, a dead body might show up."

"I'm sorry," I reached out to take his hand. "How awful this must be for you."

"It's just weird. I've never felt unsafe in my life, but now I worry all the time that I'll open a door and there'll be a dead person."

"Have you thought about talking to someone? I could ask Harold if there's someone cops go to for this sort of trauma."

"I had never even seen a dead person until LouAnn Bond," Marshall admitted miserably.

"I don't know what else to say, but I will ask Harold. Then if things don't improve, you'll have something you can do. Are you sleeping okay?"

"Not really. I have dreams about that poor girl with her head bashed in." Marshall's dark eyes were troubled. "Who would do something like that? She was apparently a nice person. People liked her. I keep thinking about her poor children."

"I know, I know." We sat in silence for a moment. "You're a good man, or you wouldn't feel this way."

"At least, I feel like I can talk to you."

"You can. Anytime. Don't ever hesitate to call me. I should have been calling to check on you, but I've been overwhelmed by this new job."

The server came back with several dishes including a selection of cheeses and a large salad with jicama. When we had served ourselves, Marshall spoke again.

"I can understand about the job, but what is this about West Virginia?"

"I need to go to an archive outside Wheeling and look at some papers. I'm thinking of driving over on Friday and coming back Sunday."

"It's got to be five hundred miles."

"Closer to four hundred actually."

"That's still a long drive for such a short stay."

"I need some information for a paper I'm writing, and I have to submit it very soon."

"Conference?"

"Yes. They accepted the synopsis but want the whole paper, and this is the only window I have. The paper's on southern women's unpublished autobiographies, and I need to look at some correspondence in this archive."

"Can't they just copy it for you?"

"Too much stuff, and some of it hasn't been processed yet."

"Will the archive actually be open on Saturday?"

"I hope so. If it isn't, I may try to get there on Friday afternoon. I hate to stay over until Monday, but I may have to."

"Are you going alone?" I nodded. "How about I go with you?"

"Really?"

"Sure. I don't teach on Monday. I don't have a class until my Tuesday evening graduate seminar. I also don't teach on Friday." He smiled slowly. "The truth is I'd like to go with you."

"Seriously?"

"Of course. I need a change of scene, and we could split the driving. Besides," he grinned, "My car is a lot newer than yours."

"A well-cared for Toyota will go 200,000 miles," I began defensively to give myself time to find a graceful way to refuse his generous offer.

"You won't get an argument from me, but you have to admit that my car has less than 30,000 miles on it. How many miles does your machine have on it?"

"120,000," I admitted, "But it runs like the proverbial top."

"Besides, I've never been to West Virginia."

"Not even to play ball?"

"Different league. We never went there. I need to complete my states visited chart."

We ate in silence for a few more minutes, and I tried to think of a way to express my discomfort without alienating this man to whom I was increasingly attracted. How was I to escape his offer without telling him any more lies about my supposed research?

"I may rent a car for the trip," I finally said to break the awkward silence.

"Celeste, I want to go with you. As your friend. Nothing more. We agreed that we'd take it slowly, and I'm not trying to work my way around that. I value your friendship too highly."

He took my hand, and I thought how much I liked his touch. It was always so gentle as if he knew his strength and size required that he take great care with others.

"I honestly wasn't thinking about that," I confessed. "I'm just so wrapped up in this project and so stressed about getting it done that I may not be good company."

"It's okay. I understand and will still enjoy being with you."

"And you won't want me to talk about my work?" I fumbled for an explanation. "It makes me crazy to talk about it when I'm involved in a project. I'm always afraid I'll blurt out the wrong conclusion and then be wedded to it." I knew that I was not making much sense, but it was the best evasion that occurred to me in the moment.

"No. We don't even have to talk. We can listen to music and look at the scenery and just enjoy being together."

"And you do need to get away." He nodded. "Okay, but you have to let me pay for the gas. I've got a research grant that will cover it."

"No argument from me," he said with a chuckle.

"And separate rooms."

"If you say so…"

"I do." I felt stupid, but he nodded in agreement, and I ignored his disappointment. "When I've talked to the archive tomorrow, I'll give you a call, and we can figure out a plan."

"Sounds great," he said and smiled.

We spent the rest of the meal talking companionably about what music we might listen to on the trip.

That night, as I fell asleep, warm with the memory of Marshall's goodnight kisses, I felt guilty about lying to him and wished that I could tell him the truth. I wanted nothing more than to share my fears, suspicions, and doubts with him. Perhaps his scientific training would allow him to perceive a different pattern. At the very least, it would be comforting to share my suspicions about Cass and Maureen, hopefully in order to have someone else dismiss them. It did not make me feel sanguine to know that Maureen feared the circumstantial case that was there for the making not only against Cass, but also against her. But Cass? Funny, flirtatious Cass. I simply could not believe that she would kill no matter how much she loved Maureen. Besides, Bond's scheme had ultimately failed: she and Maureen were still together.

I had no idea what I might find among Leonora Priddy's papers, but I hoped there might be something that would give me a clue about who had killed Bond.

The next morning, I called and talked to Felicity Krauss, Director of the Priddy Archives. Ecstatic at my interest in Priddy's papers, she offered to meet me at nine on Saturday morning and allow me as much time as I needed with them. As we said good-bye, she assured me in her soft West Virginia accent, "If you need some time on Sunday, we can meet after church."

After I hung up, to make myself feel better about the tapestry of lies I had woven, I promised myself that I would also talk to Felicity Krauss about any unpublished, women's autobiographies that might be in the Priddy Archives.

156

Chapter Fifteen

After mapping the trip and discussing the weather, Marshall and I decided to leave at nine on Friday. He proved to be a sensitive and entertaining travel companion. He told me about his visits to family in Senegal, and I, in turn, shared tales of my much less exotic Catholic girlhood. We seemed to appreciate the same landscapes and be amused or outraged by the same bumper stickers.

We took turns playing music on our iPods. Marshall introduced me to new instrumental jazz from the West Coast, and I played jazz vocalists he did not know. He also played a selection of Senegalese music for me. We argued about bebop and agreed about the Beatles, Janis Joplin, and bluegrass. I had not had so much fun with a man in a long time, maybe never. It would have been perfect had I not been worried about how Marshall would react if he ever found out I had lied to him about my position in the Provost's office, my relationship to Harold and the police investigation, and my "research" on this trip—in short, my entire life for the past few weeks.

In the early evening, we arrived in Wheeling, checked into our separate rooms, and went to a local steakhouse for dinner where I picked up the tab, insisting (yet another lie) that I could put it on my grant. Actually, I had a grant of sorts as Maureen had agreed to pay my expenses. I kept wondering: if she and Cass had something to hide, would she have encouraged me to make the trip? Maybe so, maybe not.

Saturday morning, Marshall and I ate breakfast at MacDonald's.

"I can't believe I'm doing this to my body," I told him.

"No, what you can't believe is how much you are enjoying doing this to your body!" he answered with a grin.

"Seriously, we have to find somewhere else to have breakfast tomorrow."

"If you say so."

"Didn't you see *Supersize Me?*"

"Yeah, some friends and I got a bunch of Big Macs, fries, and malts from MacDonald's and watched it."

"You have got to be kidding!"

"Not at all," he replied, laughing. "It's a guy thing. You gotta have a sense of humor."

I was reduced to laughing and spluttering indignantly, finally asking, "You don't really eat MacDonald's all the time?"

"Not all the time. Sometimes I do. Don't you?"

"It's been years."

"Now I have to ask you something," he said quietly, his dark eyes large and earnest.

"What?"

"Do you think our relationship will founder on my having a Big Mac once or twice a month?"

I laughed so hard there were tears in my eyes.

Carruthers College was a collection of red brick buildings on the outskirts of Wheeling, set in a valley among foothills with the mountains in the background. The campus, having achieved that Georgian, sequestered look that so many private colleges aspire to, was lovely. On the central quadrangle, it was easy to find the library, with predictably Greek pillars holding up a lofty front portico. We walked through the immaculate white doors into a vestibule and on through the security gate. I asked the student at the circulation desk to direct Marshall to a study area and me to the archives.

"I'll walk up with you," Marshall volunteered.

I nodded, unable to think of a way to deter him. Even if the director mentioned Leonora Priddy, I thought nervously, it would not give me away since Marshall would have no idea who she was. We climbed up the wide, marble stairway to the second floor and made our way to a door marked "Lawrence Priddy History Archives and Carruthers College Records." I pushed the buzzer, as directed, and soon the door was opened by a woman about my age.

"You must be Dr. Brinkman." She held out her hand. "I'm Felicity Krauss."

"This is my friend Dr. Marshall N'Dour. He teaches Chemistry."

"I just came along for the ride," Marshall said as he held out his hand.

"Marshall is going to work in the study area while I look at the papers," I explained, and Krauss nodded.

"There are tables over there," she gestured, "There are electrical outlets if you want to use a computer. I'm sorry, but I can't put you on our system. If you show your university identification downstairs, they may be able to give you a temporary user name and password. We do that for visiting scholars."

"It's okay. I can get a connection if I need one," Marshall assured her. "Nice meeting you, Ms. Krauss." He turned to me and said, "Come get me for lunch," and walked off toward the tables and easy chairs we could see from where we stood.

Felicity Krauss gestured me inside and shut the door carefully behind us.

158

"Now what precisely are you interested in from the Priddy papers?"

"The correspondence."

"Great! That part of the collection is in the best order." She looked embarrassed as she added, "I haven't processed the collection yet. I'm alone here with only two student workers. It takes me forever to process collections, and the one from Priddy is quite large."

"I'm specifically interested in correspondence with someone named LouAnn Bond." Krauss again looked embarrassed.

"Priddy herself kept her correspondence in an orderly fashion, but in packing the boxes, some things may have gotten scrambled. I'm so sorry."

"Don't worry. I've worked with lots of papers," I assured her, "So I won't be put off by things being as they were found. My specialty is actually unpublished autobiographies by women."

"There isn't one that I know of in Priddy's collection," began Krauss, frowning.

"No. I have Bond's unpublished autobiography, and I just wanted to do some secondary research in Priddy's letters because they were such great friends."

"Certainly." Krauss looked relieved.

"But I wanted to ask about other collections you have that contain autobiographies or memoirs by women," I said in an attempt to compensate for my basic lie.

"I know there are a couple of memoirs in other collections. Let me think, and I'll give you a list."

"Thank you so much. You don't have to do it now. You could e-mail me later," I assured her, and she smiled.

We had come to the reading room. In reality, it was two six-foot tables and some chairs.

"If you'll have a seat and complete this form, I'll go get the boxes," said Krauss. She was back in about fifteen minutes, pushing a book truck on which there were four archival boxes.

"There are two more boxes," she said, a little breathlessly. "I'll be right back with them."

"Thanks so much. I'm sorry to put you to all this trouble on your day off."

"I'm just so happy to see these papers used," she said as she headed back for the other boxes. When she returned, I handed her my university identification and the completed form.

"I'll just go copy your identification. I'm sorry, but I also need your driver's license." She was back in a few moments. "I'll be working in my office across the hall. Just let me know if you need anything."

"Can I copy papers if I need to? I notice that there's nothing about photocopying on your researcher's form."

"The Priddy family has made all the papers public so you can copy whatever you want. I'll have to charge you a nickel a page, though," she said apologetically. "The copier's down the hall."

"That's fine, and I may not need to copy anything. If I want copies of the memoirs you mentioned, can I just have you do them at your leisure and mail them to me? I'll send money to cover the copies and labor. Would that be okay?"

"Of course."

"I plan to break for lunch about twelve thirty."

"Good idea."

"Marshall and I would love for you to join us. I'd like to buy you lunch to thank you for coming in on Saturday." The invitation jumped out of my mouth before I considered its possible consequences.

"It's not necessary at all, but how thoughtful of you. Twelve thirty it is then," she said and went into her office.

I kicked myself for my stupidity as I realized that Krauss, with an innocent question or two, could expose me to Marshall.

"Friendly to a fault," I thought bitterly, but I had work to do and soon settled into it.

Someone, probably Bond herself, had arranged both sides of the correspondence chronologically and tucked them carefully into file folders marked in periods of two years. By the end of the first hour I wanted to scream with boredom. Priddy's letters, although just as formal in tone as the ones I had found in Bond's apartment, were enlivened by some local news, but Bond's were simply a report on the life she lived publicly. Priddy would share her concerns about or mention the progress of some of the students she mentored, but Bond never mentioned any personal ties. There was a break of a few months about ten years previously, and after that point, Bond reported on her mother's failing health with a lady-like non-specificity. After reading the letters, I felt an enormous wave of sadness wash over me. Priddy had worked and been much loved in her adopted community. In contrast, Bond had escaped her background into a life of sterile outward conformity and inward what? "Perversion" was the word that leaped to mind. Bond mentioned religion frequently in the latter part of the correspondence, but it was mainly to report her attendance at Bible study or lectures. She discussed none of her beliefs, and, if she had, I wondered how Priddy would have reacted.

The other correspondence had also been organized into folders by years, probably by Priddy herself, judging from the handwriting on the labels. I began to read and immediately discovered an entirely different, warmer, more open tone. I searched through the boxes until I found the earliest folder, dated more than forty years earlier and began reading through the letters from Priddy's earliest time in Mountain Valley. The correspondence with Amelia Bennington was the only one Priddy had typed. Perhaps she saw it as a journal of sorts because she had kept copies—tissue thin carbons--of her own letters. As I read, it became clear that the two women, childhood friends who attended college together, were very close. Bennington had taken part in the missionary trip that brought Priddy to West Virginia. Perhaps significantly, the year after Bennington married, Priddy came to stay in Mountain Valley for good.

"Would you like to go to lunch now?" asked Krauss and apologized when I jumped.

"Of course." I said, glancing at my watch to discover it was almost one. "Marshall is probably starving."

After I grabbed my purse and slipped on my jacket, we walked over to where he was reading.

"I'm sorry. I lost track of the time! Are you starving?"

"I'm getting a lot done, but I was beginning to be distracted by hunger."

He stretched his long legs, stood, and packed up his work.

"Where shall we go?" I asked Krauss.

"There's a diner about five minutes from here. Do you mind a walk? The food is plain but very good."

The diner, on the road back toward town, was called Minnie's, and it was a place like the neighborhood taverns of my youth. After the owner had greeted Krauss by name and been introduced to us, we settled into a back booth and ordered sweet tea and hamburger platters. They came with home-made fries, a dill pickle, a slice of tomato, and a leaf of iceberg lettuce. The vegetable soup we ordered on Krauss's recommendation was homemade, thick with vegetables and meat.

"How's your research going, Dr. Brinkman?"

"Call me Celeste."

"And you all can call me Felicity. So how's it going?"

"Fine. I may end up coming back later. I've gotten interested in Leonora Priddy who seems to have been an extraordinary woman."

"I'm sorry the collection isn't in better shape, but right when we acquisitioned those papers, I got another collection from a former governor so that took priority."

"The letters are arranged chronologically and seem to be in good order. There may not be as much processing to do as you think."

"There still needs to be an index to the correspondents and introduction to the collection," Felicity said.

"The index seems to me a job that a student could do if you could find someone responsible. I'd be happy to supply some information for the introduction when I finish my research."

"I might be able to find someone," she replied thoughtfully.

"I don't want to inconvenience you any more than I have to. When do you need to leave this afternoon?"

"I'm fine until five. I've got something to do this evening, but I'm using the time to catch up on paperwork so don't worry about inconveniencing me."

"I really appreciate this."

"How did you originally get interested in LouAnn Bond?" Felicity asked, and I almost choked on my burger as Marshall met my eyes across the table.

"It's a long story. She worked at the university where we both teach, and I became interested in her background as a woman who came from poverty and had no advantages when she was growing up. Priddy befriended her and helped her go to college. That was her ticket out. I'm hoping if I go through the rest of the letters, I may understand why Priddy went to Mountain Valley and how she began helping promising students get a college education. Bond's memoir doesn't provide any of that background."

Marshall raised his eyebrows slightly but said nothing. Anxiety overwhelmed me, but Felicity let the subject go before I was forced into further invention.

"You must have a piece of pie," Felicity said as we finished our meal.

We each got a slice of Minnie's apple pie that came warm with a scoop of vanilla ice cream. It was delicious.

"We may have to come back for dinner," Marshall said as he finished his pie.

"Not possible. Minnie closes down at three. She went into partial retirement a couple of years ago and stopped serving dinner."

"What about breakfast?" Marshall asked hopefully.

"Monday through Saturday. Minnie's is closed all day on Sunday."

"Too bad for us," I said. "Can you suggest a place for dinner? Also breakfast tomorrow."

"Sorry, but on Sundays, unless you want to drive across town, MacDonald's may be your only choice for breakfast." Marshall grinned, and I shot him a disapproving look. "There are a couple of good restaurants close to here for dinner. I would recommend Fernando's if you like Mexican food."

"Mexican?" I said questioningly.

"Actually quite good."

"Run by real Mexicans?"

Felicity laughed and assured me the family that owned the restaurant had come from Mexico a generation ago.

"I know because one of the grandchildren of the original owner worked for me a few years back."

"One more evidence that we are a nation of immigrants," I said, shaking my head. "It is truly amazing how people end up where they do."

"I know what you mean," said Felicity with a smile. "My grandfather was a Jewish peddler who married a German girl, and they settled here because his family back east disowned him when he married a gentile."

162

We paid the bill and, as we walked back to campus, Felicity gave us directions to Fernando's. Then Marshall settled down to his reading, and Felicity and I went back to the archives.

I began skimming through the remaining boxes of correspondence. As I looked for mentions of LouAnn Bond, I began to get a better sense of Leonora Priddy. She wrote often to Amelia Bennington, and both sides of the correspondence were interesting enough that I made a note to try to find information about Bennington. Several letters mentioned Bond as a gifted student with a very difficult home life. When her father died, Priddy gave her a job to help keep the family afloat. I kept skimming and finally hit pay dirt:

Dearest Amelia,

This week has brought the most terrifying and disheartening experience of all my time here in Mountain Valley. It has made me question whether I should continue here.

Jimmy King, a local man whom I knew only by sight, came into the library as I was closing last night and began telling me that I had to send LouAnn away and tell her to stay away. He said that he knew I had money and if I didn't get her away, something terrible would happen. He kept saying that her life was in danger and it would be "on my head" if anything happened to her. I told him that if I did not understand the situation, I could do nothing so he finally said that he had a friend who had cheated on his wife with LouAnn and now LouAnn is making his friend pay every week for her silence. He said that his friend has a jealous wife and is worried but is fed up with paying. He claimed to be worried this friend might hurt LouAnn if she did not leave town. I asked him if I could talk with his friend, but he said that he had promised not to reveal his name. I told him that I would do what I could, and he left.

You can well imagine my shock and dismay. I simply could not believe that LouAnn would do such a thing. She has never shown the least interest in the opposite sex, and given her father's violent ways, not to mention her own ambitions, this lack of interest is not surprising. I was shocked and upset by Jimmy King's visit. I also suspected him of being the man in question as he is a good-looking man of thirty-five who is known to be unfaithful and have a jealous wife.

LouAnn came to work in the library, as usual, the next morning. I told her the story, and she denied everything. She looked me right in the eye, but I knew that she was lying. I could not get the truth out of her so I finally gave up and sent her home, telling her that she needed to reflect on this situation and consider if there was anything else she would like to tell me.

Late that night she came to my house. She had a black eye and swollen lip and moved as if she had been beaten. She begged me to help her get away immediately, saying that if she stayed, she would be killed. Even now, I am not sure that I got the truth out of her. She said that she had "gone with" Jimmy King a few times back in the spring, and he had given her "presents." I pressed her, and she finally admitted that he had given her money and still sometimes gave her "presents." She claimed that when she saw him to tell him to stay away from me, he had beaten her up. I asked her why he had given her money and presents, and she said that he "liked" her. When I accused her of prostituting herself and blackmailing him, she denied both charges vehemently. We talked and talked, and although I came no closer to getting the whole truth out of her, it was clear that she was terrified.

That night I drove her home to pack her few possessions and say good-bye to her mother and brother. I did not go in so I have no idea what she told them. She spent the night with me. In the morning I drove her several towns over to catch the bus after calling Wilfred and Constance, my cousins who now live in Kentucky. They are good souls and promised to give her a home and find her a job until she begins college in the fall. When we parted, LouAnn cried and swore eternal friendship. Given what I now know, I will not be surprised if I never hear from her again.

After four long years, LouAnn was my first success, and I am now certain that I was deceived in her. How could I have so misjudged her? The affair I could understand, but blackmail? I cannot find words to describe how lonely, stupid, heartsick, and betrayed I feel.

How could I have been so completely deceived? I am in despair. I thought I had begun to understand this strange world I now inhabit, but now I realize that maybe I am a fool to think my calling is here. Truly, *de profundis clamavi*.... How I miss your good sense and good talk, my dear friend

I sat staring sadly at the letter. Why had Priddy appointed Bond her executor? The letter did not prove anything but suggested that Bond had been willing to take risks for money and gotten an early start on her blackmail career. Perhaps she had been infatuated with Jimmy King, bitter when he lost interest, and intent on punishing him, or perhaps, knowing he had a jealous wife, she had seduced him with the intention of later blackmailing him. I would never know, but I doubted that after all these years either Jimmy King or his wife had come after Bond.

Looking carefully at the dates, I paged back through the correspondence between Priddy and Bennington. The gaps in this very regular exchange were easy to spot. I copied the letter about Bond, returned it to the file, and then skimmed through

164

another box. In the subsequent years, more students left Mountain Valley for college and wrote to let Priddy know how they were doing. Touchingly, they sometimes included pictures of themselves or an outstanding paper or test. I glanced at my watch and saw it was almost five. I opened one more folder, read a letter from a grateful student, and laid out the enclosed pictures on the table.

I knew what I was looking at, but it took my mind a moment to catch up with my eyes: it was a picture of Stephen Hope and Pamela Rykker. They were dressed up, holding hands, and standing outside an official-looking building. They squinted a bit in the bright sunshine. I turned the picture over and found the inscription: "Dearest Leonora, Pam and I were married April 10. Love and many thanks, Pamela Rykker and ~~Bethany Ann~~ Stephen Hope." My hands were shaking. I had not seen these names anywhere in the correspondence, and I only had two more boxes to go through.

I copied both sides of the picture and went to find Felicity.

"Are you okay?" she asked, looking up from her work. "You look like you've seen a ghost."

"No, I'm just tired. It was a long drive yesterday, and I'm about ready to knock off for the day. I only have two more boxes to look through. Think you can stay another hour, or is that too much to ask? If I finish, you won't need to come in tomorrow."

"It's okay. My date is at half past seven so go ahead and finish. I could work another week and still not catch up!"

I handed her the photo.

"Can we put this photo in a separate file? It seems out of place where I found it, and I may have to locate it again."

"Of course." Felicity handed me an archival folder and a pencil. "Label it and put it at the front of the box where you found it."

After copying the front and back of the photo, I went back into the reading room and marked the folder: "Bethany Ann?/Stephen Hope and Pamela Rykker. Wedding Photo. 10 April ??" I put the folder in the front of Box #4 and noted its location. I paged through the rest of the letters. Now I was looking for anything that said "LouAnn Bond" or "Bethany Ann" or "Pamela Rykker" or "Stephen Hope." I was also looking for handwriting that resembled that on the back of the photo. I carefully paged through the fourth box and the remaining two but found nothing. I closed the last box and walked into Felicity's office.

"I'm done for now, but I would like to get you to do something for me."

"What do you need?"

"How many boxes of records are there?"

"Five, maybe six."

"I'm willing to pay for the time by making a donation to the archives or by paying someone off the books. As soon as possible, I'd like someone to go through

165

those records page by page. This needs to be carefully done. I'm going to tell you the truth about what I'm doing, but I need you to keep it in confidence. Marshall doesn't even know." Felicity nodded, regarding me curiously. "I'm actually assisting a police investigation into the murder of LouAnn Bond." Her eyes widened. "I can give you a number to call if you want to verify that I'm telling the truth."

"I should probably do that," she said quietly.

I had already written the information on one of my business cards that I now handed her.

"Call this number Monday morning. It's for the Metropolitan Police Department. Ask for Inspector Harold O'Brien. He will verify that I'm on the level. I've also written down the newspaper website for the article on Bond's death and also her obituary."

"What do you need me to look for?"

"You're going to do this?" She nodded. "I'll pay you $20 per hour if that seems fair."

"I can use the money," she said with a smile.

I handed her the paper on which I had written "Bethany Ann _____," "Pamela Rykker," and "Stephen Hope."

"I don't have a last name for Bethany Ann. It may be Hope, but keep in mind that I am not sure about the last names at all. I need a complete list of any place these names appear. You need to look at timesheets, pay sheets, check stubs, everything. I want you to call me immediately if you come across any correspondence with them or mention of them or if you find any other pictures of these people." I handed her a copy of the photo I had found.

"Were there any letters in the correspondence files?"

"No, and that's weird. There should have been."

"Do you think something got misplaced?" she asked anxiously. "I could look again."

"No, I think whatever there was had been removed before you got the collection. Priddy corresponded regularly with Amelia Bennington her entire life, and I am also sure that some letters are missing from that run of correspondence."

"I'm relieved that you don't think we lost them. I'll start looking through the stuff early Monday."

"The sooner, the better. Call me if you have any questions. Marshall and I will probably leave around ten tomorrow."

"Okay. I'll let you know what I find on Monday, once I've called the police station," promised Felicity.

"Sure. And you can tell me then what I owe you, and I'll put a check in the mail."

"Sorry to be so suspicious," she began, and I stopped her.

"It's your job." I reached out to shake her hand, thanked her for everything, reminded her to send me a list of women's autobiographies, and went to find Marshall.

"I'm ready."

"To explain?" he asked with raised eyebrows.

"Actually, just ready to go, but I guess I'm going to have to explain."

"I think so unless you want to take the Greyhound home," he said as he packed up his books and computer.

"Threatening me?" I teased, but he did not smile.

We rode back to the motel in uncomfortable silence. I felt a kind of hollow desperation. What was I supposed to do now? On the one hand, Marshall's displeasure seriously concerned me, but the secrets I was guarding were not mine. On the other hand, I did not relish the prospect of taking the bus or driving four hundred miles in angry silence. Most of all, I did not want Marshall to walk out of my life.

"Come to my room. I've got a bottle of wine, and I think we need to talk," Marshall said as we pulled up out front. I followed him to his room, watched him unlock the door, and sat down, thinking about the many things we had discussed and shared that were not related to LouAnn Bond's murder. I watched him decant the wine and pour it into two nice glasses he had thoughtfully packed. He handed me one and held up his own.

"To honesty." Our glasses touched and, without smiling, he sat down on the end of the bed facing me.

"To trust," I replied, and he muttered, "Touché!" almost under his breath as our glasses touched again.

We sipped in silence for a few moments, and I felt the wine begin to warm me.

"LouAnn Bond? An autobiography? As a research subject?"

"You have to admit she's interesting," I began.

"Not funny. I'm feeling foolish. I trusted you, Celeste. I told you things I haven't ever told anyone. I thought we were equally invested in being honest with each other."

"Please don't be angry," I began and stopped. I took a deep breath. "I have been honest with you about my feelings and my past. The stuff I haven't told you belongs to other people, not me."

Marshall quietly studied me with his dark eyes, and I made a decision.

"The Provost hired me to figure out who killed LouAnn Bond and Tareka James because she felt like the police did not have a clue. She's worried that if we don't get all of this solved soon, it will affect the high-end enrollment for the coming year. She's worked very hard to improve the university's academic profile, and she doesn't want her work to be destroyed by the public perception that there's a killer on campus."

"Why you?"

"I will pardon your entirely skeptical tone of voice," I said curtly, and he finally smiled a little. "Maureen is friends with Sam Jacoby. He's the Vice President the Director of Building and Grounds reports to. The maintenance woman in our building is married to a guy who works in Building and Grounds. He saw stuff going out the back door and wanted to tell someone. I helped him connect with Sam Jacoby who investigated. He told Maureen that he thought I was smart and willing to keep my mouth shut. This is all confidential. In fact, you're the first person I've ever told about the Building and Grounds mess."

"So the Provost came to you?"

"Yes, and invented this bullshit job for me. I started talking to people, and then my cousin Harold sent Blake Hess, the inspector on the case, to talk to me. He wanted me to sign this confidentiality form so I told him no, but then Harold came back and asked me to help on a less formal basis. Apparently the university is a hard place for the police to get any traction."

"Imagine that!"

Marshall smiled which I took as a hopeful sign.

"Everyone who ever dealt with her has a nasty story about her if you can get them to talk …."

"Which you are very good at doing."

"Sarcasm will get you nowhere," I replied and felt relieved when he laughed. "But people do talk to me so I've been trying to figure Bond out, but I nothing clear emerged from her work or church life so I got the idea of looking into Bond's past. I decided to take a look at the papers of the woman who got her out of Mountain Valley and into college. Bond identified this woman as the best friend she ever had."

"And she wasn't?"

"She probably was because Bond seems to have made no friends except the preacher at her lunatic church. Leonora Priddy, the woman, made Bond her executor, and Bond seems to have carried out her duties as expected." I mentally crossed my fingers over this disingenuous statement. "I can't figure out why Priddy trusted her except maybe she didn't have anyone else who would go to Mountain Valley, pack up the papers, and get them to the archive."

"So you found the answer to who killed Bond in Priddy's papers?"

"I wish! No, what I found is evidence that Bond was a blackmailer when she was young."

"She blackmailed Priddy?"

"No, someone else in town who complained to Priddy." I fished the letter out of my bag and held it out to Marshall. "This is a copy of a letter to the person who was Priddy's closest friend. She wrote to her in great detail throughout her life and kept copies of her own letters so it's almost like a journal."

He read the letter and then handed it back to me.

168

"Ugly way to repay trust and generosity."

"Yes, ugly in many ways, but I'm sure this Jimmy King and his wife are either long gone or too old to be operating power saws." Marshall grimaced. "So all I've found out is that we should probably look for someone Bond blackmailed."

"Hard to find since no one wants to admit they've done anything they can be blackmailed for."

"Right." I took the last sip of my wine, stood up, and reached out my hand to pull Marshall to his feet. "So let's go eat a good dinner, forget why we came here, and enjoy each other's company. I'm starved, and I bet you are too."

Marshall stood up and put his arms around me.

"Now I'm worried that you'll put yourself in danger," he said, resting his chin on the top of my head.

"Anything I find I pass on to Harold." I was glad Marshall could not see my face as I added, "I'm being very careful."

He put his finger under my chin and raised it to kiss me in a way that was dangerously distracting.

"I know you aren't telling me everything," he murmured, kissing me again.

"I've told you the important stuff, but some things are confidential. They aren't important," I lied, thinking of Maureen and Cass and the lost weekend of Bond's death. I excused myself from telling him about Stephen Hope and Pamela Rykker because I did not know for certain what the picture or inscription meant. Although I had a suspicion about their sojourn in California, I would never intentionally out anyone.

"I'm taking your word for it," said Marshall softly and began nuzzling my neck, just below my ear. Heat rushed through me as we kissed again. I tried to remember that I was hungry for dinner and not other things when he finally pulled away to say softly, "Dinner?"

This was the moment to say "No" and step away. Instead I leaned into him and let the free fall of desire take over as he kissed me and slipped both hands under my shirt. He finally leaned back and met my eyes with another slow, questioning smile.

"Life is short," I said, pulling off my shirt and moving toward the king-sized bed. "Let's have dessert first."

Chapter Sixteen

Later in the evening, we forced ourselves out of bed and enjoyed a surprisingly good Mexican meal. In talking to the restaurant owner, we learned that the family grew a huge garden each summer, froze or canned many necessary ingredients, and also had a greenhouse. To my relief, we did not talk any more about the murders or my part in the investigation. I knew that Marshall knew I had not been entirely candid, but before there could be any further questions, we were back in bed exploring each other's bodies with the slow pleasure of people who had shared a pitcher of margaritas.

Soon Marshall was sound asleep, but whether from the margaritas or worry, I lay awake. Suddenly I remembered that I had turned my phone off when I entered the archives and had not checked it since. I slipped carefully out of Marshall's embrace tucked the blankets up around him, and dug my phone out of my purse. After creeping into the bathroom and turning on the light, I saw that I had several messages from Harold. I turned the volume down and heard him saying, "Cece, where in the hell are you? Your mother says you're in West Virginia. What the hell. I need to talk to you. It's important. Call me." There were also five increasingly irate texts containing the same message. It was late to call Harold so I settled for texting him that he could call me after eight Sunday morning.

I brushed my teeth with my finger, drank a glass of water, and had just settled my head on the pillow when I realized that it would be very awkward talking to Harold while I was with Marshall. I sent a second text telling him that because I was travelling with someone, I would talk to him when I got home the next day. I had just crept back into bed and was drifting off when my phone began to vibrate. I answered it, but not before Marshall had jumped out of bed and began searching for his phone.

"It's mine," I said. He got back in bed and sleepily watched as I answered my phone.

"Where in the fuck are you?" demanded Harold.

"In a motel in Wheeling, West Virginia, trying to get my beauty sleep." I rolled my eyes at Marshall, mouthed, "Family!" and went to sit across the room. He rolled over and seemed to be going back to sleep.

"Are you alone?"

"Not exactly."

"I could make a lot of wise cracks at this point, Cece, but I'm going to restrain myself."

"A first."

"The Matthew Agency turned out to be a detective agency in California, and we finally got hold of the guy Bond tried to hire."

"Okay, tell me."

"Long process getting him to talk, but since Bond was murdered and he never cashed her check, he finally agreed to help us."

"Okay."

"She wanted to hire him to investigate someone who'd had one of those sex change operations."

"What?"

I faked surprise and was glad Harold could not see my face.

"This detective's in the Bay area, and he says that he's had a few of these requests over the years because California…"

"I know about California," I interrupted impatiently.

"You know?"

"I've actually studied gender reassignment surgery."

I looked at Marshall who was not asleep. He raised his eyebrows in surprise.

"You mean sex change operations?"

"Yes, that's what I mean." Suddenly, I knew where the conversation was going. "Who did she want him to investigate?"

"He couldn't remember the name. He was out of the office when he talked to us and won't be back in until tomorrow afternoon."

I breathed a sigh of relief.

"The archivist here is named Felicity Krauss, and she's going to call you Monday morning to verify that I'm helping with a police investigation."

"Why is she calling?"

"I couldn't get through all the papers—there were too many—so I hired her off the books to look through the financial stuff. I already went through the letters."

"Find anything?"

"Nothing except evidence that LouAnn Bond blackmailed a guy back when she was seventeen or eighteen years old and had to leave town to keep from getting killed."

"I'm not surprised. It's a kind of behavior that makes you feel more powerful every time you get away with it. Think maybe it's an old revenge?"

"No. This guy and his wife would be ancient by now. They might even be dead."

"Give me the names. Life is sometimes surprising."

"Jimmy King. I don't have the wife's name. Mountain Valley is where all this happened, but he might have lived somewhere in the area. You might want to call Joseph Saling at the Mountain Valley News. He's their archivist, but he's also a local. That's how I found out about these papers I'm here looking at."

"Okay. You will let me know if you find anything, won't you?"

I crossed my fingers as I promised that I would, quickly countering with a question.

"Why are you calling me so late? Why aren't you in bed asleep?"

"Poker night," he said.

"Win?"

"Couple of bucks."

"I'll call you tomorrow."

"Okay. Call me as soon as you get home. I may know something."

"Okay."

"Travel safe."

"Thanks."

I put my phone on the bedside table and crawled back in bed.

"Sorry it woke you. Harold got some information that he thinks may be important."

"What was that about California and gender reassignment surgery?"

"Actually, that was about a different case. Harold's pretty old school and when gender stuff comes up, sometimes he asks me questions about it."

I could not tell whether Marshall's look was sleepy or skeptical, but before he could ask any more questions, I began kissing his smooth, dark skin, beginning with the hollow in his neck and working my way down--a not unpleasant way to avoid talk.

Marshall was soon sound asleep, but I lay awake, knowing that when I got home, I would have to talk to Stephen Hope. I thought of his gentleness, what he had told me about his early life, and the smile on his face in the picture I had found. He had survived. He had crossed the great divides of class, education, and gender. What could LouAnn Bond have done or threatened to do to call up such violence? I tried not to imagine the circumstances too vividly. Of course, the murderer had neither counted on LORETTA delivering up the body so soon nor on Tareka James figuring out something about the keys. I remembered Matt Dingle's comments from the dinner I had attended about "a morally objectionable tenure case." I was now sure he had been talking about Stephen Hope. Every time I closed my eyes I could see the stack of anti-gay, anti-lesbian, anti-transgender pamphlets in LouAnn Bond's apartment. I could not help wondering how many other targets she had found, beyond the ones I knew about, in her private campaign against "immorality."

I suspected that Pamela must have killed Bond and Tareka James because I could not believe that Stephen was a violent person. I could not begin to imagine Stephen either perpetrating or being complicit in these acts. Socially ill at ease, wrapped in her strange silence, Pamela was a completely unknown quantity, but one thing was clear: she had worked in the library for years, first as a clerk in Media Services and now in cataloging where her various tasks--fetching supplies and delivering books—would have acquainted her with the entire building and its operation. I remembered her illness after LORETTA delivered up Bond's body. I had to admit that personal bias informed my opinion: I liked Stephen and was uncomfortable with Pamela.

Around four I finally fell into a restless sleep full of disturbing dreams so that I groaned unhappily when Marshall awakened me with a kiss.

"I've had a terrible night," I moaned and then saw his hurt look. "Nothing to do with us," I assured him, and was then easily convinced to provide tangible proof this was true. As a result, we were late getting away which made me even more anxious about getting to Stephen before the police did since I was sure his name would be the one the private investigator provided.

"You look exhausted," Marshall said with concern as we got in the car after another breakfast at MacDonald's.

"I hardly slept. I guess I'm not used to this much pleasure." He smiled and seemed reassured. "It may have been the margaritas, but sometimes when I'm doing research, my mind starts going, and I just can't turn it off."

"Especially this kind of 'research,'" he said ironically, and I rolled my eyes.

Marshall insisted on driving, but I only slept for an hour on the way home. We listened to Wynton and Ellis Marsalis' *Standard Time*, a series of recordings that can give simple pleasure or amply repay close attention. I chose to let the nuances slide over me as I reflected that if I were not so tired and upset, I might be worrying that the affection, camaraderie, and great sex we had shared were dying in the awkward silence of the long ride home.

When we pulled up at my apartment, Marshall carried my suitcase inside and set it down by the stairs.

"Should I carry it into the bedroom for you?"

"No, it's fine there," I said quickly, and the moment felt awkward. "Most of the clothes are going in the laundry in the kitchen."

"Would you like to get something to eat? You didn't eat much lunch."

"Maybe I'm coming down with something or maybe I'm hung over, but I don't feel much like eating. I think I'll just laze around and go to bed early."

"Sure. I hope you're okay." Long pause. Another worried look. Another opening for confession. Another moment I let pass.

"I'm okay. Probably just tired."

We kissed, and I thanked him for coming on the trip.

"It was a pleasure," he assured me, adding, "I'll call you tomorrow."

"Great."

He left after another kiss that, although brief, was very distracting.

A few minutes later, my phone rang. I didn't recognize the number, but it turned out to be Felicity Krauss.

"I've been working all day on those files," she said excitedly. "I found nothing on Stephen Hope, but Bethany Ann's last name is Fogarty. Pamela's last name is Rykker, and I found records on her too. They were both on the weekly library payroll for four years." She gave me the dates, and they matched when Stephen and Pamela would have been in high school.

"Thank you so much. Did you find any other letters or check stubs?"

"Nothing like that. Just the library pay records. Everything else had to do with obtaining books. There's no personal stuff in this part of the collection at all."

"I'm so glad you called and didn't wait until tomorrow."

"Actually, I called the number you gave me because I figured police stations are open all the time. The desk sergeant put me through to your cousin's office to leave a message, and it all seemed legitimate. I'm sorry to be so suspicious."

"Not at all."

"So is this information helpful?"

"Very. How much do I owe you?"

"It took me about seven hours."

"Okay. Tell me where to send the check." I wrote down her home address, and we said good bye after I had thanked her again and reminded her about my interest in women's autobiographies. I wrote her a check, adding an extra fifty dollars, and put it in an envelope with a note of thanks. I stamped the envelope, grabbed my purse, and drove to the nearest mailbox.

I was headed to Stephen and Pamela's house when my phone rang: Harold. I thought about not answering but decided he might have information I could use.

"Are you home?"

"Yes."

"You were supposed to call," he reminded me irritably.

"I'm sorry. I'm not feeling well and completely forgot."

"That detective in California was supposed to investigate Stephen Hope who also went under the name Bethany Ann Fogarty and his—or is it her?—I'm getting confused here--wife, Pamela Sue Rykker, who also happens to work at the university in the fucking library. Jesus, Cece, Hope's a professor in the English Department. You must know him."

"He's a friend of mine."

"Goddammit. So you know her too."

"Not well at all."

"Have you talked to him?"

"Not recently."

"Well, don't. We're going to pull him and his—or is it her...?

"Harold, stop it! Stephen Hope is a man so talk about him that way. He's made tougher decisions in his life than you or I have ever imagined possible, and you at least owe him the courtesy of addressing him and talking about him using the gender he's chosen. No one makes this kind of choice because it's easy so don't make it harder."

There was a long silence.

"I'm sorry, Cece. I wasn't thinking."

"It's okay."

"Anyway, we're going to pull him and his wife in for questioning as soon as possible."

"Why didn't the detective do the investigation?"

"He says that he has a policy of not investigating cases that involve transgender people."

"Why?"

"He says the cases are messy, and he believes that in 'matters of gender'—I am quoting here— 'people have an inalienable right to privacy.'"

"Good for him."

"I just think he's queer himself," Harold snorted, "But now we know what we're looking at."

"Don't be so sure. I'm positive Stephen didn't do it."

"How do you know?"

"He's a gentle spirit." Harold snorted.

"What about the wife?"

"I hardly know her so I can't say, but I'm sure about Stephen."

"I'll keep it in mind," Harold said gruffly, "But remember to keep away. I'd hate to have to arrest my own cousin for interfering with an investigation."

"That would be a nasty turn," I agreed. "Just let me know what happens."

I ended the call and dropped my phone into the cup holder next to me. I was only a few blocks away from Stephen and Pamela's house. I sat, lost in thought, at the traffic light until the car behind me honked impatiently. I felt blank and without expectation, only knowing clearly that I needed to talk to Stephen. I parked in front of his house.

When I rang the doorbell, he answered.

"Celeste, what a nice surprise! Come in."

He gestured me past him into the living room.

"Is Pamela home?"

"No, she just went to the market but should be back soon. Would you like to stay for dinner?"

"I would if it isn't too much trouble. What beautiful book cases," I said, moving to touch the smooth wood.

"Pammy built them."

My stomach turned over at his words, and I moved closer to the bookcase to avoid Stephen's gaze.

"She also found that old piece of wood and re-did it for the mantle. She has an amazing gift for woodwork. I need to show you the deck she put on the back of the house," Stephen said proudly. "Is anything wrong?" He looked at me closely.

"We need to talk." I turned to face him. "I know about California and LouAnn Bond."

He went white.

"You need to tell me what LouAnn Bond did, and we need to talk about Pamela."

Stephen was opening his mouth to respond when his eyes widened and my arm was suddenly jerked behind me with a force that almost took me off my feet.

"What the hell," I said, struggling to free myself.

"Don't move or I'll break your arm."

Increasing pain made me take the threat seriously.

"Pammy, don't hurt her! Celeste is only trying to help us. She's our friend." He spoke in the calm voice a parent uses to talk a child down from a tall tree.

"Your friend you mean," snapped Pamela, applying a little more pressure to my arm.

Although shorter than I by a good three inches, she was stocky and much stronger than I had ever suspected.

"Pamela, please let go. You're hurting me," I said softly, hoping she might loosen her grip so I could slip away. "Why are you doing this? I only want to talk and try to help."

"You were always after him, weren't you?" she asked, tightening her grip so that I cried out.

"Stephen and I are just friends. I wanted you to be my friend too."

I looked toward Stephen, who had not moved, and wondered if he were going to do anything to help me.

"Why did you come here?" Pamela demanded.

"I wanted to talk to you and Stephen together."

"About what?"

"LouAnn Bond."

"The bitch is dead, and it serves her right."

I could feel her hatred like a wave of heat and looked at Stephen with growing desperation.

"Pammy, please let Celeste go so we can talk. We need to tell her what happened."

176

"We don't need to tell her anything. We just need to make sure she doesn't tell anyone else anything."

"I don't know what you mean, but please! Just let her go." As he spoke, Stephen began to move toward us, and Pamela stepped back, pulling me with her so an almost unbearable pain shot out from my elbow.

"Please let me go. You're hurting me."

Stephen took another step.

"Stephen, you stay put. Stay right where you are." She spoke with an undertone of hysteria and bent my arm further up. She moved, and I could not tell what she was doing until I heard a soft snick and felt the knife blade against my throat.

"If you come any nearer, Stephen, I swear to God I'll slit her throat."

"Why would you do that? Celeste has done nothing to hurt us."

"Then why is she here?"

"She wants to help us. If she tells us why she came, will you let her go?"

"Let me go first," I whispered, and Pamela pushed my arm a bit higher so I felt like my elbow would pop out of the socket.

"You're hurting me," I whined again and glanced past Stephen toward the bay window where I glimpsed Marshall's head ducking below the sill. The image was so fleeting that I thought I might have imagined it, but then I knew he had followed me.

"I know why she's here. She knows what that bitch was doing. She was probably part of it."

"Bond was blackmailing a lot of people, but I don't know what she was doing to you and Stephen. I came, as a friend, to find out."

"She threatened me with exposure unless I left the university," Stephen said, and I marveled at his calm. Of course, his arm was not being wrenched off, and no one was holding a knife to his throat.

"Stephen's worked so hard for so many years, and that bitch was going to take it all away." Pamela sounded both furious and heartbroken.

"Pammy, I told you that she couldn't do it. I explained," Stephen replied softly.

"But she would have told everyone about you. She would have ruined everything." Pamela's voice carried a note of despair that made me shiver.

"I told you that she couldn't hurt me." Stephen's voice was soothing, and Pamela was just distracted enough that he could move closer to us. "I told you that even if Bond did out me, I didn't care. Pammy, I told you it would be all right."

"All right? All right?" Her voice rose to a despairing wail. "Everyone would look at us like freaks again! You think that would be all right? All right for you maybe, but what about me? What about me, Stephen?"

In that moment of distraction, Marshall came through the doorway behind her. I felt a sharp sting as Marshall grabbed her, but she let go and dropped the knife. I turned just as Pamela whirled around to do a high kick worthy of a karate expert. Marshall cried out and, as he fell, she kicked again, and ran. I chased her down the hall, through the kitchen, and out the back door, with Stephen on my heels, yelling, "Pammy! Stop!"

Before she got through the back gate, I lunged to grab her, missed, and went down hard.

When I came to, the first voice I heard was Harold's.

"Don't move her. Cece. Cece Baby. Come on, Cece Baby, open your eyes. Talk to me. Say something."

"Celeste." It was Marshall's softer voice. I could feel a cold towel on my forehead.

"Are you okay?" I heard Harold ask someone.

"I don't do well with blood," answered Stephen softly, and his voice drifted away.

"Stay awake. Open your eyes. Celeste, sweetheart, please try to stay awake," Marshall said, stroking my cheek, and I could hear a distant siren that seemed to be coming closer. I tried to tell them that I didn't want to go to the hospital, that I needed to catch Pamela, that I needed to tell Harold some things, that I thought Marshall was hurt, but I felt so sleepy…

"Cece, Cece Baby," Harold said impatiently, and then muttered, "Goddammit" under his breath, but I could tell he was not so much angry as scared.

"Pamela," I finally managed to say.

"She's gone. She took the car," said Harold. "Well find her, Cece. Just try to stay awake."

"Sorry. Marshall…" I wanted to tell him more, but the ambulance pulled up and soon I was on a stretcher with Marshall holding my hand.

"Are you sure you're okay?" someone asked.

As if he were in another country, I heard Marshall say, "She kicked me, but missed the real target—thank God. I think she broke a rib or two."

"Wow. Karate Kid, huh?"

"Yeah."

"Come on with us. We'll get you looked at."

"After we're sure Celeste is okay," Marshall replied, squeezing my hand.

"Stephen?"

I forced my eyes open to look at Marshall.

"Harold's talking to him. They're trying to find Pamela."

"Need to talk to Harold," I mumbled before drifting off again.

Chapter Seventeen

I spent the next twenty-four hours trying to sleep and having nurses wake me up every hour or so. The scan, of which I have no memory, revealed the hardness of my head. To this day, Harold claims they saw no evidence of a brain. When I lunged at Pamela, apparently I landed headfirst on a brick border so I was out cold for a few minutes. The plastic surgeon sewed me up and came back the next morning to tell me not to worry about my looks. At the time, my head hurt too much to worry, but a day later I was glad he had reassured me. My swollen forehead made me look like an inhabitant of the Mushroom Planet, an imaginary place I had first read about in a childhood book of my mother's. Both my eyes were black, and I had scrapes down my nose and chin from my slide on the brick walk.

The morning of the second day Marshall was sitting by my bedside when I awakened.

"I want to go home," I told him plaintively.

"I think they'll release you today."

"Are you okay?" I asked, and he smiled.

"For the hundredth time, I'm fine. I twisted so she kicked me in the thigh. I have a helluva bruise, but she missed the crown jewels," he assured me, smiling. "She did kick me when I was down—not very sporting of her--and cracked two ribs which hurt like hell, but I'll live."

"I'm so sorry. This is all my fault."

Marshall held up his hand.

"Let's hold off on that argument until we're both a hundred percent."

"How did you know to come to Stephen's?"

"I didn't know." He smiled. "Even after you confided in me, I had the feeling you were not being entirely candid so I decided to do a little detecting of my own. I hung around to see if you stayed home, and when you didn't, I followed you."

"You saved my life. Thank you."

My eyes filled, and I reached out to take his hand. Marshall wrapped both hands around mine.

"I was terrified of losing you," he whispered.

This is where we should have kissed, but I was in no shape to pucker up, and besides, a nurse came in to take my vital signs.

"Have they found Pamela?" I asked when the nurse had gone.

"I think you need to talk to Harold about that. I don't know much about the investigation."

"Where's Stephen? They didn't arrest him, did they?"

"No. He's staying with me."

My eyes filled again.

"Thank you, Marshall. Thank you so much."

"I couldn't let him go back to that house alone, and I knew that if he's your friend, he must be okay." He was quiet for a moment and then added, "I got him a lawyer."

"A lawyer?"

"When he came out of the police questioning that first night and told me what they were asking, I called my lawyer and got him to recommend someone in criminal practice. Stephen needs someone at the table with him."

"How can they think that Stephen had anything to do with what happened?" I demanded angrily, and my head immediately began to pound. I closed my eyes and lay back.

"Please don't worry, Celeste. I think they're on the right track, but there's no way around the fact that it involves Stephen."

"How much has he told you?"

"Not much. I haven't asked him many questions. We've been playing Scrabble and Gin Rummy and drinking beer."

I managed to smile at Marshall without saying, "Damn that hurts!" Apparently I had also split my bottom lip.

Later Marshall saw me through the checkout process and drove me home. When my mother opened my apartment door and threw her arms around me, I knew my convalescence would be a purgatorial return to childhood dependence and maternal anxiety.

"I've been so worried."

She winced as she looked at my face. I gave Marshall high marks for restraint when I looked in the bathroom mirror. Nothing had improved--if anything, my bruises had become more vivid. When I tried to smile, the contorted grimace—painful to make, even more painful to see--drove his marks even higher. I had a butterfly band aid on my neck where Pamela had cut me when Marshall grabbed her.

I searched my purse and could not find my cell phone. My mother denied having seen it, and when I tried to think where it might be, all I wanted to do was take a nap. I finally remembered talking to Harold and asked Marshall to go look in my car--wherever that was. He came back with my phone, and over my mother's protests, I took it and texted Harold: "I need to see you ASAP. I'm home." Within a few minutes, he texted back: "REST. QUIT WORRYING!" This response made me so mad that I saw stars. I texted him: "ASAP or I'm coming down to the station NOW." Five minutes later, he texted: "Later this afternoon when I get off. CALM DOWN. GET SOME REST." I was not happy with his response, but patience made my head ache less than anger.

I asked Marshall if he would stay with me while I talked to Harold. In the interim, I discovered that the English Department had declared a state-of-emergency, gotten funds from the Provost, and dialed up a couple of recently retired faculty members to cover Stephen's and my classes. Cass Britton had taken over my course on women's narratives, which made me worry less about my students. I relaxed enough to take a nap on the sofa and when I awoke, Harold was sitting in the armchair across from me drinking a beer.

"Hey, Cece. How's your head?"

"Best not ask."

"Can I get you something to drink?" I groaned. "I didn't mean beer."

"I think I'd like some water, and then some orange juice. Could you get me some saltines too?"

Harold grunted and rolled his eyes at me.

"High maintenance, aren't you?"

I rolled my eyes back, and it hurt.

"Please ask Marshall to come sit with us."

A few minutes later, Harold and Marshall were seated in the armchairs while I lay propped up on the pillows my mother had so thoughtfully provided.

"Where's Mom?"

"In the kitchen making dinner. I asked her to stay put while we talked," Harold said.

"Okay. No one has been telling me anything, and I haven't seen a newspaper and am not sure I could read if I could find one."

"If you rest, your head will feel better pretty soon," offered Harold.

"So you say. So says the doctor." I tried to get my thoughts in order and found it difficult. "Where's Pamela?" Harold and Marshall looked at each other. "Anxiety is not helping my head," I warned them irritably.

"We found the car this morning. It was parked in one of those new developments near the river."

"Why did it take so long?"

Harold flushed angrily.

"Do I need to remind you that the car could have been anywhere? And it's not exactly a Ferrari. We put a description on television, and last night someone finally called in. Forensic is going over it now." He paused.

"So what aren't you telling me?"

"She left a note on the front seat." Harold pulled out a small notebook and read, "'Stephen, I'll always love you. I just can't go back to being freaks. I'm so sorry for everything. Good-bye. Love, Pammy.'"

"Poor Stephen. Have you told him yet?" Harold shook his head. "Why not?" When Harold did not answer immediately, I snapped, "Surely, he can't be a suspect."

"We've checked his alibi, and he's covered, but he's not helping us at all. He still can't believe she did it. We figure she must have lifted the keys that afternoon so the chance of discovery was almost nil. We went back, questioned people who got supplies on Friday, and showed them Rykker's picture. We found a student worker who was coming to get supplies and stopped in the conference room to send a text. This student not only saw Rykker lurking outside Tareka James' office but also saw her messing with the desk. My suspicion is what you said, Cece. Tareka saw her returning the keys and put it together when the body turned up."

"We'll never know for sure, will we?" I said sadly.

"No, the dead are not very forthcoming," replied Harold and added, "Hope's told us enough that we know Rykker had a motive. The note looks like a confession as well as a suicide note."

Harold paused and rubbed his hands together, frowning.

"Come on. What else is there?"

"Rykker and Hope weren't married."

"What?"

"They came here as a married couple seven years ago. At that time, no one was required to present proof of marriage to obtain benefits. Hope finally admitted it. So your friend has been defrauding the university."

"I'd like to be with Stephen when you tell him about the note. Where is he now?"

"I think he's at my place," said Marshall.

"What's been in the papers?"

"Nothing."

"Nothing?"

"Just a report about Rykker, a library employee, being sought for questioning."

"Nothing about Stephen?"

"Not yet. I think the President called in a favor."

"Can we keep Stephen from being outed in the newspaper?"

"You know that we don't manage the news," began Harold.

"Okay. I'll talk to Maureen and have her talk to the President. No one is going to want this on the front page or even the inside page of the City section. Stephen has worked hard to get where he is today. Bond threatened to expose him unless he left the university. He refused to be intimidated, and she told him that he would be sorry. She promised to make a public spectacle of him. I don't want the local paper finishing her hate crime for her."

I leaned back, closed my eyes, and took a deep breath in an attempt to stop the throbbing in my head. Then I opened my eyes and looked at Harold.

"I'll see what I can do," he finally said, probably to stop my accusing glare.

"I need to talk to the Provost," I said, reaching for my phone.

"Don't be mad at me, Cece."

"I wouldn't sound so mad if my head didn't hurt like hell," I assured him. I put the phone back on the coffee table. As soon as I began to think about the phone calls that needed to be made and people who needed to be talked to, my head felt feel like it was exploding. "Can we please tell Stephen now?"

"It's not my case. I need to check with Blake first."

He walked into the hall to call Blake and was back a few moments later. "He said okay."

"Will you go get Stephen?" I asked Marshall.

"Are you sure you're up to this?"

"Yeah, you don't need to do this. We can handle it," said Harold.

"No. I want to talk to Stephen, and I feel like I owe him this. He's my friend."

"Okay, I'll go get him." I noticed how quietly Marshall closed the door.

"He's a good guy," Harold said approvingly, "A real keeper."

"I know. After this mess, I'm not sure where we are."

"If I'm any judge, the poor guy's in love with you."

Before I could answer, my mother came bustling in.

"Do you need anything, dear? Dinner is almost ready."

"Mom, why don't you go home and see Dad? Harold will stay with me, and we need to have a meeting that's kind of private."

My mother looked suspiciously from me to Harold and back again.

"I'm not sure the doctor would approve. Harold?"

"I think Cece is right. I'll call you when we're done, but right now we need to talk here in private."

"She isn't supposed to have any excitement," she warned Harold, giving him the evil eye.

"I'll do my best to keep things calm."

My mother kissed me gently on the top of the head, gathered her purse and coat, and went out the front door.

"By the way, I checked up on Jimmy King, that guy LouAnn Bond blackmailed," Harold said, breaking the silence that followed my mother's departure.

"What happened?"

"About five years after Bond left Mountain Valley, his wife caught him in bed with a teenage girl and shot them both. She died in prison doing a double life sentence."

"That girl could have been Bond."

"Yeah, and it would have saved a lot of people a lot of trouble."

Chapter Eighteen

Stephen walked in slowly, almost reluctantly. I immediately noticed the dark circles under his eyes. He knelt down beside me and took my hand, saying, "Celeste, I'm so sorry."

"It's okay."

"No, it isn't. I stayed back because I was afraid that she would pull the knife if I moved any closer."

"You knew she had a knife?"

"Pammy always carries a switchblade."

"Isn't that illegal?"

"It is around here," Harold growled.

"I've tried to tell her, but she doesn't care. She needs it to feel safe."

"They've found the car," I said softly.

"Oh God! Where is she?" His eyes filled with tears.

"She left a note. Harold…."

"It read…." Harold cleared his throat and then handed Stephen his notebook.

"She's dead," Stephen said and began to sob. I stroked his bent head. "I know she's dead. She wouldn't say good-bye like that unless she meant to do something."

I looked at Marshall and Harold, sitting quietly in the armchairs, their eyes full of sympathy. I moved my head very slightly, and they both rose and went into the kitchen where I soon heard them putting plates and silverware on the table. I could smell stew.

"I'm so sorry." Stephen stood up, wiped away the tears, and blew his nose. "I'm so sorry you got hurt. I've never meant to hurt anyone in my life, and now I've caused all this."

He sank down in the armchair across from me.

"'All this?'"

"Bond's death and your getting hurt, and, my God, that poor young woman!"

"Tareka James?"

"Yes. I'm responsible for all of it."

"I don't think that's true unless you knew what Pamela intended to do."
Stephen looked haunted.

"I swear I didn't even suspect what she had done until after they found Tareka James. We ran into someone from Pammy's kickboxing class, and the woman mentioned the spring tournament that weekend and how much the team had missed Pam. I realized that she had told me the tournament was a different weekend, the weekend before Bond's body was found. That weekend she was gone from Friday to Saturday evening."

"Did you ask her about it?"

"I tried to ask her where she had been and why she had lied to me, but she wouldn't talk at all. She just said that she needed some time alone, and she didn't need to answer to me. She said some other stuff."

"What?"

He sighed, giving me a look full of hurt and despair.

"Stephen, you have to tell me. I'm going to do my best to help you, but I need to know the truth, and I'm going to ask you to tell the police the truth. All of it."

His eyes filled with tears that he wiped away before speaking.

"She said that it wasn't like I was her husband so I should stop acting like it."

"I know you weren't married," I said gently. "Why?"

"I wanted to marry her, but she'd been in some trouble—there was a fight in a bar—and Pammy was afraid if we got a marriage license, the police would track her down." He swallowed hard. "She was wanted for assault and resisting arrest."

"What?"

"It happened just as I was finishing my dissertation and looking for a job. Leonora had gotten a lawyer for me, and I had gotten my birth certificate amended. Right after that we were supposed to get married, but Pammy was angry at how much I was working and how distracted I was."

I nodded with the sympathy of someone who has written a dissertation and looked for an academic job.

"Pammy left in a huff one night and didn't come home until the next day. She had been beaten up, but she never told me exactly what happened, only that someone had insulted her. She had a crazy temper. When we were in Atlanta, I suggested that she start karate as a way to make her feel safe, but I think now the karate and kickboxing and weightlifting didn't help her at all. It didn't make her feel safe. It just made her dangerous. So, you see, it is all my fault."

"What did she need to feel safe from?"

Stephen gave me a long look before he answered.

"I hate all the stereotypes about mountain people, about how they are stupid, good-for-nothing, lazy, ignorant, violent, inbred, drunken layabouts. And then there's the accent. A lot of times I tell people I'm from Atlanta so they won't start in about the mountains and incest and did I wear shoes."

He spoke with a deep-seated anger and resentment I had never seen before.

"My grandmother died when I was seventeen, and two families who lived near us and were dirt poor helped Pammy and me so we could finish high school. Out of the goodness of their hearts, not expecting anything in return, they shared what little they had to help us to a better life. They fed us when we had nothing. When I think of mountain people, that's what I think of. And my grandmother was the most generous, loving soul that ever lived. And she was smart. She only finished fifth grade, but she read anything she could get her hands on. Whatever is good in me and whatever I've achieved, I completely owe to Gran and Leonora Priddy and our neighbors."

Stephen stopped, and I waited as he gathered himself.

"Pammy and I grew up about half a mile from each other. Her mama ran off when we were little, and Pammy barely even remembered her. Her daddy was a mean drunk. Whenever he went after Pammy, she'd hide out in the woods near Gran's house, and we'd take care of her. Her daddy always came looking for her, but Gran and I hid her well. He was the meanest man who ever lived when he drank, and finally someone killed him."

"Who?"

"Never found out who, but when we were sixteen, someone found him with a bullet in the back of his head."

"And they never found out who did it?"

Stephen shook his head slowly, saying, "They didn't look too hard."

"Do you think Pamela did it?"

"It never crossed my mind then, but now I think it's possible. Pammy's cousin got her pregnant. He lived with them off and on and started raping her when she was eleven or twelve. When we were fifteen, he finally got her pregnant."

"Did you know this was going on?"

"God no! Pammy didn't tell me. The first I knew of it was when Miss Priddy sat me down and asked me if Pammy were pregnant. I knew about the violence but not the sexual part of it. I had no idea. I knew that there were things I didn't tell Pammy, but I had never realized that she also had secrets from me."

"Did she have the baby?"

"No. She actually didn't even know she was pregnant, but Miss Priddy took her away to get her an abortion. I think she also got the law after the cousin because he disappeared. Thank God, people listened to Miss Priddy. Then Pammy came to live with me and Grandma. Her daddy got shot not too long after."

"What an awful childhood."

"Mine wasn't wonderful, but I always knew that Pammy had it much worse. Mama died when I was a baby, and I have no idea who my daddy was. I think Mama may have been a prostitute from some of the stuff I used to hear people say, but Gran raised me, and I always knew I was loved. When I was born, I wasn't right.

Gran, my mother, and the midwife decided that I was a girl so I grew up as a girl. I didn't know any of this until Gran knew she was dying and told me. Everyone just treated me like a tomboy, and actually no one paid much attention to the fact I wasn't a normal girl. Pammy and I had each other through all this, and we swore from the time we were little kids that we would always be together." Stephen began to cry again, sobbing softly.

"I didn't mind being different, probably because of Gran, but Pammy always hated it with a passion. People would make fun of us in high school and ask Pammy if I were her boyfriend. We always got teased. That's when she started carrying the switchblade. She got really quick with it so the boys would leave us alone."

"But you were smart."

"We were both smart, and that probably made the bullying worse. Pammy was so shy that she could hardly say her name, but she was very smart, especially in math. I was a very good student. I could talk and write so I got the attention, but we both got good grades, and I know Pammy is, I mean, was, every bit as smart as I am."

"When did you meet Miss Priddy?"

"In the eighth grade. My English teacher saw that I loved to read and told me that there was a library in town where I could get books so she sent me there to meet Miss Priddy. Then I took Pammy there, and we started reading all the time and doing little chores for her. The library was our safe place. When we were in high school, she gave us both jobs. She also gave us money after Gran died."

He fell silent for a long time.

"So she got you into college?" I gently prompted him.

"No. Pammy didn't want to go to college. She was terrified at the idea of more school because she always associated school with bullying. I couldn't go to college without her, and I was feeling more and more confused, like I was only pretending to be a girl. Miss Priddy was very upset, but I swore to her that I'd go to school. She finally understood that we needed to make our own way so she arranged for us to go work in a restaurant in Charleston. We saved up, and then we moved to Atlanta where I finally got my B.A. and began to understand the disconnect between who I was and my physical body."

"That's when you decided to go to California?"

"I did a lot of research and felt more and more that I was male, not female, and that I needed to be male—to be seen as male—in order to be a complete person. I wanted finally to live comfortably in my own skin and in the world."

"How did Pamela feel about this?"

"She did her best to understand because she loved me and wanted me to be happy, but...." Stephen's voice trailed off, and he fell silent.

"Pamela talked about not wanting to be freaks again when she was holding me and also in the note," I said.

"She never got over the cruelty of our past, especially high school. Actually, the bullying started when we were in elementary school because we were easy targets. We were the poorest of the poor. We never had any peace at school except in the classroom, and sometimes not there. It's amazing how sly and cruel children can be. We always stuck together because that was the only way we were safe." Stephen wiped away the tears. "I always had books as a consolation and escape, as a real passion. Later I discovered my love for teaching and research so I had my work. Of course, the abuse I suffered was much less than what Pammy went through, but she never found her passion."

"What about her wood-working?"

"She liked it and was very talented, but it didn't consume her. I don't think she ever believed how talented she was because she was mostly self-taught." He shook his head. "In the first class she took, without warning, the teacher asked her to talk about her project in front of the other students because it was so good. Pammy walked out and never went back. She also never took another wood-working class."

"What about karate?"

"I talked her into taking classes when we moved to Atlanta because she felt so unsafe in the city. I tried to get her to go to a therapist, but even when she saw me benefitting from therapy, she wouldn't go. I couldn't make her do anything," Stephen added sadly. "I realized that very early and just had to love her as she was, but I guess I pretty much failed her."

"I think you tried, and that's all you could do," I said softly. "You took care of her as best you could."

"I keep thinking of all the things I should have done differently, but I couldn't make myself someone I'm not. I lived that way for too long."

"So she didn't want you to transition and do the surgery?"

"Not exactly. She loved me, but understandably, she never wanted to be around men." He shook his head. "Close as we had always been, I don't think even I understood how deep her fear was."

"Didn't she know about your physical anomalies?" I asked in surprise.

"Until I told her, she didn't know because we never had a sexual relationship."

My eyes must have widened because something hurt.

"Surprise hurts."

"Sorry. This may be hard to believe, but we were never sexual. I was so wrought up with my own issues, and Pammy had been raped. I'm pretty sure she had been molested from an early age. At any rate, sex was never on our agenda. We talked and talked before moving to California. I tried to make sure she understood how my transition would work—how I had to live as a man before the surgery. She seemed to accept what I was telling her and understand the process, but once I started transitioning and became visibly male, she was terrified—not of me, but she sensed the effect the testosterone was having and she started being scared that I would leave

188

her for another woman, for someone I could be sexual with." He stopped and looked at me intently. "You know what I'm talking about?"

"Only from reading, but I know the large doses of testosterone for transition lead to a strong level of desire."

"It was a real struggle, but I owed my survival, my life, to Pammy and our relationship. I couldn't imagine how she would survive without me or how I would survive without her." He stopped and wiped away tears. "Even when we were little kids, she was always jealous and possessive. So, as I transitioned, the jealousy got dramatically worse, but I swear I never gave her any reason to be jealous," he said in a heart-broken voice. "I tried to explain to her that even if I were outed here, we would still be fine. I tried to tell her that I wasn't afraid, but she couldn't or wouldn't believe me."

"You're a good person, Stephen. You've tried and done your best, and that's all that's required of any of us."

"I only know that I failed her in some fundamental way," he went on, as if he had not heard me, "But I couldn't face living my life as someone I wasn't."

"You weren't the source of Pamela's problems. You tried to help her, and you can't make anyone accept help if they don't want it or if they don't think they need it." I thought of Briana and her complete resistance to my attempts to help her. "As a teacher, I'm sure you know this."

"I do, but I still feel responsible," murmured Stephen.

We sat in silence for a few moments.

"I have another question."

Stephen looked up.

"Did you write to Miss Priddy very often?"

"Once a month and sometimes more. That's how Bond found out about me. When Leonora died, Bond found all my letters, and most of the story was there. When Gran died, I went to Leonora and told her what I had been told. I didn't have anyone else to help me understand. My God, she was such an amazing person. Instead of freaking out, she found information for me and told me that my journey would be to find out how I best needed to live and make a difference in the world. She gave me the courage to find out who I was. She was also the only person I could go to for advice about Pammy.

"Just before we left for Charleston, she told me that when Pammy went for the abortion, the counselor, who met with her both before and after the procedure, warned Miss Priddy that Pammy needed serious therapy. Once, after we left Mountain Valley, Leonora visited us and tried to talk Pammy into going to a therapist, but Pammy was terrified. She always said that they would lock her up if they ever knew what she thought and how she felt." Stephen smiled grimly. "She may have been right."

"So what did Bond do after she found the letters?"

"She invited me to her office for a chat."

"Did you know that she was from Mountain Valley?"

"Actually, when I got the job, Leonora warned me that Bond was here and said to steer clear of her. She never told me why, but she didn't trust her at all."

"Yet she made her the executor of her will."

For the first time, Stephen laughed.

"Leonora believed that LouAnn Bond was the most anal retentive person in the universe so she would make sure that the terms of Leonora's will, especially concerning the library, were carried out."

"But she knew Bond would see your letters."

"Leonora promised to destroy them," Stephen said flatly. "We both agreed that would be best because some of the letters concerned Pammy. Leonora was the last person on earth who would have done anything knowingly to hurt me or Pammy so I'm sure she got caught unawares--she didn't expect to die so soon."

"Was she ill?"

"She had a heart condition, an arrhythmia, but she saw a cardiologist in Charleston and took medication. It seemed to be under control."

"So what happened when you met with Bond?"

"She told me that if I did not resign, she would make sure my personal history became public. I asked her what proof she had that my personal history would be of interest to anyone but me, and she handed me a stack of papers. She had copied my entire correspondence with Leonora and some letters Leonora wrote to Amelia, her best friend. I asked her where the originals were, and she said they were safe. The worst part was she was just...." Stephen stopped and swallowed hard. "She was just so prissy and sly. It was not like she hated me for being trans—it was more like she enjoyed knowing my secret and thinking she had power over me."

"So what did you do?"

"I looked her in the eye and told her if she outed me, I would find a way to sue her ass from here to eternity. I also threatened to go to the police and charge her with blackmail."

"Good for you."

"She just smirked and said, 'We'll see about that.' I then did something I should never have done."

"What?"

"I lost my temper and told her what Leonora thought of her. She was so shocked that she just stared at me and then told me to leave. I didn't tell Pammy about the threat, and I should have because the next day, Bond got Pammy to come see her. I didn't know about the meeting until afterwards. If I had known, I would never have let Pammy go or I would have gone with her. Bond was horrible to her. She threatened to out me and told her how humiliating it would be for both of us. She told Pammy I would not get tenure, and no other college would hire me. She

190

explained to Pammy how it would be in her best interest to convince me to resign, and she would 'allow us to move on quietly.' She convinced Pammy she had total control over our future and could make our lives hell."

"And Pammy believed her?"

"Completely." Stephen shook his head sadly. "Pammy wanted to run, but I refused. I was adamant about waiting the thing out and, if I had to, fighting it. I think maybe that's when Pammy began making other plans."

"And you had no idea?"

"I didn't. Even when she was so upset when Bond's body was found, I had no idea. I didn't want Bond dead, but I have to admit that I was relieved. Pammy got quieter than usual and began having stomach problems. I think she had expected that Bond's body would not be found for a long time."

"A logical expectation, and the trail would have been much colder," I murmured softly and shuddered to think that Pamela might have gotten away with murder. Perhaps for the second time. And then what? A shiver went down my spine.

"How on earth did you know about Leonora Priddy and the letters?" Stephen suddenly asked.

"Chance. I found a picture of you and Pamela that Bond missed when she went through Priddy's papers. It was lost in another file."

"Which picture?"

"The wedding picture."

Stephen's eyes filled with tears, and he could barely speak.

"It was the only time I ever lied to Leonora. She was so happy and excited for us that I just didn't have the heart to disappoint her. I told her how much better Pammy was and how happy we were. What an extraordinary woman Leonora Priddy was. When I asked her why she had come back to stay in Mountain Valley, she told me, 'The world is saved one soul at a time, and the first soul I had to save was my own.'"

"Did you know what she meant about saving her own soul?"

"No, but I have my suspicions. She was a very private person so I never felt I could ask, but I think her best friend Amelia was the love of her life, and when she married, Leonora could not bear to stay around. You know, she paid for my surgery." Stephen was silent for a long time, and then said, his voice breaking, "My God, Celeste, what am I going to do? Pammy never understood that I needed her as much as she needed me, that I loved her as much as she loved me. Now it's all gone. Now there is no one. I feel as if my past has vanished and maybe I've vanished with it."

Knowing no words of comfort were possible, I opened my arms to hold Stephen close as he cried.

Later that evening, Harold searched Bond's office files again and found Stephen's letters to Miss Priddy in a file jacket neatly labeled "Correspondence--Priddy/Hope."

A second folder, labeled "Correspondence—Priddy/Bennington" held fifteen more letters that mentioned Stephen.

Chapter Nineteen

Late the next afternoon, over strident protests from my mother, I dressed, and Marshall drove me to Maureen's. Cass opened the door, hugged me carefully, and then led me to the den where I reclined on the leather couch.

"How are you?" she asked.

"How do I look?"

"Pretty awful. I once went over the handlebars of my mountain bike, and I looked about the way you look now. Does it hurt?"

"Only when I think anything or attempt a facial expression. Actually the headache is much duller today so I have hopes of making a recovery."

"Oh, Celeste," said Maureen, rushing into the room, "I didn't hear the doorbell. My God!"

Looking shaken, she took both my hands in hers and held them tightly.

"I still have all my teeth, and the plastic surgeon and neurologist guarantee that I will eventually be good as new."

"I'm so sorry. This is all my fault."

She sat down next to me.

"I think we share the blame for how my face looks. You put me on the trail, and I followed it."

We both laughed.

"I've made a lovely dinner. Are you hungry?"

"Actually my appetite has come back, but no wine. Just thinking about alcohol makes my head pound."

"Now that is seriously bad news," said Maureen.

I answered with my dreadful grin which made her and Cass look at me even more sympathetically.

"Enough about me," I said, "We need to talk."

"Okay."

"You need to work on the President to use his pull to keep Stephen out of the stuff about Pamela Rykker."

"I've talked to him already, and he's not sure, but he's going to try. Have the police found her?"

"No. Someone in the neighborhood where her car was found saw a woman walking toward the bridge. The description fits Pamela, but that's all there is so far. Stephen and the police are both sure what she left is a suicide note. The police I might not trust, but Stephen is very sure, and I would trust him to know."

Maureen nodded.

"You'll be happy to know the President and I have had our first truly open discussion since I came to work here. I told him everything you'd found out about Bond, and he was appalled, but I'm also sure he knows or suspects some other unsavory stuff. He has talked with Matt Dingle. They reached an agreement that the Board of Trustees will not try to micromanage tenure decisions."

"Which part of the ranch did he have to give away?"

"He had to agree that the President's office would not support Coming Out Week."

"What about the Provost's office?"

Maureen raised her eyebrows.

"It is an educational event for the academic community, and transfers of funds have been known to happen, but I also know some people who would be more than happy to make generous private donations." The three of us chuckled.

"So are the two of you a couple?"

Cass and Maureen looked at each other and smiled.

"We're not advertising it," began Maureen.

"But we're not hiding it," finished Cass.

"I've told my daughters, and they took it remarkably well. We're meeting in Colorado next month for a long weekend together."

"I'm glad," I said sincerely. "Now I need to talk to you about Stephen."

"How is he?" asked Cass. "I've always liked him, but we never did more than occasionally have coffee."

"Pamela had a lot to do with their not socializing."

I turned to Maureen.

"Once his tenure is approved, I'd like you to okay an early semester sabbatical for him."

"A semester at full pay?"

"That's the usual arrangement, isn't it?"

She nodded.

"I'm going to help him write the proposal. Also, there's something else you need to know."

Maureen sat up a little straighter.

"He and Pamela were not married. I have no idea whether this will come out, but I want you to know."

"Benefits fraud." Maureen paused. "Damn. They came before partner benefits."

"You got it, but they also came to the university before anyone was required to present a marriage certificate or prove co-habitation."

Maureen sighed.

"I'll talk with the President and see what we can do. I don't see the point in digging around about this."

"Also if you start digging, you might find some other cases of people who were or are not married."

"Possibly. Now, I have a proposition to make. Since you will be debt free as soon as I write the check…"

"I'm not comfortable with your doing that."

"I talked with your parents, and it's done."

"You talked to my parents," I began and winced.

"Now, let me finish." She spoke with authority, and I was in no shape to argue. "Even though you no longer desperately need the money, I appreciate your company and would like to keep you around."

"I'll be around. Actually, I'll be lying on your nearest couch until this headache goes away."

"No, I mean in my office. I'm offering you a permanent position on my administrative staff."

I shook my head and winced again.

"Saying no is a real problem with this head," I explained with another grimace which also hurt.

"But the answer, although I am very flattered, is no. I am a teacher and a scholar, not an administrator. Solving this has been more excitement than I need in my life. Now I just want to get rid of this headache so I can spend the summer and fall doing my research and working on a book. Then I want to go back to my teaching in the spring."

"What about that handsome guy who delivered you?" Cass asked with a grin.

"Even after our recent adventures, he still seems to be speaking to me so I'm hoping he might agree to provide the kind of excitement, other than scholarly sizzle, that I want in my life."

Made in the
USA
Lexington, KY